These are the Names

Tommy Wieringa

a novel

These
are the
Names

TRANSLATED BY SAM GARRETT

MELVILLE HOUSE
BROOKLYN · LONDON

THESE ARE THE NAMES

Originally published in Dutch as *Dit zijn de namen* by
De Bezige Bij in 2012
Copyright © 2012 by Tommy Wieringa
Translation copyright © 2015 by Melville House Publishing, LLC

First Melville House Printing: November 2016

Melville House Publishing		8 Blackstock Mews
46 John Street	and	Islington
Brooklyn, NY 11201		London N4 2BT

mhpbooks.com   facebook.com/mhpbooks   @melvillehouse

Library of Congress Cataloging-in-Publication Data
Names: Wieringa, Tommy, 1967– author.
Title: These are the names / Tommy Wieringa.
Other titles: Dit zijn de namen. English
Description: First edition. | Brooklyn : Melville House, 2016.
Identifiers: LCCN 2016015121| ISBN 9781612195650
   (hardback) | ISBN 9781612195667 (ebook)
Subjects: | BISAC: FICTION / Political. | FICTION / Cultural
   Heritage. | FICTION / Literary. | GSAFD: Political fiction.
Classification: LCC PT5881.33.I434 D5813 2016 | DDC
   839.313/64—dc23
LC record available at https://lccn.loc.gov/2016015121

Design by Marina Drukman

Printed in the United States of America
1   3   5   7   9   10   8   6   4   2

For Hazel, for Zoë

The Master said: "As long as your parents are still alive, do not travel too far. And if you must travel still, let them know where you are going."

Autumn

I

───

THE THING ITSELF

Pontus Beg had not become the old man he'd imagined. Something was missing—a great deal, in fact. As a boy, he had for a time been in the habit of walking around his father's yard with a pair of safety glasses on the bridge of his nose, his hands clasped behind his back— that was how he imagined the life of an old man to be. Sometimes he used a branch for a walking stick. More than anything else, he had wanted to be old. Slow and deliberate, a captain calmly braving the storm. To die a wise man.

When the glasses started leaving welts on both sides of his nose, he put them back beside the grinder in the shed and began waiting patiently for old age to come, instead of running out to meet it.

He had only started feeling like an old man after he developed a cold foot. He was fifty-three, still too young to really be considered old, but he could see the writing on the wall. A nerve had become pinched in his lower back. Ever since then, his left foot had gone cold. Standing on the bathroom floor in the morning, he could see that his feet were different colours. The right one was ruddy—the way it should be—but the left one was pale and cold. When he pressed his fingers against it, he felt almost nothing. It was as though the foot belonged to someone else. *The dying starts from the feet up*, Beg thought.

That was how it would be, the way to the end: he and his body, growing apart gradually.

The name is the guest of the thing itself, an old Chinese philosopher had said, and that, more and more, was the way he, Pontus Beg, found himself in relation to his body—he was the guest, and it was the thing itself. And the thing itself was now busy shaking off its guest.

The days grow shorter; life turns in upon itself. Thunderstorms at night linger for a long time over the steppes. Beg stands at the window and watches. There is a flash in the distance, and a web of glowing fissures in the vault of heaven. He stands on the linoleum, one foot warm and one foot cold, and thinks he needs to pour himself a bit of something in order to get to sleep.

The older he gets, the more sleep becomes an unreliable friend.

His apartment is at the edge of town. There had once been plans for the city to expand eastward: half-hearted preparations had even been made, but nothing came of it. His window still looks out on a proliferation of little sheds and kitchen gardens and the endless space of the steppe beyond. Maybe it's a sign of stagnation, but, as far as he's concerned, things can stay this way; he likes the view.

In the kitchen, he takes the bottle of Kubanskaya from the freezer and pours himself a shot. He is not a heavy drinker; he practises restraint, unlike almost everyone else east of the Carpathians.

Then he moves back to the window and looks, with thoughts indistinct, into the chute of the night.

He hears his housekeeper coughing in the bedroom. Once a month he lays claim to her for a night, although the phrase doesn't accurately reflect their relationship. It would be more like it to say that, once a month, she lets herself be claimed for a night. She determines which night that will be, always sometime shortly before her period. The manual to her reproductive system remains misty territory to him—something he'd rather not think about. When his day arrives, he hears about it.

Her fertile days, the housekeeper reserves for her fiancé, a truck driver ten years her junior. He pilots tractor-trailers full of commodities from the People's Republic to the capital, from whence a flood of trash inundates the country's stores. Zita waits patiently for the day when he will propose to her.

No matter how hard she tries, though, she simply doesn't get pregnant; if this keeps up, she'll be childless forever. She spends a lot of time on her knees at the Benedictine chapel. Amid golden icons and plastic flowers, she prays fervently for a child. In the confessional, the priest listens to the people's secrets; when he comes down the stairs in his black habit, his hand carves out the sign of the cross above her head, and he blesses her and the genuflecting farmwomen in their colourful kerchiefs. She feels the cross burning on her forehead; that night, the seed will blossom forth.

Dangling from the little chain around her neck, beside the golden cross, are the emblems of those saints to whom one can turn for fecundity.

Women, Pontus Beg reflects, are the pack animals of faith, carrying the world's sanctity on their backs.

He has never been able to talk Zita into turning a blind eye and granting him one of those fertile nights. For he is sure that it is the truck driver who is remiss, not her. It's the truck; so much sitting isn't good for a man. It strangles your balls.

A child? Is he trying to say that he wants a child?

'Don't kid yourself, Pontus,' Zita says.

He's not serious, she thinks. And if he is, he shouldn't be.

Beg is more appreciative of the services she performs in bed than those she renders with both feet on the floor. She is not a particularly good housekeeper. She doesn't actually *clean* the house; she picks up after him. A jar of soft soap lasts her a year. They are long past the point where he can say anything about it. Habit has locked their relationship into place; nothing can change it anymore. As it is, so shall it remain. She picks up after him, and he keeps his mouth shut.

When Zita stays over, he drinks more than usual. They sit at the table, smoking and talking. She becomes completely absorbed in the anecdotes he tells her. She laughs and shudders—she is a responsive audience. Some of the stories he has told her three or four times already, over the years, but she enjoys hearing him talk about the policeman's life. At the table with Zita, alcohol doesn't make him melancholy: on the contrary, it makes him cheerful and roguish. He looks forward to his evenings with her—they are the high point of his existence.

Then they go to bed. The light goes out.

When she is at his place, he often lies awake. He wonders whether perhaps he's been alone too long, whether it's impossible to get used to having another body beside him.

There's that, and then there's that other problem.

Zita maintains a lively relationship with her mother—in her sleep. His bed at night sounds like a henhouse. First, after making love, she sleeps for an hour, sometimes two. Then it starts. Then mother and daughter resume the conversation that death interrupted so rudely. Beg remembers the first time he heard her talking at night. He had listened in on that half of the conversation that came from this side of the void, without realising that it was her mother on the other end. These were no deep, dark secrets being shared; they talked about the price of flour, the freshness of eggs, and the unending disgrace that empty shops imply for a woman in the mood to buy. It was like a telephone call one could overhear easily, even if all you heard was what was being said at this end.

When it all became too tedious, Beg woke her.

'You're talking in your sleep,' he said.

She sat straight up in bed and said: 'Pontus, you're interrupting us! Now I'll have to go back all over again and try to find her!'

Since then, he had started getting out of bed whenever the chattering grew too much for him, the way it had tonight. On one warm foot and one cold, he stands at the window and gazes at the lightning out on the plains.

2

TO THE WEST

The sky above the steppe crackled. In the lee of a low dune, a little group of people lay huddled against the storm. Their clothes were soaked, and they were chilled to the bone. Like this, like the first humans on earth tucked away from the raging heavens, they had waited on countless nights for daylight to arrive. But the night did not end. The darkness stretched out to the edges of the world, the earth had stopped turning, and a new day would not come.

Five men, a woman, and a child. They no longer had any clear reason to start moving anew each day: mechanically as sunflowers, they followed the sun. As they breathed, so did they walk.

Farther west, farther all the time, was what the man had said.

That had been a long time ago. Drought ruled the flats then; the sun burned the earth clean. In the morning, they licked the dew from the pieces of plastic they'd spread out to that end the night before; the rest of the day, they lived with a maddening thirst. A thirst that drowned out all thought, thirst that tempted you with cool ponds, that conjured up the sound of dripping faucets. They wept for rain. Every word they spoke tasted of rusty iron. The child, a boy, pinched the skin on his forearm and pulled. The puckered skin rose up and remained in place, like a crease in a sheet of paper.

To the north, they saw clouds the colour of graphite, but the clouds never came any closer.

Then, one day, the rain arrived.

At first, only a little, a few drops they welcomed like manna from heaven. They danced beneath the clouds; each raindrop was a prayer. Their thirst was over. More rain fell than prayers arose. Then they prayed for one dry day, one night during which they would not be soaked to the skin. The boy's face burned with fever. A few times, the woman thought he would not live till morning, but he had always stood up and gone on his way. In him was a firm will to be among the stayers, to be with those who would make it.

The dreams with which each of them had left home had gradually wilted and died off. Their dreams differed in size and weight, and remained alive in some longer than in others, but in the end they had almost all disappeared. The sun had pulverised them; the rain had washed them away.

The boy saw planes in the sky. He followed their trails with his eyes. He had never seen an airplane from close by, but he knew of the miracle of travellers climbing on board in one world and disembarking in the next, with only a few hours in between. In his mountain village, planes were seen as dots against the sky that left white trails behind them. An uncle had left on a plane for America and never came back. Later, the boy's aunt and five nieces and nephews had joined him.

The boy had once made a plane from wire and wood. His brother said, 'How is a plane supposed to fly if it has propellers *and* a jet engine?'

His brother had tried to explain the different principles to him, but stopped after a time because he wasn't completely sure himself.

His brother had remained behind because he had a weak constitution. They had sent *him* instead, even though he was two years younger. He had been found fit for the crossing—not by plane, but overland. The money for the journey was tucked into the toes of his shoes. The pair he'd had on when he left home had worn out and become useless long ago. Back when there was still a whole crowd of them, a man had died along the way, and the boy had taken his shoes. He had pulled them from the man's feet carefully, afraid that the corpse would suddenly open its eyes and shout, 'Thief! Stop the thief!'

But the man remained dead, and so the boy became the owner of a pair of large, dusty sneakers.

• • •

The day came, with dirty light. They set their numb bodies in motion again. In the morning, the sand was wet and heavy, the grass whipping against their legs.

At midmorning, the boy discovered something important: a cigarette package, half-buried in the sand. Plastic bags would blow out onto the steppe and remain hanging in the brush, but cigarette packages didn't do that; people tossed them on the ground, and there they stayed. So there were still people somewhere. Maybe they had been here, and he was holding proof of their existence in his hand! The letters of the Western brand were a faded red. Drops of condensation had formed inside the cellophane. Perhaps now they would finally find the long-hoped-for village, or a little town, heralded from a distance by the glistening gold onion of a church. He shook the sand from the moist package and stuck it in his pocket—the same pocket that contained a stone in the shape of a crescent moon, and the knife his brother had given him. His brother had wrapped wire around the handle, and rust had gnawed little dents into the metal of the blade. At night, the boy held the knife tightly. Shivering with pleasure, he imagined himself ramming it into someone's heart.

His fingers slid over the cellophane. He wished he could tell the woman about his discovery, but he kept his mouth shut.

It would only break the spell. It was a sign meant specially for him. If he remained silent, it would have its effect. Otherwise not. Then they would continue to wander across the flats for centuries, and it would be his fault. Because he hadn't kept his mouth shut.

Their feet dragged through the sand. Interminable was the space they moved through. The landscape before them was precisely the same as the one behind; the one on the right differed in no way from that on the left. The only lines to guide them on the steppes were the sky above their heads and the ground beneath their feet.

Their footsteps were wiped out quickly behind them. They were passers-by, leaving no trail and no recollections.

Around noon, when the tall man shouted that he could see a village—'Houses! Over there! Village! Village!'—the boy was not surprised. He almost burst with happiness, but he was not surprised.

He ran up to the front, where the tall man was pointing his shaky hand at the horizon. 'Where?' he shouted.

'There!'

The boy saw nothing, but ran in the direction the tall man had pointed. The tall man always saw things before the others did; he was a born lookout.

The boy ran, he soared across the sand. There went a chosen one, a boy God had selected as the first to know of His intentions. He no longer felt hunger or fatigue. The grass thrashed at his legs; his lungs burned in his chest. He saw the first houses.

'Hey!' he screamed, so the people there would know he was coming. 'Hey, you there!'

It was a village sunken in the plain, round and worn as eroded rock. He ran towards a big barn. The rafters were rotten, and the roof swayed like an old horse's back. The boy ran down a street between the houses where the grass was as high as on the steppe. A soundless shriek rose up inside him, but his brain refused to accept what he saw—the vacant, mute windows, the overrun streets.

Not a living soul.

'Hello?!' he screamed. 'Is anybody there?'

His question bounced between the houses of wood and clay.

'Where are you people?'

He yanked on decaying doors. He ran into one house after the next. Empty. Empty, and the people were gone. In the heart of the village he stormed into a little house of prayer. The sparse light falling through the high windows revealed the destruction. Sacred volumes had fallen to ash and shreds; the blaze had gone cold. The boy threaded his way past charred pews and cabinets, and climbed to the altar. There he sank to his knees. He bent over, his hands covering his face, and howled like a wounded animal.

That was how the others found him.

3

ECONOMICS

At six-thirty, Pontus Beg arose. He stretched as though freeing himself from a headlock.

He ran a washcloth across his face and gargled with mouthwash. In the mirror he saw a stocky man, his chest and shoulders covered in greying hair. He thought about the boy who had swum beside the weir—the smooth, hairless body. The *lightness*; memories of an other.

The upstairs neighbours' wastewater hissed through the pipes, rushing like a waterfall when the toilet was flushed. These were only some of the building's tidal movements. In early October, they had turned the heating on, and the building began to swell; it creaked as hot water sluiced through the pipes with a sigh.

Tucked away behind a pleat in the shower curtain was the glass containing Zita's upper dentures. Beg could remember her real teeth. With the passing of time they had become stained an ever-darker brown. When she smiled, she would cover her mouth with her hand. She was ashamed of having teeth the colour of tobacco juice, but feared nothing as much as the dentist. Beg had given her money to have her teeth pulled and dentures fitted. She had asked them to put her under for the operation, and lived toothlessly until the new ones were ready.

The dental technician had done a good job: when she smiled, it was as though she'd opened a jewellery box.

I can pay for the teeth, Beg thought, but I can't make the mouth say what I want.

• • •

Zita lived in accordance with the iron regime of women. She worked hard; she stood for no nonsense. The nights with Beg she saw as a continuation of her activities around the house—dusting, sweeping, cooking, washing, ironing, and mending his worn shirts and uniforms. Each of these tasks she fulfilled slowly and attentively; in bed, he sometimes thought he heard her humming.

They benefited from each other in an easily quantifiable fashion; neither of them felt short-changed in any way. Beg considered the arrangement a perfect marriage; in Zita's mind, it was an excellent position.

He went into the bedroom, observing the sharp lines around her hollow cheeks. In her sleep, she looked disgruntled. That was the attitude her face assumed in repose, but it said nothing about her character.

He laid a hand on her shoulder and shook her.

'Yeah, yeah,' she murmured.

In the kitchen, he ladled soup from the pan and ate it cold. Between spoonfuls he took the occasional bite of dark rye bread.

'You're slurping,' Zita said from the bathroom. 'You sound like a pig.'

Beg smiled. Yes, it was a good marriage in every way.

When Beg entered the waiting room at police headquarters, two men jumped to their feet. They both began talking excitedly. One of them had run over a sheep that belonged to the other. The second man claimed that the whole herd had already crossed the road when the casualty in question suddenly came traipsing along. 'A ewe, sir,' the first one said then, 'such a lovely animal!'

Running over a sheep, Beg knew, was a complicated business. According to old nomadic custom, you were not only liable for the animal you had killed, but also owed recompense to a number of generations to come—one could say, in other words, that the shepherd had a good day when one of his herd was flattened.

'You've never seen such a lovely little ewe, so broad in the beam,' the shepherd wailed.

'That's enough!' Beg shouted.

At the information desk, Oksana was playing solitaire on the computer.

'Where's Koller?' Beg asked.

Oksana looked up. 'His wife called—an abscess in his armpit. She said it kept him awake all night. He's gone to the doctor.'

'How many abscesses does the guy have?' Beg asked in annoyance.

'That was a fistula. On his behind.'

'So who's going to draw up this report?'

Oksana looked over her shoulder at the men in the waiting room. 'Koller's actually the one on duty,' she said.

Beg shook his head. 'Call Menchov. Get him out of bed.'

He poured himself a cup of tea, then went into his office. The room was warm, and he could smell himself—his own scent, mingled with cigarette smoke. He turned on the computer. The screen did not light up. He pushed the button again, but the thing was dead. He called Oksana. After a little knock on the door, she came in. Her skirt clung to the lines of her lower body; there, where the elastic pressed against flesh, he could see the contours of her underwear. The top buttons of her glossy white blouse were unbuttoned. A person in government service, Beg felt, shouldn't walk around like that. Maybe in the brothel at the Morris Club, but not at police headquarters.

He stared helplessly at the monitor.

'Has it stopped working again?' she asked.

He rolled his chair away from the desk. Oksana squatted down and pushed 'POWER.' Then she stood up and walked around to the far side. 'Oh, okay,' she said, 'that's not too complicated.'

She held up the plug for him to see. She promised to give the cleaners hell, and stuck the plug back into the socket. The computer sighed, and the monitor blipped on.

Beg longed for his typewriter.

One hour later, Oksana came back to say that neither Koller nor Menchov had showed up. The two men were still in the waiting room.

'Tell Koller I'll break both his legs if he doesn't get down here now. He's on weekend duty, for Christ's sake. There's no reason why he can't draw up a report with a fistula.'

'An abscess.'

'Whatever the hell it is.'

'I'll tell him that in so many words.'

Beg opened the office safe. At the bottom of it lay that month's takings: money in little plastic bags, in envelopes, folded between sheets of paper, held together with paperclips, wrapped in rubber bands; money his men had garnered at roadside from speeders, from those who ignored traffic signals or drove barefooted—driving without shoes on your feet was an obvious violation. First you pulled them over, and then you asked the driver if he wanted to be registered as a traffic offender. That was the signal for the transaction to begin. No one wanted to be registered. Fines were paid on the spot.

Beg counted it all and divided it according to rank and seniority. Before him lay a large pile of banknotes, which he split into many smaller piles. He stuffed the notes into envelopes and wrote the recipients' names on them. They all came in on the first of the month to pick up their shares.

In this country, he thought, *everyone steals from everyone else. And those who don't steal, beg.* Everywhere he looked he saw outstretched hands: no house was built, no service rendered, without the hands intervening, claiming their piece of the transaction. The system was all-embracing, a colossal weave of kickbacks, bribes, extortion, and larceny—whatever else you might choose to call it. As police commander, he found himself somewhere halfway up the ladder: big hands pinched the chunks above him; little hands scrabbled at the crumbs below. Everyone took part. It was an economic system from which everyone profited and under which everyone suffered.

Around noon, he left headquarters and drove to Tina's Bazooka Bar for lunch. Michailopol: it was his city. Thirty-nine thousand inhabitants, according to the latest census. A border town, it had once been home to a prestigious nuclear-research institute and an ice-hockey team that had been promoted in two consecutive seasons and came within an inch of the national championship. Beg remembered the excitement. At its peak, early in the last century, the city had numbered one hundred and fifty thousand citizens. Michailopol station, with fifteen departures an hour, had been the gateway to the wide world. Now Beg couldn't even remember where the tracks had been. The steel had been torn up and used to build sheds and fences. The sleepers were chopped into pieces, and disappeared into stoves during the coldest of winters. The Jugendstil station itself was still there, but it had decayed beyond rescue. A mortician stored his coffins in one of the outbuildings.

Michailopol's demise had been as turbulent as its rise. There had been sixteen churches once—Orthodox and Catholic—and two synagogues as well. The services at the Armenian Orthodox church had attracted boys from far and near, like flies to honey, for there were no prettier girls than the Armenian ones.

Beg recalled the fistfights outside the church—fathers and brothers against the country bumpkins who were after their daughters and sisters.

The Armenian church, too, had disappeared long ago.

He parked in front of Tina's Bazooka Bar and went in.

'Pontus, darling,' Tina said as he settled down at the bar. Ah, Tina Bazooka—sacred icons began to sweat when she was around. She caressed the back of Beg's hand. Brothel manners never faded.

She had just come back from visiting her son, who lived with his grandmother in the south of the country. Tina put a plate of meatloaf in the microwave and tapped a beer for him. Switching on her mobile phone, she showed him pictures of the boy.

'Amazing, how fast he's grown,' Beg said.

'Next year he's coming to live with me.'

Beg slid the phone back across the bar. Heart-shaped plastic charms dangled from its fuzzy fluorescent skin.

'Sure, why not,' he said. 'We have everything here. Schools . . .'

'Yeah, and besides that?' she asked sardonically.

'A swimming pool.'

'Closed.'

'Oh?'

'We used to go swimming there with the girls. But not anymore.'

Beg searched his memory for another facility suitable for children. 'Valentine Park,' he said. 'He can . . .'

'Get chased through the woods by a rapist? Ha-ha.'

'They've got a playground.'

'He's thirteen.'

'So he can play soccer,' Beg said, feeling acquitted.

Tina turned brusquely and walked to the far end of the bar. Beg realised he'd said something wrong, and then remembered—too late, jerk that he was—the boy's foot. Tina had always blamed the deformity on the nuclear rain; her native village lay next to a notorious testing site. Her attempts to get the boy benefits as a victim of atomic testing had proven fruitless. Even today, outright monsters were being born, mutants; a clubfoot was nothing by comparison. It didn't help either that the child had been born at Michailopol hospital, and probably conceived at the Morris Club.

Beg ate his meatloaf and drank his beer. He looked at Tina out of the corner of his eye. How did they grow them like that? A heavy gold cross wobbled on her bosom. Tina had left the business; like everyone else at the bar, Beg was consumed by regret.

The joke was one her customers passed on. 'Take this bread, it is my body,' Jesus of Nazareth told his disciples at the Last Supper. 'Take this body, it's how I earn my bread,' Tina Bazooka told her customers.

When she opened the bar, most of those customers had followed her. Everyone thought her meatloaf was excellent, but her body would have pleased them a thousand times more.

It took some getting used to at first, but they all did their best.

In fact, Beg thought, the transition had been remarkably serene. No one made a fuss, maybe because they'd all had their piece of her.

4

THE ABANDONED VILLAGE

They spread out silently among the houses. They ransack rooms, kitchens, and pantries, and call out to each other from darkened cellars. The tall man falls through a rotten wooden staircase. Nothing edible has been left behind; nothing to check their hunger. Cursing, Vitaly breaks off a table leg and smashes a room to bits. He swings the wood around savagely, until at last he breaks out in a cold sweat and shivers like a man in a fever. He falls to the floor, waves of nausea racking his body.

In an overgrown garden, the woman finds potato plants that have bolted. With her hands, she digs a few wrinkled little spuds out of the wet soil. Most of them are rotten, and the stinking juice stains her fingers black.

When they find a pair of apple trees at the edge of the village, they fetch the boy. The birds and insects haven't eaten all the apples yet; there are still quite a few on the tree. Some of them are brown and flecked with mould; others, only wizened.

The boy tosses them down, and they eat old, spoiled apples until they can eat no more. The juice foams at their lips. The boy looks out over the rolling plains from that height, rips big bites from an apple, and laughs through his tears.

Later, one by one, they return from their forays. In a courtyard, they build a fire. The sky is dense and grey; the day is cold. The boy looks at his fellow travellers—dirty, starved apparitions—as though he is seeing them for the first time.

The tall man has found a huge iron lid; it will serve as his shelter at night. On his head he wears a helmet of thin ribs and fine netting. Once, it was used to keep vegetables and fruit free of gnats.

The poacher hasn't come back yet. They feed the fire with handfuls of dusty straw and planking from the high, dark shed in the courtyard. Once a low fire is burning well, they fill a dented pan with water and toss in the paltry potatoes. It takes an eternity before the first wisps of steam rise from the water's surface. After a while, the woman whips the potatoes out of the pan, and the others watch as she divides them among them. They blow and let the potatoes dance across their fingertips, then gobble them up with skin and all, and burn their mouths.

The woman wants to stay in the village—one day's rest, one dry night beside a fire—but the day is still young, and Vitaly, the poacher, and the tall man decide that they will move on. The man from Ashkhabad rinses his sore mouth with cold water.

They toss burning pieces of wood into the buildings. Before long, columns of smoke break through the roofs of sheds and houses, veined with dark-red flames. With their backs to the inferno, they leave the village.

They are already past the last houses when the boy turns and sees the smoke rising up against the sky. A bonfire—tongues of flame climbing above the rooftops. He grins. His insides cheer. The euphoria of destruction. To hell with all that rubbish.

In his pocket he finds the empty cigarette package. He tosses it on the ground and grinds it into the sand.

'Dead,' he whispers. 'Dead.'

The others are almost out of sight by then; he can't remain standing any longer. He turns his back on the burning village.

Out in front of him goes a hallucination: a raggle-taggle crew of oddballs hung with strange objects seized during their raids—the negro with a red rag around his head, the woman with the pan bobbing at her back, the tall man with the lid lashed to his own back, the plastic-screen helmet wobbling on his head. In his hand he holds a gnarled broomstick.

Despite the bitter disappointment, the village has given them new courage; they seem to be walking faster than before. This can't be the only settlement in the surroundings. Communities are never that isolated. *The next village* becomes the focal point of their thoughts. They see tractors in the fields, smoking chimneys, cattle. The friendly beehives at the edge of town . . . all they have to do is walk there . . .

Above their heads, banks of cloud slide slowly together. Mother-of-pearl light glimmers through the cracks between. A gentle rain begins. The tall man holds the lid over his head. Night falls before they can find the village of their dreams. They have seen the delicious mirage vanish step by step. Disheartened, they sit in the sand at twilight. The poacher is gone, out setting his traps. The boy is sensitive to the heaviness between them, to the coming storm; he looks at the faces one by one. Someone must bleed.

He takes an apple from his pocket and runs his fingers over the wrinkled skin. An apple: what a luxury that had seemed to them yesterday; what a meagre reward it is today.

It's almost always between Vitaly and the man from Ashkhabad. It's been that way from the start, when fate brought them together, and dominance was distributed over the group.

Vitaly and the man from Ashkhabad.

The boy sees them getting the same ideas. He knows that the will of one will bump up hard against that of the other—iron against iron.

The poacher is a lone wolf; he doesn't involve himself in the struggle for the throne. The tall man is only a vassal—he follows the strongest.

The woman, the boy, and the negro play a different role. Prey. Victim. Observer. They do their best to make themselves invisible.

Drops tick loudly at dusk against the metal lid on the tall man's head. He moans quietly. 'Why didn't we stay put? The good Lord gave us a village to spend the night in, a roof over our heads, but we didn't get it. We didn't listen.'

'You wanted to leave, too.' In the semi-darkness, it is the voice of the man from Ashkhabad.

'Not me! Him!'

It sounds as though a dog has been kicked. They all look at Vitaly—the tall man's hand is pointing at him. Vitaly sits motionless, his head bowed. His fit of rage earlier in the day has drained him.

The poacher appears from the tall, plumed grass. He sinks to the ground a little way from the rest. Wrapping his arms around his knees, he rests his chin on his chest. He rests like a mountain.

The tall man turns his attention to the boy. 'Show me how many apples you have. Come on, show me.'

'Idiot,' the boy says. He is poised to jump to his feet and run.

'Give me your apples, boy. I'm twice your size! What gives him the right to have as many apples as I do? I can't stand cheaters. Let him give me his apples!' He sits up a bit straighter. 'Empty your pockets, boy.'

'Over my dead body.' The boy slides back a bit farther.

The tall man moans. 'Listen to that! Listen to that, would you! What he needs is a good thumping, to beat the evil out of him.' He shuts his eyes, and sways his head back and forth like a woman in mourning. 'Almaty, oh Almaty! Father of all apples! All the apples in the world, blushing like a girl's cheeks. He'd rather see me die than give me his apples. What kind of world do we live in? Woe is me.'

The boy snorts. 'Idiot,' he says again.

In the dark, at a safe distance from the others, the boy rolls himself up in a sheet of plastic. He'd found it in a stall, one corner sticking out from under a pile of dried manure. After he pulled it out he used a stone to scrape off the dung. Then he folded it up and stuffed it into his coat.

Drops thrum against the plastic. He can't sleep; he's afraid the tall man will come and steal his apples. His eyes try to get a grip on the darkness, to drill through the blackness—silhouettes that change their shape, the motion that betrays the presence of an other.

He's alone. His heart is pounding hard. He clutches the knife, ready to lash out.

In the last blue of dusk, the man from Ashkhabad took the woman. Vitaly was too exhausted to fight for her. The boy covered his ears with his hands and kept them there for a while, but she didn't even scream once.

5

THE SECOND HALF OF THE EVENING

Pontus Beg ate his dinner. He ladled two bowls of soup from the pan, his forearms resting on the table, the television's sound turned off. He was listening to the radio—news and current affairs, sometimes music. A chunk of gristle lodged between his teeth. Without Zita around, his own house seemed unwelcoming. The ghost of abandonment breathed down his neck.

It had taken him a long time to figure out where the clenching in his innards came from, and when he finally did, it annoyed him. He didn't want to think about things that couldn't be changed. He didn't want to feel them, either. Feelings were for the happy.

Raindrops left glistening tracks down the panes. He went to the window and drew the curtains, locking out his reflection. He carried the plate and the soup bowl to the kitchen, mixed a little hot water and soap in the sink, and washed them. Long ago, when he'd viewed the contours of his farther existence, he had understood that it was vital to maintain a minimum of order in his home. He would cook for himself, eat at the table—slowly, not wolfing it down, as though Zita were watching him from beneath her heavy eyebrows—and then wash the pans, the cutlery, and the plate, and put them all away.

During his time at the police academy he had twice received a reprimand for having streaks of ash and spots of grease on his uniform. When his class was sworn in, Commander Diniz gave the speech. Yevgeni Diniz was a bastard, but his words glistened as prettily as his boots. And he knew a thing or two. He was interested in things of the mind; Beg remembered thinking that was unusual for a policeman.

That speech was the first time Beg had heard about an old Chinaman named Confucius. Confucius, if he were in charge of a country, Diniz said, would first set about rectifying the way the language was used. For if the language is incorrect, then what is said is not what is meant. And if what is said is not what is meant, no work can be accomplished. If no work is accomplished, arts and ethics cannot flourish. If they do not flourish, justice cannot be properly administered. And if there is no justice, the nation is rudderless. That is why language should not be used arbitrarily. That is what it all comes down to.

Diniz was verbose; the panoramas he presented were sweeping. That made Beg impatient. But in the train on the way to his parents' farm, he suddenly saw the veiled social criticism in his commanding officer's words. Diniz had not presented the words of the old philosopher as a warning to the young graduates, but as a comment on the state of the nation. Along the ladder of decline Confucius had sketched, this country was on the bottom rung. The only prospect was chaos. The social order had become specious, a layer of opaque ice of which one could not judge the thickness—not until you stood on it and fell through.

The nervous governmental paranoia of that day had probably overlooked the words of a Chinese sage.

Ever since then, Pontus Beg saw the model of gradual decline everywhere he looked. It started with one little thing and ended in total confusion. In every field of life, that one little thing had to be identified, isolated, and disarmed. That was why he cooked for himself every night, ate at the table every night, washed his dishes and put them away neatly—against the forces of neglect, the slippery slope, an ignominious end.

He must have died a long time ago, Diniz, or else he was off counting his buttons in an old people's flat somewhere, staring at the dull metal of his insignia.

Through him, Beg had become interested in Oriental philosophy; he read Confucius, Zhuangzi, and Lao Tse, and wasn't bothered by his inability to completely understand most of it.

Beg put the bottle on the table. The radio reported that the former minister of transport had been found dead in his dacha. He had shot himself twice in the back of the head, the newsreader said.

Beg poured himself a shot. The bottle cap rolled away across the tabletop. 'To you, Your Excellency,' he said, eyes raised to the ceiling. 'The only suicide in the world who has ever shot himself twice in the back of the head.'

There was exactly enough to do for half an evening. The day had slowed by degrees, and now came to a complete stop. The second half of the evening was a rest home where you waited stoically for your end to come. A bit put off, but without much hope of reprieve.

He drank four glasses of vodka—four glasses, no more than that. A lullaby. Part of his little order of things. Five glasses meant that he would stamp around the house on one warm and one cold foot, smoke himself hoarse, and go rifling through shoeboxes of letters and photos in search of things that no longer were. In his books, he would try to recover passages he'd marked, in search of an answer.

> The Master said: If one gets to know the Way in the morning, one can die (peacefully) at night.

Five glasses meant losing count.

He sank stiffly to his knees and looked around under the table for the bottle cap. Zita, he saw, cleaned optically, not hygienically. What did that say about the times in which he lived, when women no longer knew what cleaning was? What did it tell you about this day and age, when a man no longer said a word about that? When he only stared morosely at the spots on the carpet, the crumbs in the silverware drawer, the rings in the fridge, and the asymmetrically folded shirts in his closet? Did these things also fit the model of gradual decline?

The radio stayed on until he went to bed. He often forgot why he'd turned it on in the first place, until he turned it off. It was the high-pitched whistling in his ears—it had been with him for years. Two mosquitoes, one on either side. The sound rose up from the un-plumbed depths of his skull and was blown through shell-like con-volutions, where it took on that high frequency in a flat, constant tone that sometimes seemed to surge and ebb slowly. There were days when he forgot about it; but if things suddenly became quiet, he knew it had never gone away at all.

A Gypsy musician he'd arrested once thought it was a B.

'When I sing it, it's a lot lower than it really sounds, of course,' Beg told him.

'A C would have been better,' the Gypsy felt.

'Why's that?'

'Most songs are written in the key of C.'

It was at his mother's memorial service that he'd first heard the whis-tling. During the silent prayer, it made its way into his skull. He had listened in amazement. The tone in his inner ear soared above the singing and the benedictions, subjected all other sounds to its will, devoured them, and filled the sacred space all by itself. *It will go away in a bit*, Beg thought, and tried to concentrate on the pope's words.

'Verily, I say unto thee: if a grain of wheat falls not to the earth and does not die, it remains one grain of wheat, but when it dies it bears much fruit.'

During the Kontaktion for the Dead, he had wept. The tone un-dulated in the background. Pontus Beg left the church a forty-two-year-old orphan with a shrill peeping in his ears.

6

THE DOG OF ASHKHABAD

The Ethiopian lagged far behind the rest; at times it seemed as though they had lost him, but every evening he joined them again. He pitched camp for the night at a little distance from the others. He tore off handfuls of tough grass and arranged them on the ground in the shape of an ellipse. Then he lay down in the middle. Some of them imitated him, believing it protected them from snakes and the cold.

If they found brushwood or a lone tree, they built a fire. Then the Ethiopian would sidle up and warm his black hands.

His skin hung loosely around his frame. He had been underway since time immemorial, a skinny horse trotting along the earth's crust, his swayed ribs bedecked with a blanket of stolid despair. Along unknown paths he had come from Africa and ended up in their company. They knew almost nothing about him—only that he came from *Teaopia*, as he'd said, pointing from himself to somewhere in the distance and back again. The boy looked at him wide-mouthed; this was the first negro he had seen in real life. He had never heard of Ethiopia. The woman told him it was a country in Africa, the continent of black people.

None of them understood what the black man said. At the very start he had occasionally tried to tell them something, but no one knew what he was saying. He tried with wild gestures, making faces like a madman; the boy was afraid of him. When the black man saw that his attempts were fruitless, he gave up and stopped trying to make himself understood.

He had gradually become translucent. At the end of the day, when he showed up and scraped together the rest of the paltry meal, the others realised they had almost forgotten about him.

One time, the man from Ashkhabad saw him pull out a little chain from under his shirt. There was a tiny cross attached to it. He raised it to his lips and kissed it.

'Would you look at that,' the man from Ashkhabad said. The boy and the tall man looked.

'What's that he's eating?' the tall man asked.

'A cross.'

'Oh yeah? A cross?'

'He's *kissing* it.'

The tall man, nearsighted as could be, peered hard at the black man.

'A *cross*,' the man from Ashkhabad said. 'It's goddamn unbelievable.'

The tall man had thought he was eating something. Where did he get that from?

It was the first time the man from Ashkhabad realised that an African might adhere to a canonical faith. In his view of Africa, black people danced to make it rain. They worshipped weird objects. The Koran, the Bible, the book of the Jews—negroes were no part of that. And here you had the burrhead suddenly kissing a cross. Though the man from Ashkhabad was neither Christian nor Muslim, neither fire-worshipper nor venerator of the dead, he felt a deep disapproval— as though he had witnessed something blasphemous. Now he was forced to see this man from Ethiopia as a *person*, while until then he had seen him more as a harmless animal trailing behind the caravan, picking around between their feet for leftovers and gnawing down the hare's bones even farther than they had. (From outside the circle, they could hear the bones snap; he sucked the marrow out of them.)

The negro had kissed a cross. That only deepened the enigma. What kind of thoughts did he have? What kind of life lay behind him? And if the man from Ashkhabad had thoughts about the black man, then the black man also had thoughts about him. These things grated like sand in the works. They rattled his reason and heated his blood.

The shadows lengthened; the boy squatted and pricked up his ears to hear the man from Ashkhabad's monologue. The story of his escape.

In the life of the man from Ashkhabad, too, there had been no foreigners. The country he came from was sealed off from the world. The farther he walked away from it, the more insane seemed the place from which he'd escaped. No one came in; no one went out. His country was like a dark fairytale where the people lived under the watchful eye of an all-seeing sorcerer.

That sorcerer's name was Turkmenbashi.

The tall man rumbled in assent; he had heard of Turkmenbashi, who called himself the father of all Turkmen. He knew of his reputation.

After the decline of the Russian Empire, this minor party boss had knocked together a new omnipotence. The big brother had fallen, and the little brother copied all his bad habits and added a few of his own.

The women dressed in accordance with his code, in traditional, embroidered outfits. Like Peter the Great, he ordered the men to shave off their beards. After his heart attack, he forbade his people to smoke cigarettes any longer. His subjects were wild about gold teeth—a part of the world's gold reserves was gnashed to powder in Turkmen mouths. The father of all Turkmen forbade gold teeth for reasons of hygiene.

The country's fossil mineral resources were endless; as extremely poor as the soil was, so extremely rich were the treasures lying beneath its surface. At some spots, the ground was so saturated with oil and natural gas that flames leapt up from the soil.

Ensconced in thick pipelines, it flowed across the country's borders. From the revenues, the sorcerer made fountains spring up from the parched earth of Kara Kum, and refashioned himself in gold in the centre of Ashkhabad. His golden statue turned to follow the sun: in the morning, it greeted the east; at night, it laid the sun to sleep again in the west. The people suffered his self-aggrandisement resignedly. They grew accustomed to the daily portions of madness. They lived like fleas, with no say in the crazy gyrations of their host.

He gave new form not only to the daily lives of his subjects, but also to their imaginings. All imaginings—national, cultural, historical, and, ultimately, personal.

One day, the man from Ashkhabad developed an itch, locally at first, on his shoulders. In the mirror he saw red circles. They spread steadily, until his upper body was covered in them. He scratched, and watched the flakes rain down slowly on the sink. He scratched without stopping. At first, he held himself in check when others were around, but soon abandoned all shame and scratched in company as well. He groaned quietly as he did so. In the garage at the bus company where he worked, they joked about him. They called him 'the last dog of Ashkhabad'—Turkmenbashi, after all, had banished all dogs from the capital. The itching took over his life completely. Now there were two things from which he could not escape: the eyes of the father of all Turkmen that followed him everywhere, and the raging itch that covered his torso.

He scratched his skin till it bled. He rubbed himself with salve, and when that didn't help he was given pills. The red circles withdrew, but didn't disappear—at best, they bothered him less for a time. The cuts healed, and his skin was bedecked with pale scar tissue. But after a few weeks, the circles reappeared and he was cast back into the hell of hideous itching. He let his nails grow, the better to scratch himself with.

At the hospital, the doctor gnawed on his pen; this mysterious resistance was beyond his competence. Then he remembered a patient who had been cured of something similar after taking salt baths in the bay at Kara Bogaz.

Kara Bogaz!

It was like sending someone to the ends of the earth! Kara Bogaz—a lagoon containing the most highly saline water on earth.

In commiseration, he looked at the man who sat there scratching himself and moaning quietly, and felt that he could not keep from him this unscientific bit of advice.

To the west of Ashkhabad, far away along the Caspian coast, lies the mysterious bay called Kara Bogaz, the Black Maw. A saline waterfall there funnels the waters of the Caspian into its shallow basin. Under the relentless desert sun, the water in the bay evaporates almost as quickly as it can be replenished. The salt that precipitates to the bottom is called Glauber's salt, after the German chemist who discovered its laxative properties.

This miracle salt will eat clean the skin of the man from Ashkhabad.

He receives a transit pass to Kara Bogaz. His file is marked with the comment that he has one week's leave of absence, for 'medical' reasons.

The bus plods westward as the yellow heat of the Kara Kum conjures up shimmering ponds on the asphalt. The chauffeur drives with his shirt unbuttoned, and shouts to be heard above the engine's howl. 'Kara Bogaz? There's nothing out there, colleague!'

The man from Ashkhabad would rather keep his thoughts empty and stare out the window at the semi-arid landscape as it glides past, but finds himself obliged to listen to stories about salt storms. It started twenty, twenty-five years ago, when the level of the Caspian suddenly dropped. The best minds in science searched for the cause, and when they found none, the bay at Kara Bogaz was singled out as the thief of the seawater that roared through that narrow channel into the gigantic basin.

The thief was punished: the bay was dammed. The evaporation basin could no longer feed itself on seawater. The hydraulic engineers' prognoses, based on solid calculations, were that it would take about twenty years for the bay to dry up.

The bay dried up after two years.

The metres-thick layer of salt at the bottom of the bowl blew away, carried hundreds of kilometres inland by the wind. The soil became saline, as a lashing rain of salt cut a swath of destruction across the land. The powder glistened on the fields, settled on the leaves of the cotton plants, and ruined the harvests.

When the empire of the Bolsheviks fell, the dam was breached.

The water returned to its former shores.

The driver looked over at his passenger, who was scratching himself.

Still, the itch had already diminished, the man from Ashkhabad noted in surprise, as though it were keeping a low profile at the mere prospect of a concentration of salt high enough to sink ships.

• • •

The chapped earth lay motionless beneath the steely sun. The bus pulled over to the side of the road. The chauffeur walked out a ways onto the flat, planted his feet far apart, and pissed in the dust.

'Four more hours,' he said as he climbed back in.

The bus would go no farther than the port town of Turkmenbashi, formerly known as Krasnovodsk. The next day, the man from Ashkhabad would have to find a bus or taxi willing to take him to Cape Bekdash, the smattering of houses close to Kara Bogaz. With a grunt and a groan, the driver slid his backside onto the seat of faded towels.

Farther along they came to a roadblock, and a policeman entered the bus. The man from Ashkhabad handed him his pass. The driver leaned over inquisitively in his seat.

'Kara Bogaz?' the policeman asked.

The other man nodded.

'Here . . . what does this say?'

The man from Ashkhabad looked. 'Medical reasons,' he said. 'Medical reasons,' the policeman said. His silence lasted a few moments. Then he said: 'There's no hospital there. Not at Kara Bogaz.'

'It's my skin. The salt water will heal my skin.'

The itching started again. It felt as though he were rolling through an anthill. The sensation eclipsed his thoughts. He clenched his teeth and forced his hands to stay where they were; if he started scratching now, it would look like he was attacking himself.

Every destination, every movement, became preposterous under the uniformed man's sharp eye. Why do you have to go *there*? What objective could be important enough to put you on the road in this heat? Why didn't you stay where you were? What business could you possibly have going there?

The policeman wiped the sweat from his forehead. His suspicion ebbed, making way for a lack of interest.

Twilight was settling in. Onwards, always westward, the bus went. The open windows let in whiffs of coolness. Copper mountains loomed up forlornly, one by one, from the desert floor. Purple light entered at the windows; a dull section of moon was already floating on the horizon. There, too, were the lights of the port town, sparkling in the royal-blue evening. Its presence comforted him; the traveller breathed calmly, in and out.

At the bus station, the concrete exhaled the heat of the day. Spilt oil gleamed under the neon lights, and the man from Ashkhabad left the station and walked along the dusty shoulder into town. At Pension Buchara, he checked in for the night. Arms crossed behind his head, he lay on his bed and stared at the reflections of streetlights and the play of passing cars on the ceiling. Only when the girls and their sailors stopped stumbling through the hallway did he fall asleep.

The next morning, he strolled along the quay, ate watermelon, and was in no hurry to reach Kara Bogaz. He had heard that an unwholesome, sulphurous mist hung over the lagoon, that the salt deposits glistened so brightly that they blinded you; neither man nor animal held out long there.

He was in no hurry. For the first time in ages, the itching had receded.

Ships lay at anchor off the coast. The sea was in a haze; the ships seemed sketched by a faltering hand. Closer by, too, other ships were moored at piers that reached far out to sea, their names rusting. He looked at them from up close, and he looked at them from afar. A few cranes were still operating. Ladings floated through the air. A plan took shape behind his eyes—a daring deed, born in the hours that he sat in the shade at quayside, ate watermelon, and dreamed of the far shore.

As soon as a guard left his post on deck, he would slip aboard one of the ships. He would disappear down the first hatch he came across and only reappear in a port far from here. He would take along bread and water and remain hidden until they reached a far shore. He would mislay himself, roll away like a coin between the tiles, and never be found again. That's what he would do. Vanish himself into thin air.

That was how he reached Baku.

7

THE LAST JEW

The rabbi left his home covered in a sheet, relieved of all cares. The question now was how they were to bury him. You couldn't simply stuff a rabbi into a hole in the ground, could you? His wife had been lying in the Jewish cemetery at Smogy for the last twenty years, their only daughter having emigrated to Israel long ago. No one knew how to find her, to inform her of her father's death.

'So how do you even know she exists?' Pontus Beg asked police sergeant Françiçek Koller.

'The cleaning lady,' Koller said.

'Her name?'

Koller flipped through his notepad. 'Valeria Belenko.'

'The daughter's name, man.'

Koller's eyes skittered across his notes. 'Ariëlla Herz.'

'No other kin?'

'Nope.'

'No address book? Envelopes with a return address?'

'Maybe Yiri could take a look?'

'Tell him to come back with an address for that daughter, and a phone number. And tell him to find someone who knows how to bury a Jew.'

Koller shook his head. 'The cleaning lady said there aren't any left. No one has come to the synagogue for years. He was the last Jew around here.'

Koller, a bit amazed, watched his own words go.

Beg gestured to him that he was dismissed. He spun his chair around and looked outside. His window looked out onto a blank wall, and, if he craned his neck a bit, onto an airspace between the houses that admitted a view of the street. The opening was so narrow that you saw pedestrians only for a moment—a flash—and then they were gone again. Zhuangzi had said: 'The life of men between heaven and earth is like a ray of light falling through a chink in the wall: a moment, and then it is gone.'

Beg enjoyed Zhuangzi's cheerful anarchism, but when searching for direction he fell back on Confucius. The Taoists were troublesome folk, slippery, fleeting as fumes. Confucius was more a man of structure and order; he provided a toehold. Respect for the aged, the rituals and the Way, and his love of the right word: sometimes Beg truly regretted that he wasn't living in China in the days of the Master.

He drummed his fingers on the table. There was, he was sure of it, another synagogue in town. He hummed a melody from his boyhood, a song his mother had taught him. Astride the melody, the words came back. He murmured them without knowing exactly what they meant; he thought maybe it was a Jewish love song. It was about a girl named Rebecca. *'Ay, Rivkele, ven es veln zayn royzn, veln zey bliyen.'*

Lots of things from the past were returning to him lately. His childhood was so much closer than in all those years before.

He picked up the phone. 'Oksana, tell Koller there's another synagogue, on Polanen Street. There must be someone there who knows how to bury a Jew.'

The roads glistened at dusk beneath the lamps as he drove away from the station house. Polanen Street was only a little out of his way, so he decided not to wait for Koller.

It was a broad, quiet street—well-to-do citizens had built big houses for themselves here, long ago. The stained-glass windows above some of the doors were still intact; the influence of the Vienna Secession had reached as far as Michailopol.

The Lada creaked so loudly when he climbed out, the whole street could hear it. He deserved a car that didn't creak so much, he figured. After thirty-four years on the force, he had a right to better. Of course, he could commandeer a confiscated vehicle. Some colleagues did that—they drove around in rigs that had belonged to serious felons. He noticed reticence in himself, though, a certain prudishness. The people didn't need to have it rubbed in, that which they already knew: that crime *did* pay. That even a policeman was dependent on it if he wanted to drive a fairly presentable car.

He found himself standing before a tall, green door. There was no bell. He pounded on it with the flat of his hand. He looked around: the street was covered in a grey mist. The plane trees reached for the sky with their bare, pale arms. The dim taillight of a car vanished around the corner.

Beg entered the alleyway beside the building, where he found trolleys and trash barrels, and the back door of an Asian restaurant. Through a metal register, he could hear the clatter of pans. At the end of the alley, where darkness had already settled in, he discovered the service entrance to the synagogue. Something was written in Hebrew on a scrap of paper taped to the door. Again, there was no bell, and no mail slot, either. He took the steps and pounded loudly on the door. The building seemed hermetically sealed. The life of the Jews took place in concealment, in a shadow world, far from that of the others. Was the building still in use? Or were there indeed no more Jews in Michailopol?

When an old man opened the door, Beg moved down a step.

'Can I help you?' the man said.

'Beg,' he said. 'Police commissioner. Could I come in?'

The old man eyed him for a moment, then stepped back into the corridor. 'Enter.'

They sat down at a table in the little kitchen. The old man's blue-veined hand trembled as he put down the steamy glasses of tea. He had introduced himself as Zalman Eder; he was the rabbi. His grey beard was streaked with something that had the colour of nicotine.

'I'm here about Rabbi Herz,' Beg said.

'What about him?'

'You heard about his death?'

Zalman Eder nodded.

'You knew him?'

'More or less.'

That was all; apparently, he felt no need to explain farther.

'Do you know whether he still has relatives here, or friends?' Beg asked. 'The problem is . . . he has to be buried. The undertaker has to do *something*.'

'You know . . .' the rabbi said then, shaking his head slowly. 'Yehuda Herz and I . . . we didn't really get along.'

When nothing else came, Beg asked: 'For any particular reason, or . . . ?'

'Not for no particular reason. Nothing is for no particular reason.' The rabbi sipped his tea, seemingly without scalding his mouth. Then he said: 'He was a bad person. I'm glad he's dead.'

Startled, Beg asked: 'Yehuda Herz?'

'A heretic. His soul was leaky as a sieve. Now he'll finally hear that from God himself.'

Beg had imagined that an old rabbi like Zalman Eder would be a wise man, a father leading his people through the wilderness, not a vindictive old Jew who cursed other people's souls.

He asked whether services were still held in the synagogue.

'There's no one here anymore,' the rabbi said. 'Only me.'

His eyes were set far back in his skull, and his eyebrows bristled every which way. When he looked up, the washed-out blue of his eyes lit up for a moment.

Beg asked himself what could make one Jew welcome the death of another. The world never ceased to amaze him.

'I'm the last one,' the rabbi said, 'and I won't be around much longer, either.'

Beg dabbed his finger at nonexistent crumbs on the tabletop.

'Why didn't some humane doctor cut off my breath as soon as I came into the world?' the rabbi said. 'Who am I that God should demand this of me? Who's going to say kaddish for me? Who will remember me?'

His head sunk even deeper between his shoulders. The old turtle was withdrawing. 'But that's not what you're here for.'

'No.'

'You're here for Herz.'

'Yes.'

'Where is he now, the old fraud?'

In two days' time, they agreed, Eder would preside over Yehuda Herz's funeral. That was much too late, according to Eder: a dead Jew should be buried immediately, but necessity knows no law. It would have to be an improvised service in more ways than one, for there hadn't been a Jewish undertaker around here for a long time, either.

Finally, Beg asked the rabbi whether he perhaps knew the song that had popped into his mind that morning.

'Rivkele?' the rabbi said. 'I don't know any Rivkele.'

'No, a *song* about Rivkele,' Beg said.

'Why do you ask?'

Beg shrugged. 'We used to sing it at home. I thought maybe you would know what it's about, because I have no idea.'

'What song was it again?'

Hesitantly, Beg spoke the first line, the words whose meaning he didn't know. '*Ay, Rivkele, ven es veln zayn royzn, veln zey bliyen.*'

'Louder! I can't hear you!'

Beg repeated the words.

'And the melody?' the old man asked. 'Sing it—maybe then I'll recognise it.'

And so it happened that Pontus Beg sang a Yiddish song for the old rabbi.

'Good! Very good!' The old man crowed with pleasure. 'You should keep practising—you've got talent!'

Beg lowered his eyes. Even his nails and his hair felt embarrassed.

'Do you know what you're singing? "O Rebecca, if there are roses, they will be in flower . . ." A love song.'

He showed Beg to the door. The low, darkened corridors smelled of wet gypsum. Faint electric light shone on the walls. Beg thought he could still see the smoked cones left on the ashen plasterwork by old tallow candles. For more than two hundred years, with a few black-bordered interludes, this building had served as a house of prayer—and the final guardian, a love song on his lips, was leading him to the exit.

8

THE COMFORTER

They trudged in single file, heads bowed, eyes dull and unseeing. Once they had looked expectantly to the horizon, towards the land of hopes beyond that, but their gaze was drawn away less and less frequently now, until it no longer rose from the ground before their feet.

When the tall man fell, he blinked his eyes in amazement, as though he'd been tripped. The boy walked past him.

'Help me out, would you?' the tall man panted. 'You can have my shoes. Okay?'

But the boy walked on, a fathomless contempt in his eyes.

One by one, the others passed him. He looked up at them like a dying animal.

'Hey,' he said weakly, 'wait a minute.'

Their eyes swept over his body in search of what might still be useful. The shoes. His coat. His sweater full of holes. It was growing colder all the time.

Was he himself the one who had once robbed a laggard, the tall man thought with wavering conviction. So long ago now . . . so far away, as though it was someone else . . . he had twisted the man's head forcefully to one side as the others stripped the clothes from his body and ransacked his pockets. He had pressed his hand so hard against the man's mouth that he had felt the false teeth break.

That was how they looked at him now, too. As prey.

He tried to regain his footing, but his legs were so heavy. Heavier than they'd ever been, even though they were so thin.

Is this the end of me, is this what it looks like? he thought. A picture from a great height: his skin, his flesh, how it slowly became an impression in the sand, half-eaten by animals, half soaked into the earth; his bones being spread out over the steppe.

The place where he lay amazed him. Sand and tough, yellow grass; random as rain. This was how others died. He smelled the wet earth, his grave.

They had all left home on their own. Chance had brought them together; no one was responsible for anyone else. As long as you could walk, you belonged to the group; as long as you could walk, you made the group stronger. If the group had to care for its individual members, it weakened. Altruism would be the death of it. Strict self-interest improved the chances of survival. The boy, too, had understood that intuitively. He had walked past others before; he had remained deaf to the pleas, the shrieks behind him.

Sometimes there were little acts of mercy—quick, almost secretive, exceptions. Irrational. Unwise. The group disapproved of such breaches of naked self-preservation.

Panting, the tall man's breath went in and out. The killing thirst. A primal memory of pain, when his whole being was a soundless scream for his mother, for reassurance. *My sweet boy*, she cooed, *my sweet Mischa, where have you ended up this time? I can't help you like this, can I? You're alone, Mischa, alone.*

A hand brushed his arm. He smiled through his tears. So she had come anyway . . . she hadn't left him . . . so long ago, his dear mother, such an eternity.

He opened his eyes to see her.

Standing over him was the Ethiopian.

The tall man groaned in misery. He was pulled up by one arm to a sitting position. He feared the black man's intentions. He wouldn't put up a fight. He would simply close his eyes to the harm the other would do him.

The Ethiopian took a weathered blue bottle from his bag. He unscrewed the cap and pressed the opening to the tall man's lips. The coolness of stone. Water dribbled into his mouth.

'*Maj*,' the black man said, and poured another trickle into his mouth.

'More,' the tall man said.

'*Maj*,' the black man said again. The tall man repeated it after him—*maj, maj*.

He took the bottle from his hand and drank greedily of the earthy-tasting water. When it was finished, he could smell the black man: his stale sweat, his bodily fat, and the spoiled smell that rises from an empty stomach. They had never been this close before. He felt shame and gratitude.

He tried to stand up, but sank back in the dust. His fingers tingled; his vision swirled before his eyes.

The Ethiopian's hand disappeared into his satchel again. It reappeared, holding a miracle: a rusty can. Beans . . . goulash . . . it could be anything—the label was gone. He must have found it in the village, during his foray through the houses. The tall man couldn't keep his eyes off the can. A can of food. A treasure. Perverse riches.

The black man knelt. He held the can between his knees and struck it with the point of a rock. He dented the can, but couldn't open it. The agony was unbearable. The tall man leaned back and slipped his knobby, yellowed fingers into his pocket. Slowly, he righted himself again and handed his knife to the Ethiopian. Now he could murder him with his own weapon. The thought glistened behind his eyes for a moment, and then disappeared.

The tip of the knife bored its way into the flimsy can. Gouging and cutting, the blade ate its way through, revealing the jagged metal edge of the lid. The tall man leaned forward. He wanted to see what was in it—he would have yanked it out of the Ethiopian's hands if he'd been able to. When the hole was big enough, the black man bent up the edges. Now they took turns poking their fingers into the can, and ladling out the jellied substance. It had a vague taste of meat bouillon. They gobbled it down, licked their bleeding fingers, and scraped the remains from the sides and bottom. When the can was completely clean, their eyes met, big and charged, as though they were coming to their senses after having committed some ecstatic crime.

He shared his food with me, the tall man thought, *all the food he had. He is a great and noble person. He has a heart like a whale. I'm not worthy to see the light in his eyes.*

His bottom lip quaked, and tears ran down his face. The Ethiopian had shown him the light of his soul, a bright light; he felt how it had crossed over to him, the way you light one candle with another. He covered his eyes with his hands and sobbed. Once in his lifetime, a person weeps because he sees through himself completely. Once in his life, he weeps because he knows he is beyond salvation.

The black man put the can back in his satchel and looked around. He didn't seem to notice the other man's fit of weeping. He stood up and checked his pockets. The food had done him good; he blinked contentedly at the huge, black clouds over the steppes.

He licked the knife and held it out to the tall man, who snatched it out of his hand.

When the tall man awoke with a start from the delirious ravings of his dreams and looked up at the white moon, he prayed that his tribulations might end here. It had rained a bit, and the moon hung motionless behind thin, restless tatters of cloud. His gratitude towards the black man turned to poisonous resentment. He was ashamed of his thoughts, but could not shoo them away. Within the space of a few hours he had prayed to live on and he had prayed to die—it was between those polar extremes that he drifted, his long legs in a splits between living and dying. But he did not die; not yet.

Around him lay the things he had scavenged during the long journey—the metal lid, his helmet of rusty mesh, a long stick that he leaned on and that he had decorated clumsily with his knife. He leaned on it when he rose to his feet, his bones stiff and aching from the cold. The black man lay a few metres away in his circle of grass, his hands folded on his chest like a vanquished knight. He took a few steps. A crack of red light crawled onto the edge of the world; in surprise, he noted that he had come back to life.

With his stick, he poked the Ethiopian in the side. The black man had been to a wedding party in his dreams: whooping men had ridden horses into the big tent, women clapped and sang, he was happy in the scented smoke of the fire, and he had eaten as much as he wanted. He didn't want to get up at all—he just wanted to lie there, where those things had come flying to him on weightless wings.

The tall man followed the trail, half obliterated by the rain. He was carrying only his little backpack. Everything else—the objects that had protected him from the rain, the flies, and the evil—had been left behind. He shuffled ahead, the grass crunching beneath his feet. He leaned heavily on his stick, no longer trusting his legs.

As he dragged himself across the steppe, the gadflies of his thoughts stung him. He owed his life to a pariah, to a man who existed at the edge of the group. Their lifelines had crossed and become hopelessly entangled. A debt had been placed on his skinny shoulders. The pale sun climbed in the sky behind him. There, too, somewhere, was the man to whom he owed his life. He did not look back.

9

THE BROKEN JUG

Yehuda Herz is being buried on a cold, dry day; beside the grave is a mound of loose sand. A little farther along, on a bench beneath a willow tree, the pallbearers sit smoking and talking quietly. From far away comes the crack of a hunter's rifle.

The Jewish cemetery lies east of town. It is surrounded by low poplars. The wind blows through the branches, producing a soft hissing that does not disturb the silence. Here the Jews have buried their dead since time immemorial, on a plot of ground that once lay on the steppe far outside the city. Meanwhile the apartment buildings have advanced on it, pushing out in front of them a flood of kitchen gardens, sheds, and trailers.

Pontus Beg couldn't come up with a good reason to attend Herz's funeral, but he went anyway. Perhaps, he told himself, he felt beholden to Zalman Eder. It was at his request, after all, that the rabbi was now murmuring prayers of which Beg understood not a word. His caftan crinkled in the wind.

The coffin lay atop a pair of crossbeams, soon to be lowered.

Loneliness three times over, Beg thought. A dead Jew, a living Jew, and a policeman with one cold foot and a peeping in his ears. In the distance, a tractor edged across the fields. Gulls and crows lit down in the furrows.

The tall, grey stones threw thin shadows. The mason's chisel had hacked out texts in Hebrew, German, and Russian. Most of the gravestones were ancient; some of them leaned crookedly.

Beg shifted his weight from one foot to the other. As he peered through his lashes, the pile of sand beside the grave looked like a sleeping bear. His mother's maiden name was Medved—Russian for 'bear.' The wind blew a tear from his eye. He wiped it away.

He had seen countless dead, but still he was awed by the feeling that the distance between him and the dead was as great as it was negligible. He had pulled frozen hoboes from the street, alcoholics who had drunk themselves to death, victims of violent impact with a blunt object (the coroner's jargon, not his), and the old and lonely who were found dead in their homes. Every dead person he saw, he regarded as a preparation for his own death—the crossing of the final border.

The rabbi held out his shaky hands. He invoked heaven, compassion, mercy. This fallible being, too, was a child of God; this person, broken like a jug.

The bearers rose to their feet, a disorderly troupe. Only when they approached the grave did the ceremonial descend into their movements. At the pit, each of them took one end of a rope. The beams were pulled away; the ropes stood taut. Slowly, the coffin floated into the depths, the tassels of Herzl's prayer robe sticking out the sides.

'But go thou thy way till the end be: for thou shalt rest, and stand in thy lot at the end of days.'

Beg bent down stiffly and tossed a few spades of sand onto the coffin.

The rabbi wandered slowly amid the graves. Sometimes he stopped beside a stone. Mendel Kanner. Alexander Manasse.

He's taking a walk through the past, thought Beg, a few steps behind him. *He's visiting his friends.* The grass was high; the steppe had advanced to between the graves.

Zalman Eder turned to look over his shoulder. 'I'll be the next to go. At home in the house of the living.'

A few rows before the end, he stopped again. 'My wife, blessed be her memory,' he said, pointing at the stone in front of him. 'This is where I will lie. Remember that, if you please.' He laughed quietly, raspingly.

Edzi Bogen, born at Lemberg.

The rabbi picked up a pebble and laid it on the stone.

They walked to the exit and closed the gate behind them, beneath the trees full of the whispers of souls left behind.

Beg drove him back to Polanen Street. Questions about this mysterious Judaism were on the tip of his tongue—Why had he placed a pebble on his wife's gravestone? Why did he lead such a reclusive life?—but the rabbi sat beside him in silence, his hands folded in his lap. It seemed unbecoming to question him.

As they drove past the old train station, the rabbi suddenly said: 'You're a policeman . . .'

Beg looked over at him.

'You see the filth of the world,' Eder went on. 'Something else every day, I suppose. New things. The world is full of them. New things. The filth. You wallow in them, that's your job. But what do you do to cleanse yourself of the world's filth? How do you get clean again?'

Beg shrugged. 'Questions like that . . . maybe we try not to ask ourselves.'

'What a load of rubbish! Questions like that come up in any sensible mind, whether you like it or not.'

'If there's an answer . . .' Beg said, 'the answer should be, if you're completely honest, that some filth can't be washed away. It sticks to you. It doesn't go away.'

The girl—this was the second time today he'd thought about her. She'd been found that spring, in a ditch beside the road. She had broken bones, she'd been beaten or thrown out of a car—the extent of the decomposition made it hard to be sure. All they knew was that her body, before or after death, had been subject to violence.

She'd been carrying a little backpack. There were pictures between the pages of her diary. They'd found socks, panties, and a bra in her baggage, along with a blue singlet and articles of toiletry. She had been travelling in summer. Maybe she'd been hitchhiking; in her diary, they also found tickets to a rock concert. There was no wallet or ID, so they were unable to identify her. She was between seventeen and twenty-five, the coroner estimated. A few cockled photos (wet and then dried up again) showed a girl whom they assumed was her.

One of those pictures had been used for the flyers they'd posted, asking for information. No one ever responded. She had been in a drawer in the morgue for six months now. If no one came for her, she would be buried the next spring.

The face in the photograph was oval, with prominent cheekbones. Nordic. Her pale-blue eyes looked straight into the world, with the confidence of one who believes that something good and special is in store for her. Beg projected that face onto the dead girl, whose own face had turned black and been eaten away by small predators.

Sometimes he went awhile without thinking of her, and then came a period when she was in his thoughts often. With the dead it was just like with the living; some of them stayed with you; others, you forgot.

Whenever he was in the morgue, Beg would knock on the drawer bearing the label anonymous woman, to let her know that he hadn't forgotten her.

The girl they'd found only captured his interest when he saw the contents of her backpack spread out on the table before him. There was something carefree about it that touched him: the little diary, her minimal baggage. He studied it for a while, even though he wasn't directly involved in the case. He could see her hitchhiking. She trusts the people whose car she climbs into. She has always, in some mysterious way, felt protected, certain that she would be spared. She is free; each day she travels down another road.

The pages of her diary were wet, and much of the ink had run. The words that were still legible spoke of her love for a boy named Yuri, of the death of her grandmother, of her worries about the world. Beg thought she was probably closer to seventeen than to twenty-five.

The suggestion of prostitution was one he'd rejected out of hand— they would have found condoms, vaginal spray, different underwear.

He waited there until Zalman Eder disappeared through the door at the end of the alleyway. Was that where he lived, beside the synagogue? And how did he live, the old man? In his imagination, Beg saw him kneeling in an empty and shadowy house of prayer, wan-

dering through the corridors at night in search of the world that had
passed away from him.

Beg was on the night shift. Oksana brought in takeaway. He stared
out the window, at the narrow passageway between two walls that
was his view; the blueness there was deepening. Oksana popped the
top off a bottle of beer and took the lids off the plastic containers. On
a plate, she arranged a landscape of noodles, meat, and vegetables.

'Why do they say that a pig is an unclean animal, anyway?' Beg
asked, half sunk in thought.

Oksana looked up, the serving spoon poised in midair. 'Who says
that?'

'The Jews. Muslims, too.'

'Ach.'

'No idea?'

'No . . . no.'

'Me neither. Why would God create an unclean animal?'

Oksana stuck the spoon into the sauce and ladled it out over the
noodles. 'My mother always says that when it comes to God, you
shouldn't ask why.'

'Why not?'

'Ha ha.'

Beg said: 'There's nothing about a pig that . . . We had pigs at home . . .'

Oksana looked at him, but he didn't go on about his memories
of the pigs on the other side of the fence, those patient creatures, so
much friendlier and more expressive than most humans. That he had
felt like screaming whenever they had hung one of them from a beam
by its hind legs, cut its throat, and let it bleed to death in a rusty basin.
But his voice had vanished.

10

COLD ASHES

The Ethiopian stopped and pointed. He saw the others, still far away, little and sharply outlined like fidgety letters on a sheet of paper. They were shuffling on across the steppe. The tall man peered in the direction where the finger pointed, but saw nothing. Thirst foamed in his mouth. He gestured that he needed to take a rest; leaning on his stick, he sank slowly to the ground. Exhaustion had made an old man of him. He kept his eyes closed, sinking away into the darkness behind his eyelids, blissfully slipping out of the world.

A smack. He opened his eyes with a start—the black man was squatting down, leaning forward with a stone in his hand. He had crushed a lizard. He crept over to the tall man on hands and knees, and held out his hand. The tall man gave him his knife. Mumbling to himself, the Ethiopian cut open the reptile's belly and scraped out the yellow intestines. He wiped the blade on his pants and gave the knife back. The lizard he slipped into his coat pocket. Then he went and squatted again, a little farther away this time, the stone poised.

To get one, you had to be fast. First, you had to remain motionless till the blood stopped in your veins, and then you had to pounce like lightning. The tall man had never succeeded at it. The black man was good, though; the poacher and the boy were, too. They knew how to wait—to see the little animal coming closer, its tongue flickering in and out, the pounding of its heart visible through the skin, the fleshy lids sliding down over its eyes—and then to strike.

This was a little one, not much use to them. You had to get the big ones, a few of them.

The tall man had a pleasant daydream—a big fire, fat hissing in the flames. Never before had he lived with such ease in two worlds, crossed so quickly from the world where his body was painful and his thoughts desperate to the domain of the dream, delirious and happy.

The black man walked behind him, as though to nudge him along, the macerated hermit of old. He hummed a simple, repetitive melody like a prayer.

Three lizards, that's what the black man had caught. Now his gaze was shifting around in search of fuel. He stuffed blown-away plastic in his pockets. When wrapped around a stick, plastic burned quickly; you could use it to get wet wood going.

A few times they had found low trees amid the hollows, most of them dead. In the parched bushes, the undergrowth, the poacher trapped birds and hamsters. When they moved on later, they were hung about with wood, gnarled branches, and trunks—bizarre camouflage.

Now the group had split apart. Out in front went the others: the man from Ashkhabad, Vitaly, the poacher, the boy, and the woman. They would try to catch up with them. He and the black man had agreed wordlessly on that. Instinctively. The dangers of the wilderness seemed greater than those of the group.

Long ago they had heard wolves. They'd never seen them, only found their spoor the next day. On a few nights the wolves had circled their camp, they'd shivered at the prolonged howling, the growling and yelping just beyond their field of vision. The poacher said that they were little wolves, that they had little to fear as long as they stayed together.

Now each of them knew what his fate would be if he fell by the wayside. No one wanted to lag behind.

The tall man felt light in the head; he had dizzy spells. The other one gave him some water, and waited until he could move on. He always wanted more, but was no longer allowed to hold the bottle.

They walked until it grew dark and the footprints dissolved before their eyes. On the ground, the black man spread the plastic sheet he used to catch rainwater with. Pointy sticks held the corners on high, and the water collected in the middle.

He built a little fire and drove a sharpened stick through the lizards. He turned them over and over above the flames until their skin turned black. The meat on the inside was white. The charcoaled skin crackled between their teeth. They ate them up, from head to tail.

The tall man looked at his hands in mild surprise, as though wondering where his portion had gone so quickly. The hunger growled in his stomach. He watched the black man eat. Even his lips were black. He was sunk in thought, his face shining in the glow of the low flames. Scars seemed to have been chiselled into his skin. The black man was a human like him, only it seemed as though the being-human had expressed itself with a difference, like that between a donkey and a horse.

His desperate gratitude had shrivelled, so that in the hidden place of his thoughts the black man had become more and more a personal servant, a slave; a haze of injustice hung around the last half-lizard he had kept for himself.

The malformation of his thoughts went creepingly. Yes, the black man fed him, but because he also took his own share, he was to blame for there not being enough left over. The black man helped him move along and supported him when he could go no farther, but that also meant he was to blame for the way his earthly suffering dragged on. Gratitude and hateful contempt chased each other like minnows at the bottom of a pool.

How could he bear the black man's self-sacrifice? How could you come to terms with owing your life to someone? How could you acquit yourself of that debt?

The flames sank slowly into the ashes; the wood and plastic were almost consumed. The black man thrust the sharpened stick among the coals, and a flame leapt up. He cleared his throat and spat. The gob shrivelled and hissed in the embers.

In the light of the silent, white moon, the tall man awoke. He held his breath and listened—what had awakened him? He stuck his head out from under the plastic. The earth smelled of rain. Slowly he rose to his feet; the cold had crept into his bones.

The black man was asleep in his circle of grass. The tall man crept toward the plastic sheet; the moon glistened in the black water. Quietly, he dropped to his knees. He pulled down a corner of the sheet, so that the water flowed to one side. His lips to the plastic, he drank the sweet, cold water until it was almost gone. He swept away his tracks as he went back, and slipped into his lair. Only when the pounding of his heart died down did he close his eyes.

At first light, they were already on their way to follow the thread that the darkness had severed. The tall man saw the faded footsteps that the others had left behind in the sand; behind him, the black man let the paltry remains of rainwater flow into the bottle. A cold, white mist hung over the land.

By midday, they had found the others' camp: a little ring of blackened stones and the loose sand where their bodies had lain. They were catching up to them.

The black man sank to his knees and ran his fingers through the pale ashes. He sifted out the coals and put them in his pocket.

They followed the tracks. Perhaps they would find them before nightfall. So badly did they want to join up with them, they forgot how weak their position in the group was.

Later on, it rained. The tall, yellow tufts of grass seemed to give off a gentle light beneath the rolling grey clouds. The black man stuck out his tongue as he walked to catch some rain. He seemed refreshed and cheerful. Sometimes he spoke to the other man. The tall man shrugged, and the negro repeated his words more loudly this time, his yellow eyes fixed on him.

The tall man shook his head sadly. It was useless—they would never understand each other.

The black man had tried to tell him something about the journey, he thought, something about the weather or the can of food they'd devoured together. How could it be anything else? Who thought about anything else? The journey left no room for other thoughts. They had become people without a history, living only in an immediate present.

II

—

WHOOSH

Beg had gone to his dacha, seventy kilometres outside town, to ready the cottage for the winter; he spread a few last barrows of manure over the garden plots, covered the well, and screwed the shutters over the windows. He enjoyed gardening. Sometimes he thought of himself as a landless farmer. As soon as he could, he left town to prune the roses and bind up the grapevines along the side of the house.

Now he was driving home in the dark. It would be spring before he went back again. A crate of bell peppers was on the back seat. On top of old newspapers lay the last of the pumpkins, muddy and over-grown.

Approaching an intersection, he slowed. The places they lay in wait were predictable enough—and indeed, on the far side of the road was a police cruiser, hidden behind the low stand of trees. Beg crossed the road and pulled up beside it.

The patrolman climbed out, and Beg rolled down his window.

'Commissioner,' the man said. He dropped his cigarette.

'Everything in order?'

'Certainly, certainly. Quiet. A quiet evening.' A final plume of smoke escaped his lips.

'Nothing special?'

'No . . . nothing really. Quiet.'

More than anything else, his subordinates liked to hand out fines along the road. It was how they collected their take; it was their eas-iest source of income. Since the arrival of laser guns they were able to justify their extra earnings with technological precision. No one could claim any longer that they were making things up. It was there for everyone to see—digits told no lies.

'Playing the lonesome whore' was what they called this aspect of their profession, for that's how it looked as they stood beneath a streetlight, monitoring traffic.

Beg had stopped doing that when he became police inspector, long ago. With a rank like his, it was unseemly, standing there in that dome of artificial light carved out in the endless spaces of the steppes.

A policeman had been gunned down once during a speed check. They found him along the side of the road, more dead than alive. His colleagues visited him at the clinic. He was deaf and blind, he reacted to nothing. Their eyes were constantly drawn to the hole where his nose had been.

He haunted their thoughts whenever they stood along a darkened road.

Beg had prohibited his men from setting up speed traps on their own—a rule everyone ignored. You collected more when you were alone.

Whenever one of the colleagues had a birthday, a standard joke made the rounds.

'What are we going to give him?' one of them would ask.

'A microwave,' the others would say.

'He's already got that.'

'So a flatscreen.'

'Has one.'

'A new cell phone?'

'Got that.'

'What about a day off?'

In unison: 'He'd never forgive us for that!'

There were variations on the theme, but that's what it always boiled down to.

When Beg realised that he was quietly singing to himself the song about Rebekka and the roses, he clenched his teeth and turned on the car radio. Why had his mother taught him a Jewish song? He couldn't ask her anymore. The song was so much a part of the obvious in his life that only now, at the age of fifty-three, did he ask himself how it had ended up among his belongings. He had an older sister who might know, but they'd lost contact a long time ago. She, too, had once belonged to the obvious things in his life—until one day they'd had an argument that was never laid aside, and the many years that had slipped in between had rendered the silence permanent.

Far out in front of him was a truck. Beg looked at the speedometer. He was driving at a hundred and ten himself, and wasn't getting any closer.

Dilemma.

It annoyed him that he wasn't catching up. This whole worn-out-service-car thing annoyed him. And it annoyed him too that, when it came to his service car, he was such a moralist.

He pressed the pedal to the floor. Gradually, he came up alongside.

The truck driver was not only going too fast, he also kept swerving across the white lines.

Beg slapped the rotating light onto the roof and manoeuvred the truck onto the shoulder of the road. Sighing and peeping, it came to a halt behind him. There was a moment of silence, some intentional shilly-shallying—Beg liked to drag that out a little. As though you held sway over time itself.

He climbed out, all his movements equally deliberate. Once he was standing beside the car, he stuck his billy club into his belt. The truck's engine was idling. He looked up the side of the cab, and the driver rolled down the window. Beg gestured to him to climb down.

'You're allowed to go a hundred and thirty here,' the man said.

'Get out, please.'

The door swung open, and the man climbed down, grumbling. 'A hundred and thirty, I swear.'

Beg shook his head. He pointed back down the road. 'You went through an eighty-kilometre zone back there.'

'You moved the signs yourself . . .'

'While driving, you repeatedly swerved from lane to lane. Have you been drinking?'

'No, man, I don't even drink. Could I see your ID?'

He was a man of around thirty, wearing jeans, sneakers. The new generation: healthy, haughty, with an almost palpable contempt for authority. They didn't know how things had been. They had never lacked for a thing; they'd had their bread buttered on both sides.

Beg's badge gleamed in the light from the open cab.

'What's up with you guys?' the driver said. 'What do you think you're doing? You guys are fucking up everything, really.'

He turned around and placed a foot on the first step up to the cab.

'Don't do that,' Beg said.

The man looked over his shoulder. 'Gotta get my papers.'

'You're holding them in your hand.'

'Other papers.' He took another step, and was off the ground now.

Beg felt the hairs on his neck bristle. He rested his hand on the billy club. 'Get down here.'

The driver stepped back onto the ground. 'You're the third one today. The *third*. Do you understand what that means, the third? A syndicate, that's what you guys are. Organised crime. Could I see your hands?'

Beg was thrown off balance by the question. What was wrong with his hands?

'Your hands,' the man asked again. His tone was conciliatory; the vortex of rage seemed to have subsided. There was something compelling about him, something that—if he weren't a citizen who'd committed a moving violation, and Beg not an officer in the course of his duties—would make you show him your hands. Why did the driver want to see his hands? He had to resist the urge to look at them himself; it had been a long time since he'd last consciously looked at his hands.

'You were doing at least forty kilometres over the speed limit in an eighty-kilometre zone,' Beg said primly. 'While doing so, you repeatedly violated the traffic markers.' He didn't know why he sounded so weak, so fatuous. Was he already bowing internally to the man's youth? Was he already admitting in the depths of his soul to being a relic, a reject of time, ready for extinction?

'Please, may I see your hands?'

As though robbed of his will, Beg, *grandpa* Beg, held out his hands, the palms turned upwards. The man leaned down and held his face right above them, as though he meant to lick them. He studied them carefully, and then straightened up. 'See what I mean?' he said.

Beg looked at his hands. 'What?'

'Completely red with theft.'

Beg tossed him against the cab. The man laughed. 'Are you going to beat me now? For saying that you're a thief?'

Beg swiped him across the face with his billy club.

With a yelp, the driver crumpled. 'Don't, man, don't do that!'

The billy club lashed out, rage burning white behind Beg's forehead. He pounded him on the back, the legs; writhing like a worm, the man tried to make himself small, to roll into a ball, to disappear into the earth. He screamed—a high voice all of a sudden, a boy's voice still.

'Dirty'—*whoosh*—'little'—*whoosh*—'piece of shit.'

His foot bent back double when he kicked him. The sharp flash of pain sped up his shin.

Through a crack in his blinded brains came a ray of light: the realisation that he might kill him.

Stop.

Reluctantly, he lowered his arm. He leaned against the cab, out of breath. The man was lying beside the front wheel. Beg leaned down and grabbed him by the hair, to see his face. Blood and snot were running over his cheeks. Was he weeping?

'Look what you're doing,' Beg panted. 'Do you get it now? You idiot?'

He wiped his hands on the man's sweater and stood up. He rested his hands on his hips and bent his back and head as far back as he could, groaning.

The cigarettes were on the dashboard of his car. A passenger car came by from the other direction. It slowed, pale ovals at the windows. Beg gestured to it to drive on. He lit a cigarette and looked at the man on the ground. *Welcome to the real world*. Somebody had to teach them.

He coughed. His mouth was dry; the cigarette didn't taste good.

In the cab he found a roll of euro banknotes, a stun-gun, and a bottle of cola. He unscrewed the top and took a swig. There were porn mags in the net beside the mattress. He flipped through the waybills. Then he stuck the euros in his pocket, took the key out of the ignition, and turned off the headlights.

Outside, the man was crawling towards the road. Beg locked the door of the truck and lowered himself to the ground. The engine ticked as it cooled.

He lashed the driver's hands behind his back with a tie-wrap and dragged him to his car, where he heaved him onto the back seat, between the harvest from his garden. 'Be careful with my bell peppers.'

He dried his hands on his sleeves. A headache throbbed behind his eyes. The exertion had brought it on; it was happening more often lately. There came a day when you got too old for this kind of thing.

Through the tunnel of night he drove back into town. The little moon hung low above the horizon—a wan, barely discernible line separating heaven and earth. The darkness over the steppe was a substance, a night-blue stone. He thought about his sister. Maybe he should try to reach her again. She had always been interested in people's stories—especially old people. Sometimes she wrote them down. 'When someone like that dies, it's really like a library's been lost,' she'd said once. Maybe his sister knew where the song came from. She was the collector in the family: she collected stories, pebbles, paperclips, and loose ends of wool.

'I need to see a doctor,' the man in the back seat said.

Their argument had been about the parental home. She had wanted to keep it, after their father died as well, the same way she kept the stories, the pebbles, the paperclips, and snatches of wool. Maybe she would rent it out, and then live there herself after she had raised her son and retired from her job in the city. But Beg had wanted to get rid of it. She didn't have enough money to buy him out, so the house with the plum trees in the front garden and grapevines along the fence was sold.

'You broke something, man. In my back. I need a doctor, really.'

The little farmhouse with the thatched roof and white loam walls sometimes came back in his dreams—the friendly blue doors and shutters, the field of withered sunflowers rustling in the wind when autumn came and the summer was already behind you without your expecting it.

There was movement in the back seat. He adjusted the rear-view mirror. The man was sitting up halfway. 'I need help, I swear.'

'Try to forget your memories,' Beg said to the mirror. 'They don't belong to you.'

12

THE KURGAN

It is late in the afternoon by the time the tall man and the Ethiopian catch up to the others. Leaning on his stick, the tall man stands in their midst, his head bowed. The boy lets his gaze run over the grimy faces. The men with their filthy beards—how long has it been since he's seen something *clean*, something untarnished by dirt?

'We weren't expecting to see you again,' says the man from Ash-khabad. 'We thought . . .'

'My time hadn't come yet,' the tall man says.

'What are you two after? There's nothing here for you!' says Vitaly.

'We weren't chasing you,' the tall man defends himself. 'It wasn't like that. We just followed the tracks.'

Vitaly turns and walks away. 'It's getting cold. There isn't enough to go around. We're all going to die! You two should have kept your distance!'

Later, when they started walking again—the day's final stretch—the poacher told the tall man: 'I saw you two yesterday.'

Things have all gone so differently from what the tall man had imagined. They are a burden to the others. He can't rely on their patience, not when he can't keep up the pace, when things go black before his eyes and he needs to take a rest.

Maybe it really would have been better if he'd stayed alone with the black man. He doesn't push him to go faster, he gives him water and shares his food. The gratitude flickers for a moment.

The Ethiopian is walking behind him now. He and the tall man are still a pair, but the distance between them is growing by the hour.

59

The law of the group is taking over again. Their solidarity is broken; step by step, the tall man walks away from the one who saved him.

Evening. The flat land blows its cold breath over them; embers flare in a gust of wind. The black man shuffles around outside the circle; they can hear him tearing off grass for his bed. 'Pointless,' the boy hears the poacher say. The boy leans forward to hear him better. Some snakes sleep at night, the poacher says, but that's exactly when others come out to hunt. But the karakurt spiders, they're the dangerous ones. Their poison can kill a bull.

They went out digging for tubers and onions, but found nothing. That night, the poacher's snares remained empty as well.

The hunger makes you furious at first; but then, if it keeps on going, it makes you listless and weak. That's why the rages of Vitaly and the man from Ashkhabad have subsided, because of the hunger and the cold. They left again before first light. Walking would drive the cold from their bones. Gradually, the day unfolded behind them. The grass was licked with frost.

At their feet, a hare bolted. A pair of partridges flew up, cackling, in front of them. That afternoon, the poacher pointed out to the boy a herd of donkeys at the farthermost edge of their vision. There was no chance of catching one. All food ran and flew away at their approach. The poacher longed for his rifle; he could have used it to shoot the hare and the partridges, as well as the geese that babbled as they plied the heavens, but his hunting rifle was hanging on the wall at home. Home—a place that seemed pleasant to him now, not poor and desperate like when he left. There was a fire in the stove, a soft bed, his warm wife.

He had been one of the last to leave. The evenings when those who remained behind had drunk away their cares at the community hall and danced till they dropped had become increasingly rare—when the men bared their chests, giving in to that mysterious urge that overpowers almost every male once he has had enough to drink.

Sometimes they went out poaching in an old all-terrain vehicle, blind drunk, chasing away every living thing with their ruckus. They shot at shadows and glimmers, at anything that moved or stood still. Each and every one of them fancied himself a sharpshooter. They guzzled homemade hooch, the empty bottles exploding in shards against the rocks. Nikolai Ribalko shot his own dog by accident. He wept and swore that he would suffer for his deed, suffer for having shot and killed his treacherous fucking dog. They were savage, their blood boiled, but they fell asleep as soon as the action petered out.

That was the life he had left behind.

On the horizon a *kurgan* rose up, a burial mound built by a people lost long ago. They had run across these before. They tended to give them a wide berth, fearing that their presence would disturb the rest of the dead. But now they lacked the energy to swerve around the mound that lay straight across their path. The boy approached it with a mixture of dread and excitement. The hill was covered in yellow prairie grass. He longed to look far in every direction. The sole of his right shoe had come loose, and flapped as he walked. He'd tried to fix it temporarily with strips of canvas that the poacher had cut for him from an old satchel.

He climbed to the top. Dizziness. And also euphoria at being liberated from the flats, as though he had been lifted by a giant hand.

But he saw no sign of life. Nowhere was there a rectangular structure to betray the hand of man. He turned slowly where he stood: waving grass, yellow sea.

The poacher and the man from Ashkhabad joined him. 'Nothing, right?' the man from Ashkhabad said. The boy shook his head.

The man from Ashkhabad moaned. 'We're doomed.'

'You are. I'm not,' the poacher said quietly.

The boy was the only one who paid attention to his words. He knew the poacher was right, that he would outlive them all. He was a stone; he knew what it meant to endure.

Vitaly reached the top, out of breath. Then the woman appeared. The Ethiopian was the last one up the hill. Being around the tall man had changed him; he acted like one of them now. He looked around. There was no difference between the road they'd taken and the road they had to follow. The black man looked up, and the boy followed his

gaze. A flight of geese at high altitude were flying south, the forma-
tion weaving and parting and rejoining.

What does he see? the boy wondered. What is he thinking?

As they were getting ready to descend, the black man reached out
and touched Vitaly's arm. Vitaly recoiled. 'Keep your hands off me,
you pig.'

The black man indicated a dense patch of grass far away, and said
something in his indecipherable tongue. The poacher and the man
from Ashkhabad looked. There was a hint of green amid the yellow.
Maybe it was a hollow where water collected during long droughts.
Maybe they would find wood there, or wild onions.

Like shadows, they wander across the steppes, all skinny as a strap.
It won't be long before they grow transparent and disappear. Depart-
ing from their route, they head south, towards the spot the Ethiopian showed them. When they get there they find nothing but a few
bushes and tall, plumed grass. They dig like men possessed, in search
of onions and wild tulip bulbs. When they leave, the ground is up-
turned, as though a band of nomads has dug for treasure there. They
avoid each other's eyes; the blow is unbearable.

The woman weeps without tears. She falls to her knees and tosses
sand over her head. The boy sees it gliding off her hair and shoulders.

'Come,' he says, 'we're falling behind.'

He grabs her arm and pulls her to her feet. She falls back on the
ground, on her stomach now, and rubs her face in the sand. Her forehead, her nose, her cheeks are covered in dust. The boy pulls her up
again and drags her along. She takes a sudden step towards him, he
ducks too late, and the flat of her hand hits him in the face.

Then she walks away from him, after the others.

The boy remains standing. He feels each individual finger burning on his cheek.

•   •   •

They go back to the kurgan; the poacher thinks there may be wild animals there that will walk into his traps. In the late afternoon, they pitch camp in the hill's long shadow. The boy knows that the hill is hollow inside. The dead wander around in there. They will come to get him. That night, they will reach out their knobby hands to seize him and drag him by his feet into their underworld.

Vitaly walks over to the woman, who is sitting in the sand, and pulls her to her feet. He wants to take her to his bed for the night, but the man from Ashkhabad intervenes.

'Let go,' he says.

Vitaly snorts.

'Let go. Or do you want me to kick the shit out of you?' the man from Ashkhabad says.

The others watch. They expect Vitaly to give in. He steps back— not to retreat though, not like they think, but to jump at the other's throat. They fall and roll, panting through the dirt. Most of the blows miss their mark. The man from Ashkhabad rolls on top of Vitaly, and punches him hard—in the head, on the chest, right through the arms he's raised to protect himself. Vitaly is no longer the canny street fighter he was a while back, when he almost always won. Now, he remains lying on the ground as the man from Ashkhabad drags his prey along into the gathering darkness.

13

TO THE ATAMAN

The next morning, the trailer truck was empty. The slashed canvas billowed in the wind. The trucking company was informed, and sent someone to pick it up. The driver remained in custody, for having driven under the influence and resisting arrest. Sergeant Koller looked at his boss's raw knuckles, and entertained no illusions. Beg was a fine fellow, but he had his moods.

The detainee lay in his cell with his face to the wall, and didn't respond to their questions. He didn't touch his food. His lips were split; some of his teeth were broken. The doctor had come by. 'Bruised ribs, nothing broken,' he ruled. He didn't look at the man's teeth—they hadn't talked about teeth at medical school.

In the basement cellblock at the station house, the filth of the world piled up like flotsam against the walls of a sluice. Once a week, everything down there was cleaned with Lysol, but the smell of vomit and stale sweat drilled straight through it all.

At noon, Beg locked his office door from the inside and pulled a little address book from his desk drawer. It was an old one: lots of the names had been scratched out, and new ones were no longer added. In the same way that the rabbi wandered amid the headstones of his loved ones, Beg found himself leafing through pages containing the names of people who had once been a part of his life but had now disappeared from it. Under 'U' he found his sister Eva. She had divorced that talented good-for-nothing Alexander Uspensky, but she had kept his name. The name 'Beg' was too countrified for her; it had too much flatland, too much steppe to it.

He had no idea whether the number was still in service. She might have moved—people were restless, more than they used to be, blown hither and thither. Only he stayed where he was, immovable amid the wheezing heating pipes and the upstairs neighbours who tossed cigarette butts onto his balcony.

He picked up the phone, hesitated for a moment, and then dialled the number.

It rang. A man answered, without stating his name. All he said was, 'Yeah?'

'To whom am I speaking?' Beg asked.

'To whom am *I* speaking?'

Beg sighed. 'Tadeusz, is that you?'

It was quiet for a moment. 'Who's asking?'

'Your uncle, Pontus.'

Silence again. 'Mum's not here,' he said then.

'Oh.'

'Sorry.'

'When's she coming back?'

'I don't know.'

The unwillingness at the other end was almost palpable. He had probably interrupted his nephew while he was playing some computer game—a modern-day sin against the spirit.

'Well, it was nice talking to you, Tadeusz.'

'Yeah,' the boy said.

'Would you tell her I called?'

'Sure.'

'I really need to talk to her.'

'I'll tell her.'

Then they hung up. Beg sank back in his chair. Tadeusz was still a teenager the last time he'd seen him. Now he'd had a young adult on the line whom he would have liked to tell that things could turn out all right, that there was no cause for such suspicion.

Whether that was true, he had no idea.

He had known Eva better than anyone; they had been the sole witnesses to each other's youths. That one day they would turn their backs on each other in bitterness had been unthinkable. Still, it had happened. They could die unnoticed, without either of them knowing that about the other. It was something you shouldn't dwell on, otherwise it would weigh you down and make you sad.

Oksana's blond bouffant hair-do appeared above the strip of smoked glass that separated his office from the hallway. It sailed past like a ship on the horizon. With her long legs and high heels, Oksana, if she stood on tip-toes, was the only one who could look over it. Whenever she walked past she would toss a quick, almost compulsive glance inside, then turn away quickly as though she had seen nothing. Beg had thought about taping off the top section of the window, too, but never got around to it. Perhaps, he thought, he appreciated being seen by at least one person.

That afternoon, he drove to a sandy stretch outside town. After the empire's collapse, a bazaar had arisen there, a market bigger than Michailopol had ever seen. Beg had witnessed the birth of a new kind of trading place—the planned economy vanished, the bazaar shot up from the soil like a field of wildflowers in spring. Roads were built, latrines dug—replaced later by portacabins and even later by toilet blocks with running water—and there were snack bars and exchange offices. Michailopol suddenly found itself smack dab in the middle of the world, at a crossroads. The bazaar was frequented by gypsies with brown faces and scars on their scalps; traders crossed the border in their old Mercedes; farmers brought in grain and livestock; and they all returned home with pruning shears, hunting rifles, and grinders, and plastic flowers for their ancestors' graves. Old women carried such heavy loads of checkered shopping bags that it was a wonder their legs didn't buckle beneath them, like old cavalry mounts. From one day to the next, everyone became a merchant. Everyone had something to sell and was champing at the bit to buy something in turn. An old man who made ice cream said the bazaar reminded him of the market at Krakow after the Great War—the riotous outburst of mercantile fever that marked life's return after the hunger and the horrors, he had seen it there, too.

Moneychangers, ex-convicts who were recognisable by the way

they squatted with their backs to a wall—years of their lives had been spent like that in prison yards—moved between the stacked shipping containers. You smelled soap and bread, caustic cleansers, and broiled meat, you walked a few hundred yards down a street full of brightly coloured plastic toys, and then suddenly found yourself in the audio lane, between towers of cassette tapes, bootlegged CDs, and sound systems. Men used corn brooms to sweep the streets, bawled at by merchants who tossed blankets over their wares to keep off the dust.

Everyone longed for wealth, the natural end of all cares. The people hungered after money, earned with a few swift transactions. They built homes with the mortar of their fantasies, houses that said, 'Look, a rich man lives here,' wondrous constructions in every style of the world—the domes of Samarkand perched atop Ionian pillars, the fountains of Damascus burbling in the courtyards. Every day all those thousands of little hustlers came to the bazaar, waiting for the miracle.

Whenever he walked around the grounds, Pontus Beg would think about his father, about the man's impotent disdain for commerce. Commerce, that wasn't labour, he'd felt; that was making money *off* labour. The froth of trade was richer than the fat of labour—that was the bitter lesson his father had taught him. Commerce had been a forbidden city to old Beg, one he knew only from its periphery—whenever he sold milk and meat to the cooperative, whenever a truck came to pick up the grain. He never found out precisely how the price of milk, meat, and grain was established; all he knew for sure was that others earned more from it than he did.

For Beg, too, who visited the bazaar almost every week, the trading life remained a web of mysteries. How could someone who had bought a shipment of Chinese cuckoo clocks yesterday know that he could sell them for twice the price twenty miles down the road? Why wasn't the price of cuckoo clocks the same there as it was here? How did they know over there that here, today, there would be a demand for cuckoo clocks?

Those who made a killing on the bazaar disappeared from sight. They lived in big houses behind tall fences, their interests seen to by go-betweens.

In the early days of the bazaar, one such man had become breathtakingly rich, but remained true to the market nonetheless: ataman Chiop. He was the richest of them all. Pontus Beg was going to see him now. Ataman Chiop: 350 pounds dripping wet, and strong as an ox. People said he'd once mounted a sturdy horse and broken its back.

The law had a mobile police station on the grounds, but no arm reached as far as ataman Chiop's. No shylock changed zlotys for euros and grivnas for rubles without his knowledge; no article changed hands without him earning a few cents on it. In each of the thousands of transactions a day, one cent would disappear into the merchant's pocket, and one into ataman Chiop's. Taken together, all those cents added up to a mountain, and atop that mountain sat the ataman. From the summit, he kept an eagle eye on the bazaar with its myriad corridors, where everyone longed to be as rich as him.

'Well, if it isn't Pontus!' the ataman said when Beg entered his office, a café at the edge of the bazaar. 'Come, Pontus, sit down, take a seat. Vladimir, bring a glass for my guest.'

Beg slid onto the seat across from him.

Rumor had it that a secret tunnel ran from the café to a shed somewhere far from the market, and that a getaway car kept its motor running there, but Beg didn't believe it. The ataman was too big for tunnels—he would become wedged like a cork in a bottle.

'Cheers, Pontus!'

They raised their glasses and knocked them back. The ataman, Beg had noticed before, liked to call him by his first name. He had done that right from the outset, as though they were old friends. Beg could no longer ask him to stop; it was too late for that now. He addressed the other man as 'ataman,' which immediately established the pecking order. The one was his first name; the other, his position in the hierarchy.

They ate pickles and salted meat along with the vodka. If you didn't know better, you would have seen two friends running through the day's news.

Beg looked at the ataman's forehead, and the bristly grey hair above it. No one could have told you the colour of his eyes, tucked away between folds of fat.

'I stopped a truck yesterday,' Beg said.

The ataman's phone rang. He glanced at the screen and said: 'Just a moment, Pontus.'

Beg laid his hands on the table and waited.

'Round it off to thirty,' the ataman said. 'I'll accept that.'

Silence.

'Thirty, tops,' the ataman said. 'But start at twenty.'

He snapped the phone shut and put it back in the holster on his belt.

'What was it you wanted to say to me, Pontus?'

'Last night I stopped a truck,' Beg said.

'Good,' said the ataman. 'Why?'

'And this morning the truck was empty.'

The ataman raised his face to the ceiling, and then lowered it again. He sighed deeply. 'It's terrible, the way people steal these days. Thieves everywhere, absolutely everywhere. People have grown too lazy to work for it.'

The best thing to do now was to say nothing, Beg knew. He simply looked at the man across from him and marvelled at how a head could grow like that—a giant pumpkin forgotten at the edge of a field. Pity the poor mother who'd had to give birth to him, though it was hard to imagine this man being born of a woman.

'What do you want me to do about it, Pontus? I'll keep an eye out for the thieves, I'll do that. That goes without saying.'

His phone rang again. He answered, listened for a bit, and then said only: 'I can't talk right now. Call me later this afternoon.' He hung up.

Beg helped himself to a pickle, looked at it for a moment, then stuck it in his mouth.

'Where were we, Pontus?' the ataman asked.

While chewing, Beg said: 'Life's expensive these days. Everyone wants to be able to give his sweetheart a present every now and then, or go to the seashore for a vacation. When you do that, you want to feel money in your pocket—real money, not plastic. Plastic isn't money. Tell me, do you think the ataman has a credit card? Don't make me laugh. The ataman trusts only real money; he's a wise man. He doesn't trust the banks—the banks work with people, they have power failures, people looking over your shoulder. One day they might say: "Dear ataman, we don't like the look of this: the fiscal authorities want us to freeze your account until the investigation is over." Then you're stuck.'

The ataman shook his head. 'Pontus, what kind of person do you think I am? I'm in the import-export business. Times are tough. The business is flat on its arse.'

'You mind if I take the last pickle?'

'Go ahead.'

It crunched nicely between his teeth. 'We all have to make a living,' Beg said pensively. 'The ataman is right about that. That's easier for some of us than it is for others. Some people see a penny from a mile away; others wouldn't see it if they tripped over it. The ataman sees pennies everywhere. The pennies come to him almost by themselves. He's a penny-magnet; you can hear him jingle when he walks.'

The ataman slammed the tabletop with the palms of his hands. The shot glasses bounced from the shock. 'Pontus! Pontus! Stop! Where do you get this from? I tell you, I've hit a rough patch. I can't help you!'

Beg tipped the contents of the second glass into his mouth, then wiped his lips with the back of his hand. 'That truck . . .' he said.

'Was almost empty,' the ataman said, raising his voice. 'Packaging material. A couple of pallets of laundry detergent. It wasn't worth the effort. You want detergent? For the white stuff? For coloureds? It's all yours.'

'White goods and electronics,' Beg said. 'According to the waybills.'

'A little bit, almost nothing. Not worth the trouble.'

But Beg knew that in the next few days the bazaar would be flooded with washing machines, blow-dryers, and CD players. Miele, Braun, Sony; brand stuff, no junk. The ataman didn't want people asking about where it came from, any more than about the firearms and hard drugs you could get here without much trouble.

Beg shook his head slowly. 'There was a present left along the road; someone came and unpacked it. It would be unpleasant if we had to take it back.'

The ataman snorted and sputtered, then turned his head towards the bar and shouted: 'Vladimir!'

Vladimir came to the table. At a nod from his boss, he produced an envelope from his inside pocket.

'Pontus,' the ataman said, 'you're taking me to the cleaners again. Here, buy something pretty for your girl.'

Beg put the envelope away and stood up. He said: 'You know, I just might take her to the seashore.'

14

IN SEARCH OF FORTUNE

There were thirteen of them. Whispered assignations had brought them to the warehouse. The afternoon was hot and muggy. What they wanted most was to be invisible; even their shadows were a nuisance to them.

They were brought together in a little office high up at the back of the warehouse. Men came in now and then, handing out bottles of water and rolls of biscuits. They would have to make do with that, but for no longer than twenty-four hours. Each of them was allowed to take along one bag of possessions. A woman wept; she had had to leave behind a suitcase with songbooks and a tablecloth her grandmother had embroidered.

The men were brusque, unrelenting.

There was a black man in the group; the others couldn't keep their eyes off him. He sat apart from the rest and seemed not to notice their obtuse stares. He was carrying a little bundle on a strap—all his possessions were rolled into that.

His presence raised fundamental questions. Where did he come from? How did he get here? What was his name? Where was he going?

Questions no one asked him.

They were led to the truck. At the front of the trailer was the space where they would hide, a crevice left between plastic-wrapped pallets. There was a bucket in which they could relieve themselves. There was to be no smoking, and complete silence under all circumstances. Those who owned a mobile phone had to hand it over.

The boss of the operation wore a white tracksuit; gold glistened at his wrists and collar. His BMW was parked beside the truck, the door open, music blasting. Behind them, the rest of the cargo was loaded as they covered their ears against the roar of the forklift in the trailer.

Slowly they disappeared in shadow. They would not only be silent; they would hold their breath and cease to exist until they were across the border.

The voices outside became muffled, and the tailgate closed. Someone pounded on it with a hard object. They tried to fathom the darkness, but their eyes found no hold.

When the engine started, a shiver ran through the trailer. The truck idled for a while, then began moving. A sharp turn—it was leaving the lot. A little later, they were rolling smoothly down the road. Their thoughts grew a little calmer. They were all going to be fine; they would slip through the eye of the needle and act as though good fortune were a personal friend. Why should they be caught? Why not others? There were countless like them—let good luck turn its back on those others for once! No one needed it more than they did!

But every time the truck braked, their hearts leapt into their throats.

The trip would take about twelve hours, the man had said. Sometimes the luminous dial of a wristwatch would light up faintly. They had no idea how long twelve hours lasted in the dark. It was an endless, sleepless night. The clock that ticked in here was not the same as the one outside. The hour and minutes hands became bogged down; they dragged across the dial like flies caught in molasses.

A few times already, the boy has thought he is going to wet his pants, but each time the urge goes away. He shakes some life into his sleeping leg and looks down the row of others, leaning with their backs against the pallets. Shadows. Insubstantial, thin as air. He doesn't know them, these others. As far as he can tell, there is one couple; the rest are on their own.

He knows that they are blazing trails for their families, their villages, their communities. Travelling in their footsteps is an invisible company of fathers, mothers, brothers, sisters, aunts and uncles, nieces and nephews. All hope is focused on them. They are the pioneer vegetation. You can submit them to anything—hunger, thirst, heat, and cold—and they will survive it all.

The boy thinks about his father and mother, and about his brother, who isn't strong enough to make the journey. Endlessly far away, they are now. He knows he can't go back. His road travels in only one direction.

He wept when they told him. Dry your tears, his mother said. You want to be a man, don't you? A man carries what rests on his shoulders, and doesn't complain.

The boy clenched his teeth and stopped crying.

It had still been dark, the morning he left. A stranger gave him a ride; they drove down into the valley in a rattling pickup and saw it slowly grow light behind the mountains. The man dropped him at the bus station and hoped that God would be with him on his way.

The boy took a bus westward, and by that evening was already farther from home than ever. He ran through the words of counsel he'd been hung with like talismans. *Don't talk to strangers. Give policemen a wide berth. Be frugal. Avoid the company of people with red hair.*

Around his neck was a string bearing an oval of blue glass, to protect him against the evil eye.

He slept in a corner of a bus station. He sat curled up against the wall, hiding himself in the shelter of his arms.

A guard woke him. He took him along to a cafeteria close to the terminal and bought him a spicy pastry and a cup of tea. The first buses of the day pulled in as an awesome blue unfolded across the sky. The boy slurped at his tea and felt protected for a time.

The guard gave him directions and he travelled on. In the next city, he went looking for a coffeehouse called 'Darius.' Strangers pointed the way.

He asked the barman about Nacer Gül. That was the name drummed into him; if he forgot that name, he was lost.

The man showed him to the back, where he waited amid buckets and crates for Nacer Gül to arrive. Gül was the gatekeeper; no one crossed the frontier into the other world without him. The boy waited until his thoughts died down and he forgot time.

With a great ruckus—the stamping of feet, and a bossy voice—

Nacer Gül made his appearance at last. The door swung open. His head was shaven, like the children in the boy's village. Perched on his forehead was a large pair of sunglasses.

'You're late, boy. We almost left without you.'

He laughed. The boy didn't move a muscle.

'The money,' Gül said.

The boy held out the bundle to him, and his ringed fingers rustled through the banknotes. Gül stuck the wad in the pocket of his tracksuit. Money was something he dealt with offhandedly; it flew to him on obedient wings, so that he didn't have to do a thing. The boy would remember everything he saw. This was how he would be some day—the money would fly into his pockets, too, and his mother would be proud of him, of her son who had made a long journey and triumphed over circumstance.

The darkness of the trailer deepened; night must have fallen almost. A river of asphalt rolled by beneath them, the road never ending. At times they fell asleep with their backs against the cargo, but most of the time they stared wide-eyed into the darkness. *Everything will turn out all right. God is with us.*

Those who once possessed proof of identity now possessed it no longer. Nacer Gül had said they should tear up their papers. It was better to arrive without an identity in the country of refuge. A person with no name or origin overwhelms the protocol. Procedures bog down; the chance that you'll be allowed to stay increases. And so they destroyed the papers they had gone to such ends to obtain. Everything was formless now, except for the words of Nacer Gül, which were solid as coinage.

Now they are no one anymore. The woman who had to leave behind her suitcase looks back on her life in surprise and sorrow. She lives with her back to the future; the gentle glow of nostalgia has already spread over the memories of her hard life back there.

The men are willing to forget. They would, if they could, have placed not only their money and their fate in Nacer Gül's hands, but their memories, too. They want to move on. They are prepared to lose themselves, to chop their lives in two like a worm.

Countries and continents had once stood open to those seeking their fortunes, borders were soft and permeable, but now they were cast in concrete and hung with barbed wire. Like blind men, travellers by the thousands probed the walls, looking for a weak spot, a gap, a hole through which they might slip. A wave of people crashed against those walls; it was impossible to keep them all back. They came in countless numbers, and each of them lived in the hope and expectation that they would be among the ones lucky enough to reach the far side. It was the behaviour of animals that travel in swarms, that take into account the loss of individual members but will survive as a species.

The truck slowed. They saw the whites of each other's wide-open eyes. The truck crept forward; they heard voices, men's voices, and the barking of dogs when the truck stopped. The motor was still running. How could they have imagined they were invisible? Nothing but thin sailcloth separated them from the border guards and the dogs. How could the animals not smell their acrid sweat of fear, not hear their pounding hearts? At any moment the tailgate might open, and the men would come in with a flood of light at their backs. All the way at the back they would find them, drained with fear.

What was going on out there? Why were they laughing? Was it about them? Were they prolonging the torment on purpose?

A beam of light bored its way in boldly, as though taking a quick look around before the men themselves would enter. Everything resonated with the idling of the engine. The men seemed to be going away. Slowly the boy stood up; the man beside him grabbed at his arm to stop him, but the boy was already beyond reach. He squeezed his way through the crack between two stacks of pallets and stood, almost pressed against the sailcloth. On tiptoe, he looked through a rip in it, then pulled his head back quickly. A little later he looked again, longer this time. Then he crept back to his spot, careful not to stumble. His heart hopped about like a frog in his chest. He sat and held his face in the crook of his arm to muffle his heavy breathing. They heard the truck door slam. Hope sprang up. Then the voice outside came back. Dogs barked wildly, as though they had smelled blood.

The border guards were now so close that they could make out almost everything. Oh, the urge to just stand up and walk out, to put an end to the shrill fear. A sneeze, a cough, and all would be lost. Their lives had contracted to this narrow ledge: they could fall or they could reach the other side, but they had no say in it.

A shout, and the truck's door slams. Motion! The truck is moving, slowly at first, and then faster and faster. The tires zoom in abandon over the asphalt; none of the travellers dare to think the impossible.

Deeper and deeper into the night they drive. They know for sure now that they've crossed the border! Cautiously, they admit impressions of the luck they may have had.

A man leans over to the boy and whispers in his ear: 'What did you see?'

'Soldiers,' the boy whispers back. He thinks for a moment, then leans over to the man's ear again. 'A fence, and cars.'

The man passes on the report to the others, a silver line of melody going from one ear to the next, their excitement filling the darkness. It's hard to keep the joy inside their bodies.

Each of them sits in the dark with his own imaginings, impatient, wanting to trade in a life as contraband for that of a person who decides for themselves where to go and where to stop, when to talk and when to be silent.

The truck slows again, this time to negotiate a curve, and then travels along a dirt road. They crawl along a bumpy track for an eternity, until the vehicle stops at last. Someone fumblingly lowers the tailgate, and coolness billows into the trailer.

'Hey!' a man shouts. 'Come on. We're there.'

They shake the sleep from their legs, stretch, and climb over the cargo towards freedom.

It is a clear, chilly night. The driver hands out cigarettes with a grin. 'I almost pissed myself!' he says a few times in a row. 'You people thought you were up shit creek back there, but what about me?'

Awkward as cattle leaving their shed in spring, they stand beneath the freshly scrubbed span of stars, and feel reborn.

15

BEHIND THE NAMES

'Your feet,' Zita said. He lifted his feet. The nozzle of the vacuum cleaner slid beneath them.

A little later, she asked: 'What's this? Can I put it away somewhere?' Beg looked up. On the table was a package wrapped in newsprint.

'It's for you,' he said. 'A gift.'

'Pontus!'

'It's nothing much.'

Zita frowned. 'As long as you don't go figuring . . .'

'I'm not figuring anything.'

'In a few days.'

'I know.'

'All right.'

She unwrapped the present.

'A hair-dryer,' she said. 'How sweet.'

'You deserve it.'

Her hand brushed his shoulder. Then she went into the kitchen, holding the hair-dryer. Her butt had a nice wiggle to it, he thought; he liked looking at it. Her hair had once been black, but lately it had become streaked with grey. It wouldn't be long before she could forget about having a child. Sometimes he begged her for it, during the night's embrace. 'A child. Of our own. You and me. Why not?' He heard the sadness in her laugh. 'Come on, Pontus, don't say that.' She rolled to one side, he crawled up behind her and cupped a breast in one hand, beneath the nightie. More than having his lust sated, it was this he wanted: to feel her breathing slow and deepen, to wrap one hand around a breast and press his loins pleasantly against her backside. That was how he slipped into sleep, reassured. But not a night with Zita went by without him being awakened by her conversations with her mother in the other world. They would chatter about this, that, and the other. Beg could put up with anything from Zita, except for that jabbering about so-and-so's illness, 'And did you know that Vaida's got another bun in the oven? Number seven already! Poor soul. But she's holding up well. You know what they say: God fits the back for the burden.'

He couldn't sleep through that, not with all the earplugs in the world, and so he would retreat to the living room until mother and daughter fell silent. He sat in the dark, smoked a cigarette, and had another drink while Zita's voice sounded from his bedroom.

'Pontus, the phone!' Zita shouted from the bathroom. He was already in the living room, staring at the phone as it rang. No one ever called him at home. He got up from his chair and walked over to it, expecting the thing to suddenly stop when he got there.

He picked up the receiver and listened, as though to the sea roaring in a shell.

'Pontus? This is Eva.'

His sister's voice. A foolish poignancy. The only other survivor of his past, she had taught him to read; come to think of it, what hadn't he learned from her in those early years?

'Pontus? Say something.'

'Hello, Eva. How are you?'

'What did you call about? Tadeusz says you called.'

'That's right . . . I was going through my book . . . an old address book . . . I saw your name and I thought . . . well, why not.' He was silent for a moment. 'That's pretty much it.'

'Ah, I see,' his sister said. 'Well, things are going well here, thanks. All things considered.'

Silence rushed into the gap between them.

'Tadeusz is going to school to become a mechanic,' she said then. 'The security business turned out not to be his thing.'

Beg was relieved to find her less defensive than her son.

'He kept falling asleep all the time.'

'Who?'

'Tadeusz. The night shifts were too much for him.'

A lazybones, just like his father, Beg thought.

Eva still drove a streetcar; it hadn't been easy for her, working such irregular hours and raising a child alone, but now that Tadeusz was grown up she was her enjoying her independence.

'No man for me, never again,' she said. 'All a bunch of big babies.'

They didn't talk about the things that had created the rift between them; they both wanted to ignore that. Maybe, Beg thought, the cause had become trivial. Maybe she was as lonely as he was.

He brought up the song about Rebekka and the roses, and said: 'I sing it sometimes, it's so weird, it just popped into my mind. Do you remember it?'

It was nice to hear her laugh. 'I haven't thought about that for years.'

'I just found out what the words mean. It's a love song, someone told me. I figured you'd know how come Mama sang it for us. Your memory works that way. It's Jewish.'

'Yiddish,' she said. 'Mama used to sing it, that's right.'

'Where did she get a Jewish song from, that's what I'd like to know.'

She was silent for a moment, then she said: 'So that's why you called.'

Beg said nothing.

'I wouldn't know,' she said. 'It's funny, you coming up with that. They say the past comes back to you as you grow older, whether you like it or not. Is that why you've started singing old songs, Pontus?'

After talking to his sister, he felt like crawling up against Zita's broad backside and burying his nose in her hair, but it was indeed not his time. Once, when he had tried to buy that time, one extra night, she had grown cold and hard, and said: 'I'm not a whore, Pontus. What do you think, that I'm a whore?'

'No, no, of course not,' he said quickly, even though he couldn't quite have pinpointed the difference. The situation was complicated, all things considered, and one he didn't want to think much about.

The conversation with his sister had done nothing to satisfy his curiosity about the song. It didn't matter, he told himself, not really. It was just that it stuck out, like a loose thread—a bothersome thread that he couldn't help plucking at; an innocent pursuit, a petty diversion. An added benefit was that now, finally, for the first time in years, he'd spoken to his sister, the only person with whom he shared memories of the thick smoke from the burning haulms over the fields, the way it squeezed at your throat and blackened out the sun, of the sunflowers when the rain came, their heads hanging, like prisoners returning from war . . . She, too, remembered the song about Rivkele, and she, too, had no idea where their mother had got it from. The past had covered it up; both of them have to live with the realisation that there are questions large and small to which they will never receive an answer.

Koller came in to tell him that the trucking company had called. 'They want their driver back. They're sending a lawyer.'

'They've got every right to do that.'

Koller examined his boss's face, with no idea how to take what he'd just said. 'What do you want me to do?' he asked.

Beg looked up from the monitor. 'He can't leave without being booked, can he? Has he been booked? Has he even talked? No. So he's not going anywhere.'

Koller thought about the man in his cell. Just as bullheaded as Beg. Hard against the grain. Two furies. Beg would break his will with neglect and, failing that, by force.

When Koller came in the next morning, Beg said: 'He's ready for questioning.'

When Koller came into the cell, the driver was lying on his cot, in a foetal position. The sergeant slammed his billy club against the metal door, but the man didn't budge. He shook him by the shoulder, half expecting to find him dead, but the driver raised his head from the protection of his arms. His eyes had disappeared behind contusions and clotted blood. It had been by force, after all. A deep cut scored one eyebrow. Koller held up a glass of water. The man sat up slowly and took the glass. He raised it to his lips, his hands shaking. 'We're going upstairs in a minute for questioning,' Koller said. 'Then you'll be a free man.'

He took the glass back. A grimace of pain. Koller couldn't believe his eyes, but he had seen it clearly: the man shook his head. No. He pressed his split lips together. Koller admired his toughness, and said: 'You're only making things harder for yourself. Not smart, not smart at all.'

The man looked up at him. 'Injustice,' he said.

Later, Koller peeks around the corner again, into his boss's office. He keeps his hand on the doorknob, his body in the corridor. 'The prick won't budge.'

Beg nods and says tersely: 'Well, that's too damn bad.'

Koller withdraws from the doorway. He shuffles down the hall to his desk, tired as a field where armies have fought to the death. *Tomorrow morning*, he thinks, *I'll call in sick.*

Beg waits till Koller's shadow disappears from behind the smoked glass. Then, from the desk drawer, he takes the sheet of paper bearing the words that have been filling him with great excitement all afternoon. It is a page copied from the book *Behind the Names*, by Professor Janosz Urban. He'd found it in the little district library, run by a few old women. In grey light through the windows, they sit reading, their spectacles bound behind their necks on beaded metal cords. When was the last time he'd been in a library? It was such a strange parallel world, so far removed from daily life.

One of the women showed him to the Genealogy shelf. The book by Professor Urban was old but unread; the glue along the spine cracked as he opened it. It was a study of the origins of the most common surnames—where they came from and how they had assumed their present form. Beg followed a possibility the way a hunting dog follows an old spoor. In the drifting moments before sleep, it had moved into position in his mind. Otherwise, he had not taken the possibility very seriously; he had paid it little heed. But now that the trail had run cold in the person of his sister, this was the last resort.

He flipped through *Behind the Names,* looking for the M.

Markowski. Martyn. Maslak. Matula. Then came the name he was looking for: Medved—his mother's maiden name. Commonly encountered in large parts of Eastern Europe, it was also used as a nickname:

> medved; bear. Referring to a large, strong, and clumsy person.
>
> In some cases a *reductio* of the Ukrainian or Byelorussian *Medvedev.* Also Jewish. (Ashkenazi).

Sitting at the desk, his eyes were drawn again and again to the little phrase that closed the lemma so nonchalantly. *Also Jewish.* This was what caused his excitement, what made his ears burn. *Also Jewish* . . .

He is no specialist in onomastics, no genealogist either, but he thinks now that his mother was an assimilated Jewess who had hidden her Jewish roots—except for a nursery song and that surname.

He will go with this to Rabbi Zalman Eder. He will ask him what he thinks about it, about his discovery—for if his mother was Jewish, then he is a Jew. That much he knows, at least, about Jewish law.

16

VITALY

Vitaly was born a cur and was bound to die one, too. In the meantime, he pursued a lifelong strategy of violent intimidation, bluff, and sarcasm, or, if the other person was stronger, of sly opportunism and avoidance. No, there was not a lot of good to be said about Vitaly, except perhaps that he had survived thus far. Every scar told a story. Here a knife, there a baseball bat; the fractures from being beaten and left for dead. But he was alive, a damaged man, capable of no feeling other than sentimentality.

His territory was the city, the human clot. He needed it the way a parasite needs a host. The other person meant nothing to him save the opportunity to reap a benefit. If he remembered your name, it was time to watch your back.

Within his social class he was among the success stories. In his world, every year you aged was a victory over circumstances. Many like him had died in the mouldy cellars of wrecked buildings that had never been cleared after the Great War; they had gone mad from glue, speed, and heroin, died of aids, overdoses, and methyl spirits— in short, the usual tableau of life in the gutter after the empire's fall.

Vitaly realised early on that it was better to be a supplier than a customer. He was an addict, true enough, but he kept his wits about him. He carried a pair of pliers at all times. Those who welshed on their debts had their gold teeth yanked out. Those without gold teeth had a finger cut off. They were allowed to keep the finger as a souvenir.

He himself had lost two fingers after stealing from the big boss. Weeping and writhing, he had declared remorse, but a few months later he stole a kilo of heroin, sold it to someone the same day, thought in vague amazement, *I really am incorrigible*, and hightailed it out of town.

In Nacer Gül's truck, he had crossed the border and knew, like the boy, that he could never go back to where he came from—the only road lay straight ahead.

Along the way, he kicked his habit. Which explained his chronic rotten mood.

He had sores on his legs from vitamin deficiency, large bruises where the needle had entered—on his arms and groin mostly—and inky blue clouds beneath the skin. Shivering in the truck, he had occasionally thrown up bile. When they left the trailer, he had walked away from the others and vomited his guts out.

The driver pointed them in the direction they had to go, westward. Two or three hours farther, civilisation was waiting. Along the roads were checkpoints, guard posts; better to arrive on foot and then spread out through the city.

Trails of mist floated over the flats. A little later, a reddish-blue stripe of light appeared on the horizon behind them; the wavering, ethereal purple of dawn was overtaking them. They were lightheaded with exhaustion and euphoria, unsure of themselves and happy. It would not be long before they entered the new world. The sun catapulted into the sky, the coolness of the morning yielding to its immediate heat. None of them had brought water. In silence they walked beneath the hot, open sky, their eyes red from peering at the horizon where their dreams stubbornly refused to materialise. They had already been walking for much longer than the man had said.

Doubt struck—first soundlessly, but soon openly. 'We've been screwed!' one man shouted.

His words were received with relief. Now they could set off against their worst fears. 'No!' they said. 'We just went the wrong way. We have to go *there*!'

They all pointed in different directions.

Everyone talked at the same time now, their ears attuned only to comfort and affirmation.

'What did you see?' they asked the boy. 'What *exactly*?'

'Barracks,' he said, startled. 'The dogs. And soldiers. They were wearing pistols here.' He slapped his hip.

'What else?'

'Lights, cars. How should I know?' All the eyes turned on him made him shy.

His answers reassured them: he had described a border, no doubt about it. The driver had pointed them in the wrong direction, that was all.

On purpose, one of them figured.

He didn't know any better, said another.

Some of them said: 'We need to go back to where we started, then we can follow the trail back.'

Others were against it: 'We've been walking all day! If we keep going straight, we have to end up *somewhere*!'

The black man kept his distance from the bickering. He stared across the flats, his chin held high, as though he saw things approaching that were still invisible to the others. The boy couldn't keep his eyes off him. The Ethiopian was the first of the wonders that awaited him. The black man's kinky hair was drab with dust; no one knew how long he'd been on the road. Did he himself have any idea where he was going? Who had shown him the way? And how had he ended up in their company? With every new question, the mystery deepened. He was a fairytale figure, a mysterious transient, but whether he was a force for good or for evil, the boy had no idea.

There was yelling behind him. To go on or to go back, that's what it all came down to. A couple of men strode off ostentatiously to the west. 'There's nothing out there,' they shouted over their shoulders. 'It will be the death of all of you. Suit yourselves!'

The couple followed reluctantly. Then the woman and the boy.

Two men went in the other direction. No one followed them.

Those who headed west bunched together again to form a group. The black man, too, had joined them, the boy saw when he looked around.

• • •

These things had happened endlessly long ago. Just as they forgot the individual days, so they forgot those they had left behind on the plains. The woman who had mourned for her abandoned suitcase was given a grave; her husband dug it with his hands. The others, they had simply left where they lay. The cares of the living were greater than those of the dead.

What did they know about Vitaly? His tattoos spoke of a life on the fringe; his mannerisms, of a city boy, rough and talkative. You didn't want to know too much about him, out of fear for what might show up.

He was the first to rob a corpse. The next day, he had an extra pair of shoes hanging around his neck. A disgrace, some mumbled; some turned their backs on him. The next slacker, a man who could no longer struggle to his feet, was robbed by three of them very early in the morning. They had stood looking at him for a while, at the way he wriggled in the dust. 'Help me, would you,' he had said quietly. 'It's no problem . . . once I'm on my feet.' He fell back again, staring up at them in mortal fear. 'I can . . . I can,' he panted. They pounced on him—Vitaly, the man from Ashkhabad, and the tall man. The latter twisted the victim's head to one side and held his hand over his nose and mouth. The others stole his coat and shoes, and the money and valuables from his pockets. Lighter. Money. Cigarettes. The body struggled with the strength still left in it, the assailants snorted and cursed, and then it was over. The predators took to their heels.

A half-naked body lies on the steppe. Tears dribble from his eyes, trickle down past his ears and into his hair. The sun climbs in the sky. Red light shimmers behind the closed eyelids. Flies wander across his flesh. They plant eggs in the corners of his eyes, in his ears and nose. They walk over his lips; the man weakly tries to blow them away.

When he dies that afternoon beneath the high, hellish sun, all manner of invaders—yeasts, fungi, and bacteria—begin proliferating on the corpse. The next morning, the fly eggs have already reached the pupal stage; maggots swim through the subcutaneous tissue, their food. The body has become the stage for a bacchanalia, converted into energy by micro-organisms that reproduce at lightning speed, by thousands and thousands of maggots that drill their way through the softened tissues, until the little red fox comes and eats its fill. The body has become a marbled purplish-blue; the skin is already separating from the bones. His lips are eaten away. He grins obscenely at the expressionless sky.

Now Vitaly is weakening, too, after the fight for the woman he has lost to the man from Ashkhabad. The sores on his legs are open, bandaged with strips of cloth that he sometimes rips away with a shriek when they become melded with the flesh.

He knows the smell. He knows it all too well. He has smelled it in the cellars and the little rooms where junkies lay rotting away under coarse blankets. It is the odour of despair that had told him he could now 'do business.' Most customers came to him; some, he visited himself—those who were so badly off that they could no longer get to the door. Hollow-eyed as the *Häftlinge* from the camps, they lay waiting for him. He could have started a pawnshop with all the things they offered him in return for a shot. Antiques made him uncomfortable—he didn't know their value—and so he stuck to plain old cash and precious metals. His clientele's mortality rate was high, but their ranks were always replenished. It was a good line of business to be in; no need to advertise, wheedle, or grovel.

The poacher leads the way more often now. His stamina is exceptional. Never has he become involved in the struggle for dominance; he is sufficient unto himself. Fanning out through the tall, plumed grass, the others follow. Vitaly scratches at the sore on his upper arm. He took his sweater off this morning and looked at the deep, leaking wound. It had come up suddenly, as though he'd been shot with a phosphor bullet. There is a bright red ring around it. At the spot where the sore is, that's where the black man touched him a few days ago—atop the hill, when he pointed out something to them in the distance. Right there is where the sore came up, not anywhere else, not on his stomach or on his arse; no, right where the one body touched the other. With his finger, the black man had burned a festering crater in his arm. Vitaly stays far away from him now; the man's eyes alone are enough to do harm. He doesn't want the darkie to touch him again, or even look at him. He's got the evil eye; his hands are charged with magic powers. He's the one who brought disaster down on them—their misfortune is all his fault. Hadn't their luck been rotten right from the start? From the start of the journey all the way up till now? They should have beaten him to death right away, crushed his head—but instead they had wandered farther and farther off course, until the steppes had almost killed them.

To the rhythm of his footsteps, Vitaly's mind churns round and round: a dying machine that generates only fear and hatred.

17

A NEW SOUL

'The point,' said the rabbi, 'is whether or not you came from a Jewish womb. That's what it all boils down to. The rest doesn't matter. There is no other way, except that of the *giyur*, the process of converting to Judaism. But that's not something I'd recommend. It is extremely hard. We would never encourage that. Better a good goy than a bad Jew, as Rabbi Stiefel said. The chance that he will obey the seven laws of Noah is greater than that he will subject himself to the six hundred and thirteen laws of Moses.'

Pontus Beg, feeling uneasy, said: 'All I want to know is whether my mother . . . whether she was a Jewess.'

There it was—his barely noticeable hesitation in using that word, the way it rubbed up against the epithet, as though he'd cursed in front of the rabbi. The word dragged a world of suffering behind it. Mockery is a cover for a fundamental lack of understanding. For condescension. That's how the word came to him. But here, in Rabbi Eder's kitchen, it is washed of the world's filth and goes back to what it means: a daughter of the people of Israel.

The rabbi shook his head impatiently. 'You can't just ask that about your mother! When you ask about her, you're asking about yourself. I explained that to you already. If that's what she is, then that's what you are. Then you even have a right to an Israeli passport, whether you like it or not.'

Beg straightened up, as though trying to wriggle out from beneath the role of the slow learner. 'And if you're not much of a believer? Even then?'

'Reason can bring one to God as well,' the rabbi said. 'Did you

know that a child in the womb assumes a position like it's reading the Torah?'

'I read Eastern things. Books without God in them.'

'A Jew is a Jew, even without the Eternal. We . . . we are a braided rope, individual threads woven to form a single cord. That's how we're linked. What ties us together is what we are.' He raked his fingers through his beard.

Beg suddenly realised where his heavy-heartedness came from: there were no windows in this room. The only light came from bare bulbs on the ceiling. No ray of sunlight ever entered here; no breeze ever blew through the rooms. Here and there, the plaster formed bulges on the walls. Moisture made the building smell like a cadaver.

Beg was curious about the other rooms, about the floor plan of this labyrinth. The door facing the street opened onto the synagogue; the rabbi lived in the rooms beside it, which one reached from the alleyway. The building was as mysterious as an oriental bazaar. The old man had to have a bed somewhere, just as, somewhere, there had to be a door that led from the inside to the house of prayer.

'Rabbi Eder, who cooks for you?' Beg asked.

'The neighbours,' the rabbi said gloomily. 'Chinese food, every night. It's making my eyes go slanty. When my cook died, I stopped being a Jew. The kitchen is the cathedral of the Jews, my good man.'

Beg nodded.

'It takes me three days to finish one helping,' the rabbi said.

Could he still comply with the dietary laws, while eating Chinese food every night? Beg didn't dare to ask. Maybe the whole thing is crumbling away, now that there are no successors, he thought. *Maybe he doesn't care much anymore, now that there's no one breathing down his neck.*

'I can't tell you whether or not your mother was Jewish,' the rabbi said suddenly. 'You'll have to find out for yourself. Ask the people who are still alive. That's where the answer lies. What made you think so, anyway?'

'Her surname, Medved.'

'All right.'

'And that song.'

91

'What song?'

'The love song. About Rebekka.'

The rabbi shook his head. 'I don't know any song about Rebekka.'

'I sang it for you!'

'Sing it again, then I'm sure I'll remember it.'

And so it happened for the second time that Pontus Beg sang a Yiddish love song for the old rabbi.

'Very good,' he said contentedly when Beg was finished. 'Singing brings us closer to God.' He rocked his head back and forth, light-heartedly, as though at a dance party. 'So your mother used to sing that to you? When you were little? But that's very unusual! Why would she sing a Yiddish song? Do you have any idea?'

Beg wiped his eyes with one hand. 'That's why I'm here,' he said.

'You really should have a little more than that to go on. Indications.'

'Like the name,' Beg said. 'Her maiden name. Here . . .' He pulled out Professor Urban's book of names, found the right page, and slid it across the table.

'What am I supposed to look at?'

Beg put his index finger beside his mother's surname.

'I can't see anything without my glasses,' the rabbi said grumpily. 'Where did I put my glasses?'

'There,' Beg said.

The rabbi slid his reading glasses down from his forehead and mumbled: 'Old man, keep yourself together.' He bent over and read the word in the book that Beg held up for him. 'Also Jewish, indeed,' he said. 'Ashkenazi, um hum. High German.'

He looked up. His washed-out blue eyes slid over Beg's face. 'Your mother received her surname from her father. That doesn't mean anything. If her mother was Jewish, then she was Jewish, and so are you. What interests me is your maternal grandmother—if she was Jewish, then you are, too. What do you know about your grandparents?'

'Not much. I never met them. Patriots, my mother said. My grandfather died . . . the last year of the war, on the Neisse, the last big offensive. My mother was raised by her mother. My grandmother married again, but I don't know much about her second husband . . . I can't remember him so well. An officer, if I'm not mistaken.'

'How can you live like that? Without any history? We Jews . . . we're touchy enough as it is, and our memory goes back four thousand years! Some people . . . they don't care about where they belong anymore. They hide it away, they don't talk about it, and when they die, someone suddenly says: "Shouldn't we be giving him a Jewish burial?" General consternation, no one knew, all this time. Why? There are so many reasons. The Eternal not only blessed us, he cursed us, too.' He was silent for a moment. 'What do you want to do with this knowledge, anyway? A Jew, a Gentile—does it really make any difference to you?'

'Yes,' Beg said resolutely, without knowing what else he was going to say. 'There's a difference.' And, after some hesitation: 'Even though I couldn't tell you what it is.'

To arrive at an answer, he needed to delve deeper into himself than was his wont. He had a sneaky feeling about what he would find there—the loneliness to which he'd grown accustomed, like having a cold foot and a peeping in his ears. Long ago he had decided to tolerate life and demand from it nothing that was beyond his own capacity to fulfil. Eastern schools of thought advanced resignation as a way of life, too. But a seed might sometimes sprout, even in a crack in the pavement—it shouldn't have been there, yet still it grew, its roots stuck right through the concrete . . .

It had become a longing, to know where he came from.

'There's no hurry,' the rabbi said. 'The only right answer is the answer at the right moment. It will come of its own accord.'

He stood up and shuffled to the sink. His hands shaking, he poured himself some tea concentrate and added hot water from the samovar. Blue veins lay beneath his thin, yellow skin. Long nails. Liver spots on the backs of his hands.

'We're going to need a bit more—documents, perhaps. Something irrefutable. Paper is the best proof. Can you get hold of documents?'

'What kind of documents?'

'Something that proves you're descended from Jews. The problem is that the system here keeps track only of the paternal line. That can complicate matters.'

• • •

The rabbi asked whether Beg would like to see the synagogue. He shuffled out in front of him, across the grey tiles. The place looked like an underground bunker complex where the sun never shone—a phantom realm where you became less and less a body and more and more a shadow, an erased pencil stroke. The rabbi stopped in front of a door, felt around under his coat, and pulled out a bunch of keys. He held them up to the light of a bare bulb and ran through them one by one until he found the right one.

'Wait here for a moment,' he said.

He came back with a yarmulke. 'Put this on.'

Beg wormed the thing onto the back of his head and followed the old man inside. The high, open space was a hallucination—after the darkness, it was as though the heavens had opened. The pillars bearing up the roof were inlaid with royal blue and gold mosaic tiles; the late-afternoon light fell through high windows. The smell was of a space no longer animated by any human presence. The wooden benches and cabinets along the walls were hung with webs of grey light. The rabbi, his hands behind his back, stood looking around, a tourist at an antique ruin. Beg walked past the podium in the middle, a cupboard draped with curtains, and the stone steps leading to the platform above it all. He knew nothing of what had been said and done here, in this mysterious world where the memory of a journey thousands of years old was kept alive. This, then, was where that journey ended, and there stood the last traveller, waiting for him to get his fill of looking.

The rabbi gestured to him. They passed through a door and down a narrow corridor. At the end was yet another door. He opened it; behind it, all was darkness. When the light clicked on, Beg saw a landing the size of a little room, with more wooden benches along its walls. It resembled a dressing room. The rabbi led the way down the stone flight in front of them. The steps were worn hollow. Deep in the ground, a long rectangle had been hewn from the rock—a bath beneath a brick masonry arch. And standing motionless in the basin: chimerical, clear water. The steps disappeared below the surface and on to the bottom of the bath. It was a descent to a place that seemed more vital than the synagogue itself: the sacred heart of a mystery cult. The light from the landing above reflected off the water's surface. Beg would have liked to touch it, to set it in motion, but it would scald his unclean skin, as punishment for that act of blasphemy.

Water trickled down the walls. The grey stone gleamed.

'The forefathers built the house on a source of living water,' the rabbi said. 'Like Moses, they struck it from the rock.'

Here a Jewish man or woman went down the steps, naked and alone. There was to be nothing between the body and the water. No clothing, bandages, jewellery—even the paltriest crumb under a nail was to be removed. Only then were you cleansed.

'A sort of baptism, in other words,' Beg said.

The rabbi looked up at him, displeased. 'Those three little drops of water! You have to go all the way under, all the way! And not just once—again and again. How else could you be purified?'

In silence, they looked at the glassy water. Deep in the earth was where they found themselves; the world was far away. The rabbi's voice sounded quiet now. 'It's not a baptism; it's not a bath in the sense of soap and water. He who is immersed in the mikveh becomes a new person. He gets a new soul.'

A drop fell. Beg's heart cringed; it had been so long since he'd heard such a serene sound. The ripple in the water died away quickly. He wished he could undress, go down the steps to the bottom of the basin, let his body go under, and cleanse it of the world's filth. Even the filth that did not wash off, he would scrub that away, too. A new soul—there, deep in the earth, with this magic water, that kind of thing seemed truly possible. What a pleasant, comforting thought . . . to shed his old soul, that tattered, worn thing, and receive a new one in its stead. Who wouldn't want that? Who would turn down something like that?

18

THE JUDGEMENT

Vitaly bared his upper arm to display the wound. The boy turned away in disgust; the sore, covered in a green film, made him nauseated.

So the black man possessed powers. He'd suspected as much, always had. Yet he still hadn't decided whether he was a good sorcerer or an evil one; harming Vitaly could very well be the act of a miracle worker. Mean dogs are there to be kicked.

'He says he touched him there,' the woman told the others. 'That that's what caused the sore. Something like that is . . . well, it's . . .' She searched for words, without finding them.

The boy didn't respond; he hadn't forgotten the slap. He looked around, but saw the black man nowhere. Just to be on the safe side, he would avoid him. And keep his eyes open in the meantime.

Look, he told himself, you have to look carefully.

He remembered something his mother had told him once, a memory of him as a little boy. A little sister was born and, according to his mother, he had said: 'Babies can't talk because they're not allowed to tell secrets about heaven.'

All right, he thought now, *I may not know about heaven's secrets yet, but I'll sure find out about the earthly ones.*

During the journey, he had already seen and understood more than in all the years before. If he survived, the trip would shape and scar him.

'He was the last one to show up,' the man from Ashkhabad said.

'What if he touches us, too?' the woman said. 'In our sleep?'

The man from Ashkhabad shook his head, unable to answer. 'He wasn't the last one to show up,' the boy said. 'He was there from the start. Along with the rest of us.'

'Why do you say that?' the woman said bitterly. 'Why are you lying about it?'

'He was the last one,' Vitaly said. 'No one knew where he came from. Suddenly he was just there, to bring us bad luck . . .'

'Like a djinn,' the woman said.

It was the first time the boy saw her talk to the man from Ashkhabad, whose prey she was at night. Once she had spat on him—she had said she would kill him if she got the chance—but that all seemed to have vanished now. The boy kept his mouth shut; this sudden unanimity allowed for no dissent.

It was not his custom, but now the poacher joined in, too. 'You're the one who brought him back to us,' he told the tall man. 'We shook him off, then you showed up with him again. That's the way I see it.'

'All I did was follow him!' the tall man protested. 'He was the one who found your trail.'

The poacher shrugged. 'I'm only telling you what I saw.'

Vitaly nodded furiously, fever and mortal fear in his bulging eyes. The life will go out of him soon. His breathing is agitated. There's only one thing he longs for now: someone on whom to pin his misfortune. He needs to punish the black man, drag him along in his fall. That's what he still has to do. All the venom left in him he will apply to that end.

Evening. As they sit in the wet sand, a host of fat, round clouds converge above their heads. At the edges of the steppe, bolts shoot down from the violet sky.

'Hey, beanpole!' Vitaly says. 'What did you two get up to back there anyway, you and that nigger friend of yours?'

The tall man shrugs reluctantly.

'We leave you behind for dead and suddenly you're back, nothing wrong with you, fit as a fiddle. How about you explain that to us, how that's possible.'

The others chimed in. Yeah, what exactly *did* happen?

The tall man looked at the ground. 'Nothing,' he said quietly.

'Bullshit,' Vitaly said. 'One minute you're kicking the bucket, the next minute you come prancing in.'

The woman pulls her coat tighter around her. The boy looks down the row of emaciated male faces, the jutting cheekbones above their beards, their eyes sunk deep in the sockets—an inquisition in rags. They glare at the tall man. He should never have returned from the plains. For that he was being condemned. The deepest suspicion still had to be pronounced, but it floated out in front of the rest, waiting for the right moment to descend: the suspicion that witchcraft was at play here, a conspiracy with the darkness. That was the line of accusation the tribunal would choose, inexorably; the boy sensed it. The tall man could not escape. There was no possible defence; suspicion and verdict were one. The dark shapes before him, a tangled-up ball of fear and rage. The tall man slid back from the circle a little. His hand rested on a pebble. He picked it up and raised it to his myopic eyes: a smooth, white little stone, bleached like the shells on a beach. Had the steppe once been a sea? Black fish slipped noiselessly past his body. Dark waves of kelp bobbed before his eyes, the eyes of a pitiful drowned man at the bottom of the ocean.

'He gave me something to eat,' he said.

'So what did you two have to eat?' Vitaly mocked. 'Soup and white bread?'

'He had a can with him.'

'And what was in the can? Caviar?'

'Dog food. I think it was dog food.'

'And where did he get that from?'

He shook his head. 'How should I know . . . ?'

'He's your friend, isn't he?' the woman shrilled.

His quiet voice: 'He's not my friend.'

'You mean he helped you for *no reason*? *Just like that?*'

Behind them, a flash of lightning broke the clouds. Thunder rolled across the sky. Gently, after that, came the sound of rain around them.

Pointing at his upper arm, Vitaly asked whether the black man had touched him, too.

'For Christ's sake,' the tall man said, 'what do you mean by that?'

'Here!' Vitaly hissed. 'Here, this is where he touched me with his finger!'

Pulling his sweater up over his head, he showed them his arm. They looked in dismay at the wound that lay like a burning sun between faded tattoos. The ring around it had widened, and the crater seemed even deeper.

'No,' the tall man said, 'he didn't touch me. Or wait, when he helped me to my feet.'

'Show us,' Vitaly said.

'Fuck off.'

'Show us!'

'Aw, man, knock it off.'

But his plea was weak. Vitaly stood up and began yanking on the man's clothes. 'Show us, damn you!'

The tall man flailed his arms wildly and edged back even farther. Beyond Vitaly's reach, he slowly pulled off the layers of sweaters and T-shirts. A little later, he stood before them like that, a shivering blade of grass in the rain. They were shocked by the look of him. They knew: they were this skinny, too. His sternum stuck out, and the ribs rose and fell beneath the papery skin. The tall man looked down at his own body, inquisitively, in search of marks. 'Hey,' he said when he spotted the infected fleabites on his stomach.

'You see, you see!' Vitaly crowed.

The others could not keep their eyes off his offensive nakedness, the face of starvation. Skin, nails, and hair.

Slow as a cold reptile, the tall man put it all back on.

A web of forked lightning illuminated the twilight.

'And that one over there'—the man from Ashkhabad pointed to where the black man had built his nest—'has been stuffing himself and laughing at us the whole goddamn time.'

This was an unbearable thought, an insult to their desperate hunger.

'Has he got grub or not?' Vitaly asked the tall man.

'I didn't see any.'

'He gave you something to eat, didn't he? That means he's got grub, doesn't it?'

'Maybe, yeah, I guess.' The tall man flapped his arms wildly now. 'How should I know!'

The man from Ashkhabad rose to his feet, and he and Vitaly

walked over to the Ethiopian's camp. The others followed. They approached him cautiously, fearful of the power they had created in their minds.

'Hey, Africa,' Vitaly said, kicking at the prone form. The tarp moved, and the black man stuck his head out.

'Food!' Vitaly said. He raised his hand to his mouth. The black man laughed nervously.

'You've got food there,' Vitaly said. He kicked at him again.

The black man crawled out from under the tarp and backed away from them.

They dumped the contents of his satchel on the wet ground and lifted the plastic to see if anything was hidden there. Uncomprehendingly, the black man watched as they rummaged through his possessions—the empty can, a Bible they couldn't read (they saw the silver cross on the cover), a roll of newspapers, his empty lighters, and his jingling collection of tin bottle caps. They had counted on finding a secret food stash, and now they looked in disbelief at his paltry possessions. They kicked apart the ring of grass, but found nothing. The Ethiopian looked at the tall man—a look that asked for help, a mitigating word to break the tension—but the tall man averted his eyes. Dark pillars, dripping with rain, they looked in silence at the African. They turned and went back to their places.

19

ANONYMOUS

Nagged by regret, Beg followed the rabbi up the steps, back from the hollow in the earth to the surface world where his old soul rejoined him. It was dark in the synagogue now; the vibrant blue had faded from the pillars.

Humming, the old man straightened a cloth that hung before the cabinet containing the Torah. Beg felt like going away, like leaving behind the questions without answers, and resuming his life. The rabbi stood with his back to him, nodding his head slightly now and again. Beg sat down in the front pew. Who had sat here before him? What had those people been like? How unthinkable, suddenly, that he should be one of them! He knew nothing about them; they were as remote to him as the Eskimos. Or the dead. That was more like it, he thought, for there was only one of them left: the captain, who would be the last to leave the ship.

He crossed his legs. No sound made its way in here. He heard only the crystalline singing in his head—inside his head, it wasn't quiet at all. It would never be quiet again. It was in surroundings such as these that the metallic whistling had started. He tried not to think about it, that was his strategy; he lived around his burgeoning defects. But now, in the synagogue—where, just like on the steppes, the absence of sound came across as a gentle murmur—he felt a light, serene sorrow at the loss of silence.

For a long time he had feared that the whistling in his ears was a harbinger of deafness. He was afraid of going deaf. The deaf man seemed lonelier to him than the blind, because his world was limited to what he could *see*. A blind man could hear what happened behind and above him; for the deaf man, the world behind was an abyss. A deaf person could tell you less about the world around him than a blind person; he had proved that to himself at work one time by sealing his ears with balls of wax. The bustle of police headquarters had disappeared as if by magic: he could barely hear the phone, or the knocking on doors. The conversations in the corridor, Oksana's silly chatter, the lowing of a drunken prisoner—all vanished. As did doors that opened and closed, cars in the courtyard, snatches of conversation, the cooing of pigeons on the sill. The world without sound was a flat surface; all depth disappeared.

The rabbi straightened and turned around. He gestured to his guest to follow. At the exit, Beg saw a tapestry woven with gold thread and depicting a candlestick. He stopped in his tracks. There was a memory he was groping after, but couldn't quite reach. He strained his eyes, as though that might help him squeeze out the memory. Suddenly, in his mind's eye, he saw his mother emptying a bucket of potato peels into a trough. She was perspiring, and the hair at the back of her neck was straggly. It was a *living* memory, so different from the pictures he had of her; photographs tended to overgrow living memories, and finally to replace them. But now he was *seeing* how she put down the bucket, straightened her back, and rested her hands on her hips; with the back of one hand, she brushed away the hair that hung in her eyes from beneath her kerchief.

The first thing he forgot after she died was her scent. Then it was her voice. And soon enough after that, he could no longer summon up her looks and expressions.

Words had moved in to take their place. That she was loving and hot-tempered, maternal and dominating. At her funeral, he recalled, they had said that she worked like a horse, and had a will of iron. Without her stamina and financial insight, people said, the family would have gone to ruin. (*Because the head of the household was a financial nincompoop*, he heard them think.)

Gradually, his mother was put in a nutshell of a few traits: a life in catchwords.

The words had replaced her.

Now there she stood, squinting as she looked out over the fields;

behind her, her son snuck into the house, an intruder in his own memories, through the kitchen and into the dark hallway, on stockinged feet into his parents' bedroom, the planks creaking beneath his footfalls—forbidden territory. There is the corner cupboard with its glass doors; she stores her valuables behind panes of cut glass. Her wedding photo in its silver frame, the picture of her parents beside it: her father in the infantryman's summer uniform; her mother in white, a coronet in her raven hair. A jade cameo, an ivory hair clasp—the riches of a farm wife. At the back, covered by the veil she wore at her wedding, is a little candleholder with seven branches.

A candleholder exactly like the one he was looking at now.

Beg stood in the alleyway and put on his cap. The back door of the restaurant was open, and an old woman was peeling onions in the doorway. The skins fell into a bucket between her knees. A cigarette dangled from a corner of her mouth; she kept one eye closed to keep out the smoke. The woman followed his every move, but her hands went on peeling mechanically. Behind her, under fluorescent lighting, Asians were at work in the kitchen.

Beg entered the restaurant from the street side, passing through a curtain of tinkling beads. A man and a girl behind the counter looked at him as expressionlessly as the old woman had.

Sitting at a little table by the window, he flipped through the menu, which featured pictures of the various dishes in strange colours and attitudes, as though a pilot had squeezed off a random series of aerial landscape photos. The caramelised duck glistened temptingly. Beg looked up at the girl and pointed to the duck: 'This one.'

She nodded.

'And a coke,' he said.

He watched her go. The Chinese were every bit as enigmatic as the Jews. His legs were shimmying under the table.

'That thing, what is that?' he'd asked Zalman Eder, after they had stood looking at the candleholder.

The rabbi explained to him that the menorah, along with the Ark of the Covenant, was one of the most important attributes of Judaism.

Beg thought about the poignancy he'd felt—the same thing he'd felt when he talked to his sister. So much had been lost, he thought; sometimes you could survey that loss in its entirety. His sister's voice had carried him back to where he came from, to the days when everything still had its natural place, and none of them had foreseen a future in which your rightful spot on earth was a thing half forgotten. Condemned to years of air and dust, the inconstancy could only be combated with ironclad routine. There was less and less difference between him and the nameless ones they sometimes found—the anonymous ones committed to the soil with a modicum of formalities. His sister's voice was a lifeline tossed to him from the past, to keep him from forgetting who he was and where he came from.

The candlestick showed him his place in the past and awarded him a place in the present. It reminded him about the child he was, sneaking through his parents' bedroom and taking in the objects in the corner cupboard, and told him that he had been born of a Jewish woman who had concealed her past—just as she had hidden the menorah beneath the veil. He had no doubts anymore. He must be a Jew—no, he *was* one. That was his place in the world, part of a people, of a community. A community extinct, but for one.

That he belonged somewhere, that was the poignant thing. Sitting in the Chinese restaurant, he looked back over his life. The boy taking a swan dive from the bridge by the weir: a Jew. Pontus the son: a Jew. The cadet: a Jew. Commissioner Beg: a Jew. This time, history, that process of erosion, had won something rather than lost. Nothing had changed, yet everything was different. He belonged to another people now, as chosen as they were doomed, as the rabbi had said.

The last century had roared over their heads with such brute force that now only one of them was left—or, in fact, two. When Zalman Eder died, Beg would be the last Jew in Michailopol. The shuddering of his legs made the table shake.

After the pogroms came the camps. In Michailopol, there had been a *Lager*. People spoke of one hundred thousand to two hundred thousand prisoners who had been executed there: mostly Jews, but also Red Army prisoners. In 1943, the Germans had started destroying the evidence: the mass graves were opened, and *Sonderkommandos* piled the bodies high and burned them. The fires burned for months. After the war, a Soviet report noted that the ground and substrate were saturated with the juice from corpses and melted human fat.

The girl put a hot plate on the table, and lit the tea-warmers inside it.

Little was left of the camp itself. It had become overgrown with trees and bushes. Years ago, a little monument had been set up beside what were once the gates to the *Lager*. Later, it was set on fire and plastered with swastikas. The brick walls still standing were daubed with the angled cross. In Michailopol, there was no such thing as a respectful nod to the past.

The Chinese girl placed the platters of noodles and duck on the hot plate. Beg served himself, tilting the platter to let the bird and its juices slide onto his plate. He had arrived at the age when only sex and large quantities of food provided him with sensations of happiness. All the rest was extinguished; the heart was a motor that lost power with the years.

Still, undeniably, the discoveries about his past produced in him feelings that seemed like happiness; the right word for it, perhaps, was excitement, an edgy kind of anticipation. As though something was about to start—a sensation he remembered from childhood. The only thing was: he couldn't for the life of him figure out *what* it was that was about to start. He was a Jew, that was all. It changed nothing and solved nothing. He would harbour no expectations. He would follow it, of course, but without assuming that it would add anything to his life.

It was a strategy the Chinese people behind the counter might have had something to say about, had they not made silence towards outsiders such a part of their nature. They lived behind a screen of enchanted silk, invisible and impenetrable.

In Michailopol's crime statistics, they were almost entirely absent. He couldn't remember a Chinese person ever having been arrested. If he went into the kitchen, of course, he would be sure to find a few people working without the proper documents, but there was no cause for him to check. They weren't bothering anyone. Chinese people seemed to avoid even the most minor of public infractions.

If more ethnic groups did that, his work would be a lot easier. In fact, it would make him pretty much superfluous. He would show up at the scene of accidents, settle minor territorial disputes, and lead an existence otherwise as calm as that of a civil servant at the court of Lu, in the sixth century before Christ.

The curtain tinkled. The rabbi came in and walked to the counter without looking around. He placed his order. Beg ate his duck mechanically and watched him. The old man stood at the counter motionlessly until his meal came sliding through the little trapdoor. The Chinese man wrapped the containers in drab paper and dropped them into a plastic bag. Slowly, the rabbi counted out the change from his wallet.

As he was heading for the door, Beg raised his hand and said: 'Mr. Eder.'

The rabbi looked up, roused from his thoughts. He came over to the table.

They spoke, the rabbi standing, his gaze fixed on the debris on Beg's plate. Only then did Beg tell him about his mother's candleholder. He heard himself talking. The bedroom, the glass cupboard, the veil. Then the rabbi said: 'The menorah is hard for us to part with. It's something . . . very important. Seven arms that draw us back to our origins.'

He looked at Beg's plate again and said: 'Your first meal as a Jew, and already you're in violation.'

Beg looked at the remains in surprise.

'Ham,' the rabbi said. '*Treife*.'

Beg didn't understand.

'Not kosher,' the rabbi said.

There were strips of pink ham between the noodles; Beg hadn't noticed them.

The rabbi looked despondently at his own plastic bag of food. 'But, oh well . . . ?'

He was almost to the door when Beg stood up and said: 'One more thing, one more question.'

Zalman Eder came back, his movements impatient.

'I was wondering,' Beg said, 'what if all those things are a mistake? The directives. All happenstance. What then?'

A sly smile appeared on the rabbi's lips. He said: 'Let me ask you this: in a city there are ten butchers, nine of them kosher. Then, on the street, you find a package of meat. Nice meat; you're glad you found it. But is it kosher, or isn't it? You go to the rabbi for counsel. How great is the chance, do you think, that it's kosher?'

'Nine out of ten,' Beg said.

'The chance that it's kosher, I would say, is so great that you can eat it with a clear conscience.'

'And what if it's not kosher?'

The rabbi laughed. 'Then we pretend it is! And anyone who tries to prove differently had better be pretty damned sharp.'

The Chinese laughed quietly along with them, behind their counter, without understanding a word.

20

THEN THERE WERE SIX

The boy crawled out from under the tarp. He stared into a day of ground fog and water—nothing but gusts of rain and a train of clouds as far as you could see. His travelling companions lay scattered around him in dark clumps, unrecognisable in their night-time shrouds of plastic sheeting and old coats. The man from Ashkhabad and the woman lay farthest from the rest. The boy looked in the direction they would take later, at the flat band of earth, the monotonous view, as though this journey began anew each day, the eternal return of the same. The steppe was a repetition, a dull-wittedly looping melody; it ground them down and wore them out, took another little piece of them every day, and would finally pulverise them all. Sometimes he thought about going on alone, about trying his luck without the others—how much of a chance was there that he would be the only one to reach the far side? And how much of a chance was there that they would arrive without him?

Had he learned enough from them to establish his bearings? Could he imitate the poacher's techniques? Did he know where to dig to find edible tubers? He needed to pay more attention, so that he, too, could survive on his own someday.

Once, long ago, they would have been on their feet before sunrise. They had been conquerors back then; these days, wild horses couldn't drag them from their beds. They abandoned their dreams with a curse. They scratched at their fleabites and rubbed their eyes. Never did they seem more lost than when they arose and the dispiriting flats rolled out before them.

They packed up their sleeping gear, tossed the bundles over

their shoulders, and entered the new day. The wet grass of the steppe soaked their trouser legs. No one said a word. The gaping sole of the boy's right shoe scooped sand. They spread out and moved through the tall, dead grass.

The boy looked back. Africa and the tall man were missing. 'Hey!' he shouted to the others, then ran back to the campsite. His shoe flapped. It made him dizzy, but he kept running.

Foreboding.

The black man was kneeling beside the tall man's sleeping space. The plastic had been thrown back. The tall man's mouth had fallen open, as though he'd choked on a word he would never pronounce again. His beer-yellow eyes were riveted on the sky above, drops of rain trickling through the grey hairs of his beard.

The black man was murmuring a prayer with his eyes closed. In his hand he held the cross that hung on a cord around his neck. The boy began pulling away the plastic at the tall man's feet, cautiously, ready to leap aside. The trouser legs were pulled up a bit, and he saw his skinny blue shins, bitten to pieces by fleas. The others were coming; he had to work fast. They were filthy old gym shoes and they stank like the plague, but they were still whole. He had the left one already, but it was the right one he needed most urgently. The shoe wouldn't budge; it was lashed tightly to the foot. The boy was in too much of a hurry to untie the laces, so he pulled hard on the heel. The tall man's body shook beneath his efforts.

Almaty, oh Almaty! This is what has become of the world! Oh woe is me!

When the shoe shot loose, the boy fell on his back. The others were almost there; he quickly grabbed the left shoe as well and ran off. He wasn't strong, but he could outrun them all.

From a safe distance, he looked back. They were standing around the body. The black man, still kneeling, was looking up at them. The boy pulled off his own shoes and put on the tall man's. They were much too big for him, but sturdy enough, if he pulled the laces tight.

Shoes were vital. Without shoes, you were lost. Within their little economy, shoes represented great wealth—more than trousers or a coat. Water came first, then shoes. He was proud of his catch. He had been smarter than the others, faster. Above all, it was a victory over Vitaly, the slyest of them all. He had beaten him hands-down.

Once, he had shared a pair of shoes with his brother. The son with shoes could go to school. He wore them one day; his brother, the next. When he left, they had given him the shoes. Now his brother couldn't go to school anymore.

These were his third pair since he'd left. In the distance, he sees the man from Ashkhabad lash out at Africa with the tall man's stick. Did he hit him? The black man rolls over, leaps to his feet, and picks up his satchel on the run.

The boy follows him with his eyes—the running that seems almost like fluttering, an awkward bird that can't get off the ground.

Vitaly and the man from Ashkhabad pull the plastic off the tall man and search his body with practised movements. They apply force to bend the stiff arms away from the man's chest. The body doesn't give; it shudders beneath their brusqueness. It looks as though they've found nothing of value. The man from Ashkhabad takes only the stick. You could use it to poke up a fire, or to swing at Africa.

The boy waits till they're out of sight, then starts moving. In passing, he glances at the violated corpse: the shirt is torn open, the trousers pulled down to its knees. Bones. Nails and hair. There isn't much left for the other predators. The pale genitals against the grey pubic hair make the tall man more a *thing* than the boy likes to see.

The thing lies there helplessly, an invitation to be torn apart. The boy realises how much his own life has come to rely on defence—the *clenched* position with regard to everything that could happen to him. Comfort does not exist. Everything has danger as its shadow. He is a nervous animal: he has to cross the open field in search of food, but flight is built into all his movements. It has become second nature to him. That is what the road has taught him.

The boy looks back from time to time, and sees Africa pop up amid the tall grass. He is a dog in the caravan's wake. No matter how much they beat him, he keeps coming back, begging for attention and mercy. They will hit him even harder, and keep on until he finally understands that he doesn't belong with them. That he is a stranger, the bearer of enigma. There is no place for him in the group any longer;

he will have to complete the journey alone. Especially now that the tall man is dead. He needs to understand that it is more dangerous for him to be with the group than to wander lonely across the flats. He needs to finally understand that his time is almost up.

The boy admires and despises his stubbornness. Why does he go looking to be humiliated? Why doesn't he realise that they want to hurt him? He turns around and shouts: 'Go away! Go away, would you!' The black man waves to him. He approaches. The boy hisses, 'Ksst! ksst!,' the way you would at an annoying herd of goats. The man nods and smiles.

The boy turns his back on him again. *Well, then, it's up to you*, he thinks bitterly. *I warned you. You can't say I didn't warn you.*

He looks at his new shoes—the shoes of a grown man. There are almost no holes in them; the soles are unbroken. Who did the tall man steal them from? He racks his brains, but has almost no memory of those who remained behind. Whatever the case, he's wearing them now. He rescued them from the heat of the battle. His mother would be proud of him.

Don't think about Mother now. Better not.

Her hands were often hard, but sometimes soft, too, like when she used them to cradle his head.

Bad thoughts. Stupid thoughts. He hates his tears.

It was important to keep getting closer to them, unobtrusively, to make it seem as though you'd always been there. If you popped up all of a sudden, they would remember why you'd lagged behind; someone might say: 'Give us those shoes, you little thief!' and take them away from him. But they didn't even look up, didn't notice the little spurts with which the boy kept getting closer. He tried to read the expressions on their dark backs: were they tense and aggressive, or simply resigned?

If Vitaly tried to take them off him, he would hit him on the wound, bite into it. Yes, biting him would be the best thing—right through the sleeve of his sweater, sinking his teeth into that filthy wound. The shrieks would be deafening. Revenge for the blows, the insults, the times that he ate the boy's portion—Vitaly, the lowest of the low. That's right, let him try to take his shoes away. The screams would be music to his ears.

Against the other men he was defenceless, although he had little to fear from the poacher, who was neutral as a corpse. The boy couldn't count on the man from Ashkhabad, who had his moods. He didn't give a damn about anything most of the time, and then suddenly things went haywire. He was strong; his wrists were thick. When they left, he'd been overweight—he'd had a round belly. He would sigh all the time, the way fat people do. But the steppes had taken away his belly. Now he was as skinny as the rest. His skin lay draped in folds against his bones, like a carpet.

Once again, they had no fire. The snares remained empty; they rooted around in the earth without finding a thing. It had been so many days since they'd eaten, they envied the dead who had no share in their concerns.

The woman, her face in the shadows, said: 'He was just hunched down there, bent over him. It was hideous, as though he wanted to drink his blood.'

'That's what they do. Defile our bodies,' said the man from Ashkhabad.

'Hell is the last thing he saw,' said Vitaly.

'Terrible,' the woman sighed.

The poacher appeared from the twilight. He had found rabbit warrens. And he had seen Africa, he said. He was lying not far from here.

The woman moaned softly.

'Where?' the man from Ashkhabad asked.

The poacher pointed. 'He saw me. I just kept walking.'

'Did he try anything?' Vitaly asked.

'What are you talking about, man?'

But they all knew. How he had fed on the dead, and with a single touch turned Vitaly's arm into a withered stem. For them, everything was getting worse and worse. For him, everything was getting better. They saw it clearly, the sorcerer's circle. The black man was slowly drawing it closed, like a net.

21

LEAH

The rabbi asked him which district his family was from. Oblast Grünewald, Beg replied. His mother's family was from Brstice; that, as far as he knew, was where they'd always lived. The rabbi nodded. He had heard of Brstice; he would write to the rabbi there and ask for more information about the Medveds. Maybe that would produce definitive proof.

'If that's how it is, then that's how it must be,' he said cryptically.

For reasons he himself didn't fully understand, Beg was giddy with happiness.

When was the last time he'd been so full of hope and anticipation? The question took him far back in time. Sergeant Beg—he had shot up through the ranks. He wore the decorations proudly on his claret-coloured lapels. He walked hand in hand with the girl with whom everything started. There were others like them on the promenade, but the limelight shone only on them. Below, along the quay, the dark river hurried to the sea. There were slow, glassy vortexes in the water, as though a huge beast was roiling just under the surface. In front of a café, on the pavement, a quintet was playing, the notes of the clarinet sounding like the good cheer of a swarm of sparrows. The heat of early summer had left everyone carefree and happy. She took him by the hand and said: 'Come on, Pontus, let's dance.' He refused. The couple of lessons he'd had at the academy had not been enough to make him a good dancer. She took the glass out of his hand and simply said: 'Come.' She led him along under the little lights in the plane trees. The bear danced; there was nothing she could not make him do.

She reached around behind and loosened his grip a bit.

'Sorry,' Beg said.

'Close your eyes,' she said. 'There's no one else here.'

He closed his eyes. Behind his lids, the lamps slid by in a red blaze.

She had studied mining engineering; in Murmansk, she had spent part of her university days in a factory lab where the mineral apatite was converted to superphosphate. The way she spoke those words—Beg had never heard music any lovelier.

Her father was chairman of the regional party council and managing director of a steel mill on the Volga—part of the new nobility, risen after the collapse of the old regime and the redistribution of all resources.

Woe to the lover who believes this enchantment to be his actual, his natural state; what an injustice that it should be denied him so often. How could he have lived without it? Now that the scales have fallen from his eyes, now that he knows the way it really is, he will never let go. From now on, this will be his life. In this blaze, in this daze, he will go on.

The smile on the lover's lips says that he has plumbed an important secret: he is an initiate; the opiate of love has let him look behind the drab veil of daily life. This is the time of anticipation. The same kitchen smells still waft under his door, children still scream in the hallway, and above his head the neighbour listens to loud martial music, even though he is much too young to be a veteran. But all these things are already different now. Isn't it true that it annoys him much less than it used to? Don't the sounds already seem much less loud, and isn't the stench of roasted meat and herbs from the Tadzhiki refugees next door somehow already less penetrating?

Twenty-eight years later—at another house, in another city—Pontus Beg sits at the table in his living room and stares at his reflection in the darkened window. *A happy life*, he thinks, *is always marked by a certain anticipation, no matter what the Chinese sages may say about emptiness and the absence of expectations.* Beneath rustling bamboo beside the rushing stream, it is easier to disengage than it is on the sixth floor, with the heaters gurgling and water rushing through the standpipes, carrying away his neighbours' bowel movements. Under the table, his stockinged feet shuffle on the carpet. His only memories of a certain hunger for life are accompanied by those of expectation and longing—the elation at yet another day. He, too, was capable of that once. No one can imagine it these days; but he, too, sang love songs when he thought no one could hear, and on occasion he jumped for joy on a deserted street.

Things like that happened a long time ago; he can barely imagine it anymore. After being driven out of paradise, he had—gradually, so that he barely noticed it—set up his life as a barrier against pain and discomfort. Suppressing chaos: washing dishes, maintaining order. What did it matter that one day looked so much like the other that he could not recall a single one; he keeps to the middle, equidistant from both bottom and top, although he is sometimes envious of the alcoholics and junkies with their trampoline lives, from low to high, high to low, on and on until they have no more teeth in their mouths and die a lingering, miserable death. He protects the citizenry from them. (He likes the word 'citizenry'—it summons up a world in which everything has its place, like the stars in the firmament.) The desperate plunder homes and shops, and rob passers-by at knifepoint in secluded places; they disturb the peace with their ecstasy and despair. He, Pontus Beg, defends the right to an undisturbed life in the middle, for better or for worse. The world is insane, people heartlessly pursue their own interests, and only the middle provides the guarantee of a modicum of peace and quiet.

Does he still have her letters? Of course he still has her letters. Four glasses an evening; he drinks no more than that. He doesn't want to go stamping around the room on one cold foot and one warm, opening letters, looking at pictures, sighing beneath the false memory of melancholy. The alcoholic born of wistfulness. They're the worst; Pushkin says so, too.

There had been other women before her. He had fallen in love at times. None of them kept him interested for long. One had stale breath; the other laughed like a hyena. He remembered bitter regret and disappointment in the face of the imperfect. It was such a very fine line.

From one day to the next, therefore, he started keeping his mouth shut. Only the absolutely crucial came out of it.

When he was silent, they talked. Oh, such questions!

What are you thinking about? Why don't you say something? Why are you so quiet?

He saw their disappointed, drawn faces, the uncertainty eating away at them. But he remained silent. It was too painful. Let them draw their own conclusions. Followed by a lingering period of argumentation and feints, then it was over. He was alone at last.

Leah did not have stale breath. She didn't laugh like a hyena. Nothing about her annoyed him. She was perfection. Eloquent and well raised, but with a certain wildness still, a spontaneity, that drove them to the darkened riverbank to make love. At night they listened to Radio Free Europe. It was illegal and exciting; he knew he was breaking the law, but how could this delectable girl do anything wrong?

Summer arrives. She gives him *Eugene Onegin* and *First Love*—he reads literature for the first time.

He is a country boy. His father works for the kolkhoz; in the late afternoon and early evening, they garden on their own land. A quarter of a hectare, they eat from it.

Pontus goes out with a sledgehammer and drives fence posts for all the farmers in the surroundings. His shoulders have become burly; his chest, broad and muscular.

When he walks into his father's yard, the chicks go running to their mother and disappear, zoof-zoof, beneath her; clucking quietly. The hen ruffles her plumage and settles onto her haunches. She follows him with quick, choppy movements of the head. All those chicks are underneath her now; the young Pontus can imagine no greater sense of security.

In the winter he slaughters the hen, and in the cloaca he finds eggs in various stages of development. The final one is nothing but a yolk. Everything goes into the frying pan; nothing edible is wasted.

Ah, Leah. He nudged his loins up against her buttocks, and she turned her head to him and whispered: 'Don't squeeze so hard.' He relaxed his clasp around her torso, the clutch of a drowning man around a piece of wood. He didn't understand himself.

'It doesn't matter,' she said when he apologised again, 'as long as you let go.'

He was alone again with his thoughts, and her breathing grew deep and regular again.

As long as she didn't think his breath was stale, or that he brayed like a hyena! He tried being silent, to camouflage his lack of refinement. But when they drank, he forgot to be silent, and it was precisely then that he made her laugh so much. She thought he was funny, she said, and he could imagine nothing better than to make this girl laugh.

'I think humour is an advanced form of intelligence,' she said.

'There are humourless people who are very smart,' he said.

'My father!'

He doesn't know her father; she hasn't introduced him to her parents yet. And she doesn't seem to be in any hurry to do so.

'And stupid people with a sense of humour, do they exist?' she asked.

He thought about most of his colleagues, who seemed to have a lot of fun together at times. He shrugged. A different kind of humour, maybe.

'A different kind of humour . . . Yes, I guess that's possible. But fortunately, you're very funny.'

If she thought he was funny, then maybe she thought he was intelligent, too. It was a conclusion he arrived at by fits and starts. He had never thought of himself that way. At the police academy, he had advanced easily into the officers' training program; they tested your intelligence beforehand, but it mostly had to do with assessment skills and reaction times. In those respects, he was among the best, but he attributed intelligence to the biochemists in their labs and the rocket scientists at their bases—not to a police sergeant with only six years' experience.

In January, in the third season of their love, she grew quiet. 'It's the winters here,' she said. 'They last so long. It makes me gloomy.'

Often, she didn't answer the phone. Sometimes, after it had kept on ringing, she would answer and say: 'I was just getting ready to call you back.'

He longed for spring, when his ice queen would thaw and they could continue where they had left off. Her eyes would shine again when she looked at him. She would laugh again, for no matter how he joked these days, her broad laugh had vanished. A regretful little smile had taken its place. She often felt more like staying at home alone. 'I don't feel so good, Pontus; I'd rather be alone tonight. Maybe I'll feel better tomorrow.'

When she wasn't alone, she went out with girlfriends whose names he'd never heard before.

'Tomorrow' became the pivotal point of their relationship, comparable to the jokester who had written 'Tomorrow, free vodka' on the wall behind the bar at the academy. If only the damn winter would pass. If only spring would come. Tomorrow. Tomorrow, free vodka.

He said: 'You're so quiet' and 'What are you thinking about?,' and knew that she would never thaw. Even before the ice melted on the river, she would dispose of him.

When at last she told him on the phone that she'd had enough (in fact, she'd said: 'I can't go on anymore,' as though she'd been engaged in hard physical labour), he saw it as nothing but a formality, and knew that he would never again be so happy.

22

EARTH

In the deepness of the night, the boy awoke to a cloudburst over the steppes. The rain hissed. He peeked out from beneath the plastic, but didn't see the slight glow that announced the day. He pulled his head back quickly. The tarp was leaking in a few places, so he tried to lie down in a way that would keep him from getting wet. Fat drops drummed on the plastic. The cold had seeped deep into his bones; he never felt warm anymore. It seemed as though there was no limit to what they could endure. Only death could keep them from wandering off each day anew through the vastness.

He thinks about the tall man, but the memory of his obscene nakedness is already fading. Already the sand has almost covered him.

The boy rolls up in a ball and waits with open eyes for morning.

Little by little, the black man came closer. He added himself to the group again bit by bit—first an arm and then a leg.

But his approach did not go unnoticed. The woman looked back often. She stayed close to the man from Ashkhabad.

Rain. Nothing but rain. No one had had a dry piece of clothing on them. The boy saw the hunched silhouettes behind him—the ghosts of the deceased, awakened from the sleep of ages.

The dark, shuffling forms returned in his fearful dreams.

How far can you walk without ever coming to a road or village? It's as though they've begun circling the globe all over again. Maybe the world has perished without their noticing. *Are there still people?* the boy wonders. *Where are they hiding?* Coming across a goat or a cow would be a major miracle in itself! The joy! First they would cover the cow with kisses and blessings, then slaughter her and devour her whole. A cow—oh, if only they would find a cow. If he was the first to find her, he would hop on her back and ride off. He would leave the others behind and enter the new world on the back of his cow. He could see the streets strung with banners, people coming out of their houses to cheer on the one who had survived the steppes—the cow's back festooned with cookies and banknotes, sweets and garlands. The cow stopped before the house of the woman with gleaming hair; that's where it lived. The woman bathed him, swathed him in soft linen, and tucked him into the softest bed he had ever lain in.

He would sleep for seven days and seven nights . . .

Without noticing it, he had moved out far ahead of the rest. He looked back. The man from Ashkhabad was waving his arms wildly, the tall man's stick in his hand. Another fight? Were they ever too tired to fight? Someone left the group and walked on. The poacher. The woman followed, then the other two. The boy squinted—at a little distance from the others, he saw movement. The black man. He wasn't giving up. It was a pointless pursuit. He would never be one of them anymore; the fear had acquired the force of law. They would beat him to death if he came too close.

The rainwater gathered in pools. Leaning on his left hand, the boy scooped up water with his right and raised it to his lips. After each sip he looked up, then drank on. He heard a voice—there were the others. He saw the hollow-eyed skulls emerging from the grey rain, their hair in strands against their scalps. They walked past him in silence.

The boy walked a little ways behind the woman, alone with his thoughts.

Sometimes the woman stopped. She leaned over and picked something up. She raised it to her lips. When she bent down again, the boy was on her in one giant step. 'What have you got there? What are you eating?'

To his dumb amazement, he saw that she had scooped up a handful of wet earth and was eating it. Sand stuck to her lips. She swallowed with difficulty and took another bite. The boy seized her by the shoulders, his face contorted in disgust. 'Stop that!'

She ignored him.

'You can't eat sand! People don't eat sand!'

The woman wiped her lips.

He tried to reason with her. Why was she eating sand? It was bad for her; she had to stop. Was she trying to kill herself?

She smiled faintly and looked at him without seeing him. 'Let me go,' she said. 'It will be all right. If that's what God wants.'

Inky clouds rolled together and parted again above their heads. The boy walked on alone once more, heavy with gloom. They were doomed. There was no hope for them anymore.

Yet still, yet still.

Inside him was the strange conviction that he would survive. He would be among the saved.

But the woman scooped up sand. She was lost. You shouldn't eat sand. It was admitting defeat.

A few families lived in his village. For as long as anyone could remember, they had built terraces on the mountainsides, stone walls chest high, filled with dirt. Without those basins of piled stones, the soil would have washed down the rusty slopes right away. No fertile soil could be found at those altitudes, so they bring it up from the valley. They load the fertile soil onto the backs of donkeys, in the beds of pickups and little trucks, and even fill their pockets with it before starting on the long, windy road up. Bit by bit, they carry their land into the mountains. All the land they possess they have carried up themselves. Nothing is more costly to them than that dark soil which produces scanty cabbage, pumpkins, potatoes, and onions.

Boys keep watch on wooden scaffolding. The wind rustles in the dry leaves of corn; with slingshots, they fire stones at crows. When they hit one, they hang it upside-down on a stick as a warning to its comrades.

And if anyone asks them why they do that, why they live in a place suited only to carrion crows and vultures, a place that has to be *overcome*, they shrug and say that's what they've been doing for as long as anyone can remember.

The mountains produce tough, bent people. They live and die just as their ancestors did, while in the valley the new century has begun. The new era makes its way uphill in bits and pieces; it reaches them in strange, convoluted morsels, free of the surroundings that explain it and lend it its logical status. It generates fear, but also hope—it means they won't have to go on lugging burlap bags of earth up the hill till kingdom come, to replace the soil lost to wind and wash.

A family equips a pioneer to make the journey to the distant world. Another follows. Never before have young people left the village to make such long trips, for such uncertainty.

Those who remain behind watch and pray; they wait tensely for the first reports of plenty.

Far away, a boy carves his way in the world. He has traded in the alliance with the soil for a wandering existence; the wind blows him across the steppes. Today he saw a woman eating dirt. He has carried so much soil uphill on his back, but *eat* it? Never. It's filthy, it's not done, it can't be anything but sinful. And along his way he has seen almost every sin you could imagine—there are so many more of them than he'd ever realised!

He knows that he can never go home again. He has crawled out through the keyhole, and can never get back in.

'Goddamn it,' the man from Ashkhabad said that evening. He stared in amazement at the tooth he held between thumb and forefinger. Now there was a gap in his gold-plated incisors. Cautiously, he felt at the others. 'I could pull them right out of my head,' he said sadly.

Vitaly lay down and rolled himself up in plastic and rags. He was withdrawing into himself, further and further. He hadn't said a word all day; the pain had gained the upper hand. His being was concentrated around the burning blemish; he wrapped himself around it and no longer thought of anything else. The pain was unshareable and solitary.

From not far away there came a sound. They stood up. In the distance they saw the black man, a shimmer of rain between them. 'Goddamn it,' the man from Ashkhabad said again. He held the stick tightly in one hand. 'Africa!' he screamed. There was no reply. He held his hands to his mouth like a megaphone. 'Hey, Africa!'

The black man unfurled his plastic and disappeared beneath the horizon of grass.

'What do you want from us?' the man from Ashkhabad yelled.

The plain sang out.

The poacher and the man from Ashkhabad took a few steps in his direction, but there was no energy in their movements. The woman and the boy looked at their wavering backs.

'Finish him off,' came Vitaly's voice from under the plastic. 'For Christ's sake, just fucking finish him off.'

The man from Ashkhabad wheeled on him. 'Shut up, slum rat. Why don't you come out here and do it yourself?'

'Sniveling shits,' they heard from beneath the dark pile.

The boy felt a burning desire rising up—that the man from Ashkhabad would take his stick and pound the pile of rags until the flux of filthy, blasphemous words came to an end. To see the blood flow out from under it, silenced at last.

The poacher stared at the spot where the black man had vanished into the grass. He just stood there, and no one knew what was going on inside him. Motionless as a donkey, he was. Maybe he was thinking the same thing.

23

A THEOLOGICAL DEBATE

'Why don't you just start reading?' Rabbi Eder said in annoyance. His guest never stopped asking questions. Beg took home a pile of books from the synagogue. At the table in his living room, he started reading. It wasn't long before his legs started shimmying. His scalp started itching. Because the rabbi had failed to point him in any direction, he read without system until it made his head spin. A four-thousand-year-old history was laid out in those books, along with all the popular superstitions, the parables, and rabbinical counsel. There were, on occasion, things he thought were funny. He now knew, for example, that you could identify a virgin by sitting her down on a wine barrel and smelling her breath—if you smelled wine, she was no longer a virgin. That's how they did that, those old rabbis.

At the theological level, he became entangled in the cacophony of standpoints, interpretations, and commentary on commentaries; there wasn't a single subject they agreed on, not a single question that received an unequivocal answer. It was like a rummage sale. He couldn't figure out whether you were allowed to mention God's name or not, and was it G-d, YHWH, or HaShem? They mixed it all together; it was a mess.

It was a mystery to him how they had come up with the Torah.

One scholar wrote that they had been chosen by God; the other, that He had forced them to accept His sacred book. He threatened to have a mountain fall on them if they refused, and they agreed under duress. But the mystic Judah Halevi, he read, said that the people of Israel had enjoyed His special favour from the start.

With pleasure, he read Halevi's book *The Kuzari*, a dialogue between a Jewish sage and the king of the Khazars, who was converted to Judaism along with his people. But before the king accepted the new faith, he submitted the rabbi to an extensive interrogation. He was as ignorant as Beg; his dialogue with the Jewish wise man was witty and funny. When the king countered with a claim that the Jews had once worshipped a golden calf, the wise man replied that it was God's very anger about this that showed how important they were to him.

Yeah, right, the king said. Worshipping the calf is the worst sin of all, isn't it?

Have patience, the rabbi answered, and I will show you why God took Israel as His chosen people.

> Any Gentile who joins us unconditionally shares our good fortune without, however, being quite equal to us. If the Law were binding on us only because God created us, the white and the black man would be equal, since He created them all. But the Law was given to us because He led us out of Egypt, and remained attached to us, because we are the cream of mankind.

Beg read through this argument again and concluded that it was the same old song and dance: anyone trying to define himself did so in principle at the other's cost.

> Now we do not allow anyone who embraces our religion theoretically by means of a word alone to take equal rank with ourselves, but demand actual self-sacrifice, purity, knowledge, circumcision, and numerous religious ceremonies. The convert must adopt our mode of life entirely. We must bear in mind that the rite of circumcision is a divine symbol, ordained by God to indicate that our desires should be curbed, and discretion used, so that what we engender may be fitted to receive the divine Influence. God allows him who treads this path, as well as his progeny, to approach Him very

closely. Those, however, who become Jews do not take equal rank with born Israelites, who are specially privileged to attain to prophecy, whilst the former can only achieve something by learning from them, and can only become pious and learned, but never prophets.

It had been a long time since he'd pored over texts this way; Beg read on till the letters danced before his eyes. Leaning back in his chair, he blew a stream of smoke at the ceiling. This was the wondrous company to which he had been added; the exclusivity flattered and irritated him. A Christian, you could become; a Muslim, too; but not a Jew. Never completely. And for the rest, they made you work awfully hard—for as long as it took you to become pious or learned, and then they kept that coveted final piece for themselves. Therein lay the injustice, but he bathed in the warm light of chosenness. He was the fruit of a Jewish womb; he was part of the family without having done anything to deserve it. From the mother lode of his memory, a silver bubble had risen. It had burst on the surface, and his ears had caught the melody that escaped from it.

So much had come back to him since he'd developed a cold foot. In dreams and musings, he had relived episodes and places. There was no direct connection between his cold foot and his memories, although you might also say it started with that cold foot, and now here he sat with a pile of books, studying Judaism.

It was after midnight. The radio had been silent the whole time.

Polanen Street grew accustomed to the white Lada parked at the curb. Even the Asians had stopped being startled by the policeman in the alleyway. A plastic sack in hand, Beg stood waiting at the bottom of the steps to the synagogue. He often brought along tea and cookies for the old man. One discussed matters of faith along with sweet cookies and aromatic black tea from Krasnodar.

He wanted the rabbi to tell him why a convert could never completely become a Jew, but always remained inferior.

'There are different views on that subject,' the rabbi said, once they were seated at the kitchen table.

'I was afraid of that,' Beg said despondently.

'Generally speaking, the opinion you expressed is one found mostly among the orthodox.'

'I read Halevi's book.'

'The great Halevi.'

'I finished it last night.'

'An important work.'

'He says that, too.'

'I agree with him,' the rabbi said. 'The proselyte is a ninety-nine percent Jew. There is still something missing.'

'A prophetic element, that's what he calls it.'

'That has been passed down to us from our forefathers. From Adam to Seth, from Lamech to Noah, from Abraham to Isaac, and from Isaac to Jacob. From Jacob to his sons. Moses and Aaron carried the light through the desert for forty years, and passed it on to their heirs. How could a gentile possess that light? After all, he's not related to the patriarchs.' He looked up. 'Inferior, you said. When you say that, you're engaged in polemics. All I'm saying is that it's a trait that can only be passed on by inheritance, the way red hair shows up in some families and never in others.'

Beg closed his eyes; he had to think hard about this. 'In fact, what you're saying . . . is that a distance remains. The prophets are Jewish, they are close to God. He gives them their visions. The proselyte doesn't possess that sensitivity; he can get close, but never make it all the way. That percent, that's the distance God maintains between himself and the non-Jew. And that cannot be bridged.'

'God is close to us, so that applies the other way around, too. The goy can cross the bridge, but never reach the other side. Rabbi Halevi in Andalusia and Reb Eder in Michailopol are in agreement on that. Would you like some more tea? You always bring tea with you—I assume you're extremely fond of tea?'

Beg nodded.

'Don't you see that?' the rabbi said. 'That's precisely what makes it so hard for others to bear. God who watches over us and sends plagues to Egypt, who shows us the way in a pillar of cloud and a pillar of fire, and talks to us on Mount Sinai—what a pact! What a pronouncement!'

He poured some more hot water into the cups. It was the little movements that caused his hands to shake most.

'When a father has a favourite son,' he said with his back to Beg, 'it always leads to jealousy in the household. Jacob loved Joseph most dearly—his brothers tried to kill him. Jealousy! Joseph also had a prophet's dreams; he dreamed the truth that was yet to come. The prophetic element had been passed on to him, and even though he was persecuted, it's not easy to extinguish a light like that. His light shone from the dungeon all the way to the pharaoh's chambers . . .'

Beg remembered the Old Testament stories that his mother had read aloud to him and to his sister—most of them had coagulated into a mood, a couple of names, half-histories, but he remembered the story of Joseph in the well, and the storehouses he built for the pharaoh to stockpile grain for the lean years to come.

'The first thing you need to do is read the Torah,' the rabbi said. His breathing sounded laboured. 'Everything is in there. The rest is interpretation.'

Hot tea splashed on his fingers when he put the glass on the table. 'Moses never entered the Promised Land, but Joseph's bones are buried there. He made the children of Israel vow not to leave his bones behind on the day of their return. They carried them with them in the desert for forty years, until they entered the Holy Land. Our memory is also what produces our faithfulness. But most of us . . . we won't reach the Promised Land, not until the Last Day. You saw how I sprinkled some sand over Rabbi Herz's grave? That was sand from Israel, a sign of our covenant. Our bones are scattered all over the world, just like Ezekiel saw in his dream:

> Then he said unto me, Son of man, these bones are the whole house of Israel: behold, they say, Our bones are dried, and our hope is lost: we are cut off for our parts.

> Therefore prophesy and say unto them, Thus saith the Lord God; Behold, O my people, I will open your graves and cause you to come up out of your graves, and bring you into the land of Israel.

And ye shall know that I *am* the Lord, when I have
opened your graves, O my people, and brought you up
out of your graves,

And shall put my Spirit in you, and ye shall live, and
I shall place you in your own land: then shall ye know
that I the Lord have spoken *it*, and performed *it*, saith
the Lord.'

'And see,' the rabbi whispered, 'they form an exceeding great
army.'

He wrapped his crooked fingers around his glass and said in a
thick voice: 'I shall place you in your own land . . . I have spoken it,
and performed it . . .'

24

AND THEN THERE WERE FIVE

The tall man looked like an insect. He strode through the world on giant legs—a hundred thousand times life-size, his legs reaching to the sky. High up above there, you saw his face, the gloomy, drooping face, anticipating the disappointments life had in store for him. His footsteps left craters that filled with water. One by one, they drowned in his footsteps, struggling, sinking until they hit the bottom. Waving grass.

With that dream the boy had woken, lying on the soaked ground, in the rain that blew across the earth in gusts. He stood up. The sweat was beaded on his forehead; wobbling, he waited till the dizzy spells withdrew.

He lifted his nose to the wind like an animal. Out on the steppes, his senses were piqued, a nervous sensitivity amplified by hunger and exhaustion. He left the circle of sleeping forms and walked to a rise in the landscape a little farther along, a sort of dune. The sand slipped beneath his feet as he climbed. He looked around. At the edges of his vision, the earth wavered, a flowing transition from earth to sky, like the misty spurs of a distant mountain range.

Then he hopped back down and searched amid the grass for something edible. He'd found the cadaver of a hare once. He had gnawed off the dried remains.

In smaller and smaller circles, he wandered around the camp, until he saw the barrier of grass in which the black man took cover at night. He stopped. Within a short time, the distance between them had become unbridgeable. Not long ago, he had still been warming his hands at the same fire.

'Hey!' he called out faintly.

'Hey, Africa!' he shouted again after a few minutes, louder this time.

The boy picked up a stone and threw it at him. It landed beside him. He dropped to his knees and felt around on the ground for more stones, his eyes glued on the sleeping body. Fear and excitement coursed through his body when he hit his target. But the man slept soundly and did not move. The boy took a few cautious steps in his direction. 'Hey, Africa!' A few more steps. His torso was bare. The boy yelled, but the yell never passed his lips. In the sand lay a dead man. One eye socket was filled with blood; the other eye had burst and emptied. The boy forgot to breathe. Behind the torn lips he saw the splintered teeth. The blood had clotted, but deep inside the wounds the flesh was as red as his own.

This was the information at a glance. Then he fell onto the sand. From the corner of his eye, he saw a chunk of stone, and the blackened blood. He tried to scramble to his feet, but the ground was pulled out from under him as though it were a carpet.

Gasping for breath, he crawled away from the dead man. His heartbeat rang in his ears. They had got him—Africa! The word reverberated loudly inside him, as though he was hearing it for the first time. No one had travelled as far as he had! His head, now crushed by a stone. Dawn had brought the crime to light.

He, of all people, had been the one to find him. No one but him. Once again, that mysterious knowledge of being elected!

The others had risen and were getting ready to leave. The boy appeared from the plumed grass and came to stand beside them. He squared his shoulders, and said in his deepest voice: 'Africa's dead.' He pointed back over his shoulder. 'Someone finished him off.'

The poacher and the man from Ashkhabad looked at him and at each other by turns; the woman fell to her knees and shouted with joy, 'God be praised!'

Vitaly sat on the ground, his teeth chattering. His forehead gleamed. His upper body swayed back and forth, as though he were listening to distant music.

'Didn't you hear him?' the woman said. 'The black man is dead.'
Vitaly rubbed a pinch of sand between thumb and index finger.
'God bless the hand that killed him,' the woman shouted.

Vitaly's eyes shot nervously back and forth. He licked his lips
with his white tongue. He was in a place where no one could follow
anymore. In his weakness, the boy detested him more than ever.

He led the men to the spot where he had found Africa. The flies were
awake, the scouts in their gleaming corselets. They crawled into his
eye socket and walked across the torn eyeball; it made you itch. It
would not be long before the black man was covered in a buzzing carpet of flies. The man from Ashkhabad picked up the stone and looked
at it. None of them said a world. They left the corpse alone. This was
a different kind of dead.

The woman had come up behind them. The boy heard her snort
loudly. She spat on the dead body, white gobs flying from her dirt-
smeared lips. She kicked at him; his corpse shuddered. 'Ape!' she
panted as she kicked. 'Filthy ape!'

This is the first time she's ever touched him, the boy thought.

The poacher pulled her away, but she kept kicking at thin air.
'That's enough!' the poacher said. 'He can't hurt anyone anymore!'

She stopped moving in his grasp. 'Burn him,' she said. 'Make sure
he never comes back.'

The poacher gave her a shove, sending her back in the direction
she had come from. 'With what? With sand and grass? Are you out of
your mind, woman?'

The man from Ashkhabad was not distracted by the fuss. He
never stopped looking at the dead man. He took in the tattered rags,
the dull, black skin—his gaze wandered along the trail of scars on
his arms and chest, the wizened neck and grimy beard, and on to his
ruined face.

Oh, loathsome flies. He scratched red furrows in his neck and
breastbone. His whole life long, he had been swatting flies away
from his face, his hands, and his ankles, but then one day they finally
claimed the body they had been tasting for so long. He squatted and

put the stone down beside him. Slowly he reached out to the black man's chest and pulled the cord from under his shirt. He took the little cross that had slid into the man's armpit, and dangled it between thumb and forefinger. The crossbeam was attached in the middle. The wood was oiled with body fat. It was tooled; if you looked carefully, you could see a sort of interlacing pattern, almost obliterated now by the friction between shirt and skin.

He had once seen the black man kiss this cross. It was a pious ape he had seen. It had insulted him. God was not for donkeys and dogs and apes.

Little remained of his distaste now. He rubbed his thumb over the grooved wood. In the same way he used his stick, so had the black man worn his cross, holding it up to ward off disaster.

What were the differences between them again? He couldn't remember. It had to be there, that bottomless difference, but his hands clutched at air. Now that the delusions had lifted, he saw only how alike they had been in their suffering and despair.

He laid the cross back against the man's chest. What good were such thoughts when you'd had no experience with them before? He used his arms to push himself to his feet. The boy had been staring at him all this time. Maybe he understood what he was thinking. Maybe he could tell him what these thoughts were supposed to mean.

They moved on through the day that never grew light, each with his own thoughts about the black man they were leaving behind on the plain. One of them had crushed his skull. The others imagined how that had gone. How the killer had snuck through the grass, heel-toe, heel-toe, to keep from making a sound, the stone in his hand, how he had raised his arm.

Sacrificed himself. Set them free.

The following straggler was revealed now. They heard a faint lamentation at their backs, sometimes punctuated by raging monologues. Vitaly was being visited by his demons. Deep within him, a primal force was spurring him on to follow the others, but the shades around him had already begun pulling him back into his past. Their grip was stronger all the time; he fell farther behind his companions all the time. Their pace slackened nonetheless. Vitaly had never given any cause for compassion; an act of charity would be lost on him. They would leave him behind and forget him as quickly as possible.

The wind stirred; rain fell, too. The woman stuffed her mouth with dirt. Her jaws ground slowly. The boy walked as far from her as he could, in order not to see how she devoured bite after bite of earth, her eyes as blank as a blind woman's.

Far away, where honey-yellow light fell from behind the clouds, tumbleweed danced across the earth's surface—translucent balls of thistle and kali, driven by the wind. High as a house, the wheels rolled slowly across the steppe, a series of slow-motion, dreamlike images. The travellers' hearts leapt whenever one hopped into the air and was then chased away. They reached out their hands to touch them, but one by one, the rollers vanished from sight and left behind a yearning. Where were those wheels rolling to so light-heartedly, so far away in that yellow light?

But before evening comes, the travellers' heads are once again bowed to the earth. The eternal repetition has rocked them to sleep. The nimble dance of the tumbleweeds is forgotten. Everything is forgotten.

Winter

25

HUNGER

The first call came in early that evening: a woman complaining about drifters knocking over garbage cans in the street. Just before eight, there was a second one: another woman, weeping this time; the group of drifters she'd encountered had thrown her into a panic. 'They're the dead,' she'd said.

Car 37 took the call. At a quarter past eight, patrolman Ivan Budnik turned into the street. *Fucking transients*, he thought. *Give a couple of them a good thumping every once in a while—that's all you can do.*

Halfway down the street, between the flats, where the street-lights were dim, he caught them in his headlights. The glow from the rotating light reflected off them. His brain didn't understand what his eyes were seeing: shadows, separated from their bodies. He had been planning to bark an order at them through the megaphone, but his breath caught in his throat. It was as though he saw tears glistening on their filthy cheeks. Weeping phantoms. Great God. Skin, lashed tightly around their bones, mummified almost. Black eye-sockets.

In rags worn to threads, they had appeared from the darkness of centuries past. Two of them were sitting on the ground, rooting slowly, mechanically, through the garbage bags in front of them. Their jaws ground the frozen slops. Plumes of vapour rose around their heads. Because his brain was locked up tight, Budnik started classifying what he was seeing—the beginning of understanding. He saw a child, probably a boy; he saw two men and a woman. He saw that they were not reacting to his presence. Another one came out of the bushes—a man, an emaciated saint with a beard down to his chest. He looked teary-eyed into the headlights—then his hands, too, began rooting through a garbage bag.

Why were they weeping? What sorrow was it? Or was it something else? Budnik had no intention of leaving the vehicle. He called the dispatcher.

'I can't read you, Car 37,' the woman at the desk said.

'Send backup, goddamn it!' he whispered.

As he watched, the situation remained largely the same. They emptied garbage cans and tore open the bags. The road was littered with trash. The occasional pedestrian came by, on the other side of the street, and then went running off.

At nine, a second patrol car came down the street. It parked beside him. Patrolman Toth climbed out. Only then did Budnik leave his car, his Makarov clenched in one hand.

'Holy Mother of God,' his colleague stammered. 'Who are these people?'

Budnik nodded in a way that said he was already familiar with the situation. The fact that he had been here for a while gave him a jump on things. That authority gave him the right to lead the operation—if only he knew what to do.

They stood in the light of their high beams, a few metres away from the scene. 'Who are you people?' Budnik shouted. They heard the crackle of frozen plastic; sometimes, the gasping breath of someone weeping.

'Not from around here,' Budnik said quietly.

'I think . . . arrest them,' his colleague said.

'Yeah, sure,' Budnik said absently. He looked over at Toth. 'But for what?'

What a disgusting thought, to have to touch those decrepit bodies. To sit in the car with them, to breathe the same air. In fact, yes, for what? A couple of garbage cans. Once you started down that road, you could go on all night. He tried to focus. To assess the risks. What were they failing to do that could later be held against them?

'What are they crying about?' Toth whispered.

Budnik shrugged. He tightened his grip on the pistol. Indecision was weakness. Capitulation could pass for wisdom. He took a step back—the step with which the retreat begins.

'Come on,' he said, 'we're going to Tina's.'

In the days that followed, there were sightings here and there. Their appearance prompted a shudder of excitement. The untouchables became a persistent rumour; in the alleyways of the bazaar and the streets of the city, it hopped like a virus from one mouth to the next. The descriptions were so vivid that it seemed as though everyone had seen them with their own eyes. No one knew who they were or where they had come from; the general assumption was they had come in from the steppes. It was as though victims of the plague had walked into the city. Their numbers varied from five to fifteen. They seemed to be everywhere, all at the same time. In the collective imagination, the armies of the undead marched through the streets of Michailopol. They were gawked at and stared after, and no one dared speak to them.

Thefts were reported. Chickens disappeared from their coops; geese were plucked from behind fences. At night, when the temperature fell to twenty degrees below zero, no one knew where they stayed. The lock merchants at the bazaar did good business. It was mid-December; a cold sun lay on the icy-blue horizon. In Pontus Beg's office, the phone rang. 'The mayor, for you,' Oksana said.

Semjon Blok was in the midst of his second term as mayor of Michailopol. He had built his empire on slot machines. You saw his one-armed bandits everywhere. He had gone into politics to gain status in the straight world, the world of people who attended the Bolshoi and rarely saw a slot machine. His nickname was Mister Cash—during his campaign, he had paid his staff in rolls of coins. As Mister Cash, he was elected by a wide majority; the tough materialism he embodied was an example to the man on the street. Whether he'd actually gained access to the circles of those who attended the Bolshoi was up for grabs.

'Pontus, I'm hearing things,' he said.

'I'm listening,' Beg said.

'Transients, Pontus. A group of—how shall I put it . . . starving people. I see reports about them. They're going around stealing. People say they've never seen anything like it. Who are they, you know what I mean? What are they doing here? We need to find out, Pontus. We don't know them—it's an impossible situation. We *have to* know who's who around here. Transparency, Pontus, that's my motto. Bring them in, do something. Don't ask me what.'

Like ataman Chiop, Blok had the irritating habit of addressing him only by his first name—the way you might piss on a puppy's head to make it obey. Could you ask someone to stop doing that? In writing, maybe. He wasn't sure.

'We've had the report here, too,' he said. 'We have an eye on them.'

A deep sigh. 'What do you guys do there, anyway? Arrest these people. Get them off the street.'

Beg knew that the mayor would prefer to send a couple of guys from his own club to deal with it. There was a real chance that he actually *would* get to them first. Free enterprise is so much more efficient than the public sector.

He said he would give it top priority, and hung up.

Budnik and Toth told everyone at Tina's about their encounter—a ghost story. 'Hunger like that,' Budnik said. 'You've never seen anything like it.'

'The way they were crying,' Toth said, 'that's what I thought was . . . it was *real* crying. You only cry like that when you . . . well, yeah.'

Their listeners stared into space. 'Things like that happen,' one of them said. The others remained silent because they didn't know what to say; two of them had witnessed something they couldn't explain, and had run away from it. They had described a forlornness that seemed beyond this world—a sense of horrors that couldn't be told.

Things beyond their control.

'Tina!'

Tina came over and filled all their glasses.

'Cheer up, guys,' she said. 'It can't be all that bad.'

Budnik and Toth smiled wanly, and knew there was comfort in the sight of her bosom. So, too, when she walked back and forth behind the bar, in the tight leather skirt into which she had wedged her flesh. They were too young to have known her in her capacity as a trollop, but in the course of time their imaginations had been set afire by the stories their colleagues told—stories that made their blood run hot and made them mourn lost ground that could never be recovered.

The razzia began by order of the powers that be—vagrants were picked up all over town. The basement cells were packed. Fights broke out. One detainee was stabbed in the neck with a pen that the guards had overlooked. Almost every transient in town was swept off the streets, but the ones they were looking for weren't among them. They seemed to have vanished from the face of the earth. The sightings that were reported were too diverse to all be true.

Maybe, Beg and Koller reasoned during a meeting, they had moved on and were trying to cross the border.

'Then we'll be hearing from them again,' Koller said.

The border was locked down tight. Every car, every truck, and every train was searched twice—first on this side, then on the other. The technology on the other side belonged to the domain of science fiction. They had heartbeat detectors, carbon-dioxide sensors that betrayed people's presence by their own breath, infrared cameras, and night-vision equipment—all their technological ingenuity was applied to catching illegal migrants. Visas were awarded only very rarely; anyone headed for the other side took refuge in illegality. Countless of them became stranded at the border. Michailopol was home to many of those who had been picked up and sent back. They often remained drifting, and never returned home.

He had a predilection for problems that solved themselves, but Beg still felt regret at the idea that he might never know who the emaciated transients were. Budnik's report had made him curious.

'Like they were standing beside their mother's grave, that's the way they were crying,' the patrolman had said.

Beg asked what they were crying about.

'About nothing. I racked my brains trying to figure it out, but I couldn't see any reason.'

'No pain, no visible injuries?'

'Pain, yeah. But not like someone who's just got a beating. It was different.'

'Could you describe what they looked like?' Beg rested his chin on his clasped hands and closed his eyes, so he wouldn't have to see how the patrolman swayed back and forth in his chair.

'Like the Jews in the camps, sir. That's what they looked like. I don't know how else to put it.'

Beg opened his eyes. 'And what did *they* look like, in your view?'

He saw the man—in fact, still only a big boy—searching for words to match the pictures in his head.

'You know, terrible,' he said then.

'Where are you from, Officer?'

'Barsan, sir.'

'That's Oblast Grünewald, isn't it, unless I'm mistaken?' The constable laughed shyly.

'Yes, um-hum, Grünewald, that's right. Twenty kilometres from Brstice. You know it?' Beg withdrew the hand he'd held out and told him he was dismissed. The young man saluted and went. In fact, Beg had been meaning to upbraid him for his negligence on the street that night, but his heart was softened by the dialect of his native region.

He would have Koller do it. Frightened patrolmen were no good to anyone.

26

THE UNDEAD

Grey wood smoke was coming from the shed close to the old train station. A metal pipe had been stuck through the window, so the smoke rose straight up to the rooftop before it blew away. Lev Krasnik, a scrap-metal dealer, leaned his motor scooter and its trailer against a wall and walked over to the storage depot. He pressed his nose against the windowpane. The glass was dirty; something had been put in front of it on the inside—he couldn't see a thing. Krasnik went to the door and gave it a little shove. He pushed harder, and something behind the door gave a bit. The crack was wide enough to look through now. It was a dim, deep space, and it stank inside.

'Hello?' he said. 'Anybody there?'

He leaned against the door with his full weight, and then he was inside. The dank smell of rotting, faeces, and smoke took his breath away. Beside the window was a makeshift woodstove; the flickering glow from its belly illuminated the coffins someone had stored here. In front of it lay two long bundles. He strained his eyes to make them out— people, those were people lying there. In two lidless coffins on the floor, he saw human forms as well. He wanted to run, but was frozen to the spot in the semi-darkness. Then he saw the eyes looking at him from beside the stove: they belonged to a man sitting on the floor. He was wrapped in blankets, looking at Krasnik motionlessly. 'Holy Mother of God,' the scrap dealer whispered, and made the sign of the cross.

The man leaned forward and swept together some splinters from the floor. He tossed them in the fire, and it flared up. Krasnik saw splintered wood all over the floor; they had chopped coffins to pieces for firewood.

The mouth of the man by the fire formed words that Krasnik couldn't make out. It was an old voice, like cracked dinnerware. Krasnik swallowed a lump of saliva and said: 'Sorry, I didn't get that.'

'Close the door,' the man said. 'It's cold.'

'Yes, of course, yes. Sorry.'

He took advantage of the moment to hurry out of the shed. His hands shaking, he tried to pull the door shut from the outside, but the lock had been forced and the door wouldn't close completely. Krasnik stepped inside and took a wedge of wood from the floor.

'Sorry,' he said, bent over and peering into the darkness, 'but it won't stay closed.'

Then he was outside again, where he jammed the splinter between door and threshold. Now it remained shut.

On his scooter, decked with frozen autumnal mud, he drove to police headquarters as fast as he could. On the way there, he tried to figure out why he had said 'sorry' so often. Apparently you couldn't help but be apologetic when you stood face to face with creatures of the twilight.

Five patrol cars pulled up to the old train station—not all at the same time, but still, five in total, giving their occupants a rare feeling of urgency. Sergeant Koller was in charge. He had gone to work that morning with a nagging pain in his lower back; he had been planning to consult a physical therapist about it later in the day. But before he could leave the building, the unpleasant news came in that someone had apparently found the drifters.

The police station buzzed like a hive, stories large and small zooming around constantly. Koller knew he was about to play a leading role in one of the big stories of the day—one told with the relish of sensation but also with a superstitious sort of concern.

Still sitting in the car, he watched the smoke rising from the chimney pipe. *Action*, he thought, but the word only made him feel abysmally tired. For a moment he considered firing a teargas canister into the shed, but there was nothing to justify such overkill.

Minutes later, six men stormed into the shed. The beams from their heavy police flashlights swept around the half-darkened space. Koller was the last to enter. He flipped the switch beside the door. A fluorescent tube popped on overhead.

One policeman stood waving his gun and screaming in mad fear at a woman in a coffin. 'Get out of there, goddamn it!'

There were five of them in all. The men were handcuffed; the woman and a boy were dragged out of their coffins and pinned to the floor. They had lined their beds with straw and rags.

'Man, does it stink in here,' another policeman said. Koller nodded. The room gave off a deadly stench.

The boy's wrists were as thick as sticks. A wolf boy—he struggled so hard they could barely restrain him. He spat and cursed.

'Tape him,' Koller said.

The boy's mouth disappeared behind a strip of duct tape. The others submitted calmly to their arrest. None of them spoke a word. The only sounds were the guttural noises coming from the boy's taped mouth. Koller shook his head. What was the world coming to when children behaved like that?

That afternoon, the hive buzzed even louder than usual. Everyone wanted to see them; the cell block was a popular attraction. It wasn't the state of neglect that shocked them—after all, human flotsam washed up here all the time. No, it was the face of starvation.

After they'd all had their turn, Beg went down to the basement. His footsteps echoed in the stairwell. Pieces of the concrete steps had broken off, so you had to watch your footing. Beside the cells was the shooting range. You could hear the shots through the walls. The red warning-light above the door, which was supposed to be lit when the range was in use, was still broken.

He rang, and the door to the cell complex opened with a click.

'Okay, show me what we've got,' he said to the guard.

The man removed his earplugs. 'What?'

'The transients.'

The guard walked out in front of him. He turned to Beg. 'I have two of them in here. Well, see for yourself.'

The door swung open.

'Holy Christ, what a stench,' Beg mumbled.

'Koller said I shouldn't hose them down. Not till you'd seen them, that's what he said.'

Patrolman Budnik's comparison with Jews in the camps had been accurate. The men were alive, and that was all you could say. When they came in, one of them lifted his head from the cot and looked at him, his eyelids red and inflamed. The other one remained motionless. Death's heads. Cheekbones jutting sharply from beneath their beards.

'And what about him?' Beg asked.

'Him? He just lies there.'

'Have they had anything to eat?'

'They're lying here just the way they were brought in. Nothing different.'

'They haven't eaten anything?'

The guard glanced at his watch. 'They only came in a couple of hours ago.'

Beg looked them over. Multiple pairs of trousers tied with cords around their skinny loins. Around their emaciated necks he saw the collars of numerous T-shirts and sweaters—all frayed ends, rips, worn patches. But they had survived the cold.

They gave off a bitter stench.

An automatic pistol rattled on the shooting range. Beg turned in annoyance. 'Tell them to cut out that noise.'

His gaze wandered over the rags, the filthy hands and faces, the sight of their shoes. The shoes, lashed together with bits of wire and rope, had almost rotted away on their feet. The shoes told him that they had undergone deprivations that were different from those of the city's homeless—deprivations in the wilderness. Had the cold forced them into town? Were they a family? What did they have in common?

'Who are you people?' he said under his breath.

The automatic fire stopped. The men were sick, febrile; he could hear their laboured breathing.

When the guard came back, Beg left the cell. He looked through the peephole in the door of the next cell. 'You're kidding me,' he said.

The guard looked up.

'I thought he'd gone home already,' Beg said.

'Him? No, the gentleman's still keeping us company.'

Beg looked again at the man in the cell. He was lying on his cot, his hands folded under his head.

'That's too damn bad,' Beg said.

'Were we supposed to let him go? I didn't see any release papers.'

'He can go,' Beg said. 'Then he'll be home for Christmas.'

'Barefooted. They took his shoes.'

'Who?'

'The drifters. They stuck him in the neck with a pen, and stole his shoes.'

To his own amazement, Beg remembered those shoes—fancy white sneakers. A wild surge of annoyance almost made him change his mind about sending the man home. He took a deep breath. 'He can go,' he said. 'Make sure he has enough money for a bus ticket home.'

In the next cell, a boy was sitting on a cot. His cellmate, a man, was asleep.

'Well, young man?' Beg said.

The filthy boy's eyes spat fire. There was more life in him than in the others; no doubt about that. His hair stood straight up on his head, like an emaciated lion cub's.

'My name's Pontus. What's yours?'

The boy sniffed loudly and stared at his toes.

'I bet you're kind of hungry,' Beg said. 'I'll have them bring you something to eat. What do you feel like having?'

The boy's eyes lit up. Then, right away, he hugged his knees in shame and bowed his head, hiding his wide-open, traitorous eyes.

His cellmate had razor-sharp features beneath his dingy beard. His teeth were chattering.

In the corridor, Beg said: 'Bring them blankets and food. And where the hell is that doctor?'

'Was the doctor supposed to come? I never heard anything about that.'

'Where are your brains, man?'

Behind the last door was a woman. 'Help me,' she said.

She had her forearms wrapped around her belly. Beg was relieved to hear at least one of them speak a few words. 'How can we be of assistance?' he asked with exaggerated politeness.

She was sitting hunched over, tears cutting trails down her smudged cheeks. 'Help me.'

Beg looked over his shoulder at the guard. 'What's wrong with her?'

The guard shrugged. 'She says she's pregnant. But I can't really believe that. I mean, you tell me . . .'

27

GUSHING AND BURSTING, EVERYTHING COMES TO THE FORE

'Now that's good news, Pontus,' Semjon Blok said on the phone. As he spoke, he seemed to be doing something else—something that required effort, with the receiver clenched between shoulder and chin so that the rest of his body could go on with it. 'That's what I pay you for, for good news.'

Beg couldn't tell him who they were or where they came from; they had barely spoken a word yet.

'So they're not talking? Is that what you're saying, Pontus? Foreigners, man, they don't understand you. That's the problem with people like that. In their own language they might even be kind of useful, then you can at least tell them to do something, but otherwise . . . picking bell peppers, that's about as far as it goes.'

In the background, he heard a man laugh. *When you've got power*, Beg thought, *you always make people laugh*. Koller and Oksana often laughed at things he didn't mean to be funny.

'You're not much of a talker either, are you, Pontus? Maybe we should go fly-fishing sometime, you and me, get to know each other better. What do you think?'

'I'm not much of a fisherman.'

'It's not just about the fishing—it's all the other things that go with it,' the mayor said. 'I know the best spots. Trout, man, you've never seen anything like it. You ought to see me, hooking one after the other. Those guys who go in for sport fishing, we make them look like amateurs, I'm telling you. Or are you more of a hunter? You go in for the heavier artillery? Then we'll go shoot a bear. You ever shoot a bear, Pontus?'

Beg wondered what the mayor was up to the whole time. Was he chopping wood with his free hand?

'I've never shot a bear,' he said.

'Aw, man, I've shot so many bears, I've lost count. I just might be the best bear-hunter you ever met. I can *think* like a bear, you know. You have to be patient. Waiting. Waiting. And then waiting a little more. You've only got one chance to squeeze off a shot. A bear's a lot more dangerous when it's wounded. Where do you think you have to hit him, in the heart or between the eyes?'

'In the heart, I guess.'

'Yeah, okay, but *where* do you have to hit him—you know that, too?'

'I don't know anything about bears.'

'Okay, but where do you *think* you have to hit him?'

Beg said nothing. He looked out the window, at the narrow alley-way between two buildings. One single step, that's how long a passer-by lasted.

'So, Pontus? Tell me the first thing that pops into your mind. Just say it.'

'A man's life between heaven and earth is like a ray of light falling through an opening in a wall: one moment, and then it is gone.'

'What's that?'

'Gushing and bursting, everything comes to the fore; slipping and flowing, it all recedes. One change and he is alive; another change and he is dead.'

'Have you been drinking, Pontus? I'm asking you where you have to hit a bear.'

Beg glanced at the receiver. 'I'd hit him straight from the front. In the chest.'

'Wrong!' Blok crowed. 'That's what everyone says who's never shot a bear before! From the front you've only got a fifteen-to-thirty percent chance of taking him out right away. Then you're in trouble, buddy. Aim for the shoulder, above the front leg. Left or right, makes no difference. The chest cavity—heart, lungs, all at one go. Boom, bagged another one!'

· · ·

Semjon Blok was his own standing ovation, Beg thought after they had hung up. He produced his own applause in deafening quantities. One ear to bellow his triumph into—that was all he needed to be happy. It was an extremely unpleasant thought, to go fishing or hunting with this man who 'knew the best spots.' And what did he mean by 'all the other things that go with it'? He sounded like a goddamn faggot.

It was snowing slightly: light, monotone grey. Oksana came in with his lunch—noodles and meat, and a glass of kvass. 'No pork,' she said. She had accepted this minor dietary law as one of his eccentricities. To show that he had heard, Beg looked up from the notepad on which he was drafting a letter.

To the mayor, the honourable Mr. Blok,

In response to our recent telephone conversation ~~about bears and fly-fishing~~, I would like to ask you to ~~leave my first name unmentioned~~ no longer call me by my first name. It is ~~an annoying habit~~ good custom among friends and family members to call each other by their first names, but ~~as far as I know we are neither of those but~~ for friends we do not know each other well enough.

I would appreciate it if we could maintain a certain formalism in our dealings, in order that the separation of powers might remain clearly visible, also for our subordinates.

Etc., Etc.

Late that afternoon, the draft letter still unfinished on his desk, he went down to the cell block again. They had eaten, the warder said. 'Like wolves.'

The first prisoner undressed in the shower. 'Clothes in the bag,' the warder said, pulling on a pair of thin plastic gloves. They were too small for his fat fingers, so he blew into them to make them stretch a bit. The prisoner was sitting naked on a stool, the electric shears vibrating above his head. The humming bounced off the concrete walls. The sharp teeth of the machine drew red strokes across the scalp; filthy clots of hair fell to the floor.

'Chin up.'

The shears revealed the sunken features, the toothless mouth. When all the hair had been removed from head and face, the warder showed him the corner where he was to stand. The man stood there, bent over, the bright white light on his pale, pleated skin. Skin and bones. The deep depression in the pelvis, like a bowl. The warder tossed the gloves in a bin and turned on the fire hose. Shivering, the man bent over even farther, his hands crossed in front of his genitals. The force of the blast pushed him against the back wall.

'Turn around!'

He no longer had a backside—only folds of skin.

The jet of water stopped.

'Lather up, friend. There's the soap.'

With feeble hands, the man soaped himself. He was as stiff as a plank. The hand holding the bar of soap reached to his knees. He could bow no deeper; he would break in two if he bowed any deeper. The warder threw the lever, and the blast hit him in the balls.

When it was over, the warder tossed him a towel. His kneecaps were broader than his thighs, his tendons in sharp relief beneath the thin skin.

He received togs from the mission: a fisherman's sweater and a faded tracksuit. The logo on the back of the jacket said ENERGIE COTTBUS.

The woman was the only one exempted from the nozzle; the rest were shaven and hosed down. Beg waited in his office for the doctor to arrive. He read the newspaper and smoked a cigarette. Lying on the table was an ad asking for security guards. Security was the future. And that future had been going on for a while already. The pay was better, for starters. Security guards had a more limited jurisdiction, but also more possibilities. More and more of them were needed; the wealthy couldn't count on the police for much, so they had to protect themselves. And there were more rich people all the time. Blossoming in their shade was the guild of men with earpieces and heavy-calibre Desert Eagles under their jackets. He had lost a lot of his men to that. Sometimes he thought about becoming a turncoat, too, but it never got further than a daydream. Habit kept him where he was—the comfort of his position.

The warder came to get him before dealing with the last one. They looked at the pale body covered in tattoos. An ex-con. A church was etched into the skin between his shoulder blades, a swastika on his calf, and hearts and barbed wire everywhere else—the code language of the slammer. Beg knew that each dome on the church on the man's back represented a conviction, but the meaning of most of the other symbols was hidden to him.

The doctor was a new one, a woman. Beg had never seen her before. Well-educated women tended to make him feel uneasy.

She came out of the woman's cell almost right away and asked agitatedly: 'Latex gloves—do you have any of those around here?'

A little later, she came back into the office in a rage. 'She's heavily pregnant! She shouldn't even be here!' She was trying to contain her anger, but Beg recognised the signals.

'She has to be hospitalised right away. How long has she been here?'

'A couple of hours,' Beg said.

'I want to see the other ones.'

When she returned from the cellblock a little later, she seemed subdued. 'Do you have anything to drink?' she asked.

The warder opened a bottle and poured some water into a mug.

'Who are these people?' she asked.

Beg shrugged.

'The boy should be in the hospital, too. He's malnourished. All of them are, but he and the woman need intravenous feeding right away. The others can remain here, at least provisionally. They're sick; I've already given them anti-pyretics. They should be on a special diet—feeding them normal food is too big a risk. Does that telephone work?'

Later that afternoon, the boy and the woman were taken from their cells to the psychiatric hospital, where they were to remain under lock and key. The doctor left dietary instructions for the others, and said she would come back the next day. The clicking of her heels echoed in the stairwell.

'Tough lady,' the warden said.

The news that really set the beehive abuzz came in around that time. In the transients' baggage, a man's head had been found. Only when a gruesome stench had filtered through the corridors and offices did they get around to searching the bags and finding the thawed head. Shielding their nostrils with an arm or a handkerchief, they examined the purplish-black, mutilated thing. It was wrapped tightly in plastic; and when they stripped that away, the nose and lips kept their flattened look. One corner of the mouth was curled up, revealing a pair of broken yellow teeth. The eyeballs had burst and emptied down the face. One man vomited.

When the commissioner came in, they all backed away from the table. Beg took the towel that was handed to him. The head had rolled over backwards. No matter what you did, no matter how you tried to steel yourself, you never got used to it. You could adopt an attitude towards it, but the inner shock could never be avoided.

Where the neck had been separated from the body, you could see rough incisions.

There was nothing but a head; they found no other body parts.

A head, damn it, Beg thought. Who goes around carrying a severed head? A pitch-black, malignant thing. It looked like a cancer. It stank like a cancer, too.

Was this a black man, or had the colour been caused by decay?

There weren't many blacks in this part of the world. Conditions here were not favourable for them. If one did happen to come to town, he was beaten up all the time. A black DJ at the Tarot Club had been stabbed on the street. Black people didn't have an easy time of it around here; they didn't stick around long.

Beg examined the head carefully—the wounds on its head and cheeks, the shattered ocular ridge. The cold and the plastic's tight grip had slowed the decomposition, but from now on it would go quickly. It wasn't until he got to the hall that he took the towel away from his face.

28

THIS SHALL BE THE SIGN OF THE COVENANT BETWEEN ME AND THEE

Beg had fallen asleep while reading the directives that the Everlasting had given His people. He had resolved to read everything worth knowing, and then decide whether to be a practising Jew or simply a Jew by birth. He lived in the naïve hope that the answer would emerge of its own accord from all those books and documents. It was a Herculean task. He read slowly, not wanting to miss a thing; everything was potentially important for his final decision.

And now he had fallen asleep above the third book of the Torah. An odour of mould and incense rose from its pages. With pleasure, he had read the accounts of the lives of Abraham, Isaac, and Jacob. The sun of the Holy Land burned on his face, he heard the bleating of sacrificial goats, and he laid his head to rest on a stone.

But Leviticus did not hold his attention for long. The Eternal had been fairly detailed in His directives; He left nothing to chance. It was his tough precision that had rocked Beg to sleep. A trail of saliva dangled between his lips and the tabletop. His breathing was laboured, and it was the discomfort that finally woke him. On the silent TV screen, a man in drag was being laughed at by an audience with wide-open mouths. What was it that made everyone so wild these days about a man dressed as a woman? In how many shows did that pop up? The one-man carnival, that failed clown, loud and boorish, the born victim. He was a punching bag and a scapegoat—you could hit him and abuse him as much as you liked, he shrieked and writhed, but seemed essentially immune to the violence done him.

It was past eleven. Beg wiped his lips with the back of his hand. He walked over to the television. His Achilles tendons had started hurting recently whenever he got up. They seemed to become too short in his sleep; he was afraid that one day they would tear off completely. He turned on the sound, and the room was awash in laughter. The transvestite ran through the studio, but before he could disappear into the wings, he was seized by a bodybuilder in a ridiculous gym suit. The roughing-up began all over again. 'Gentlemen! Gentlemen!' the host cried. And then, leering at the camera: 'Or should I say *lady* and gentleman?'

Again, the laughter came rolling down from the gallery.

Sometimes Beg thought that the need for cruelties and the perverse delight at the other's expense was part of being an impoverished people that had suffered a great deal itself. The pain of others was a distraction from one's own suffering, from existential worries. But Koller had told him that, in Japan, there were much crueller programs on TV. He had seen a few examples on the Internet—and the Japanese were a civilised, prosperous people. Nowhere else in the world, said Koller, did people laugh so loudly at someone else's pain. That was the end of Beg's theory: tested against reality, it collapsed like a bad soufflé.

Brushing his teeth, he looked at his face in the mirror. He rolled his eyes and opened his mouth. He turned his head as far as he could to the left and to the right—everything was still working. That was all you could say about it, though: everything was still working.

The coroner's report had come in late that afternoon: the head they'd found was, indeed, that of a black man. Forensics noted that the insect damage showed the head had been outside for quite a while. Exactly how long, it was hard to say. What was certain was that the cause of death—here it came, Beg thought, his favourite formulation—was violent impact with a blunt object.

Tomorrow he would interrogate a couple of them, whether they were in a weakened condition or not. They'd been detained as a public nuisance, but with the addition of a crime the temperature of the case had skyrocketed.

In bed, his thoughts were still jittery and alert. The crime had brought them together, or kept them together. They had carried the evidence, a head, along with them. It reminded them of the crime. Why did they want to be reminded of that? What was the point? The question kept him awake. His eyes wandered over the ceiling to fix on a pale spot, which could be a kilometre away, or, just as easily, a couple of metres. They might have known that the head would be found, at some point, one day. They had accepted the consequences. The consequences were subordinate to another, greater interest. The head symbolised something; it stood for something.

In the course of the years, Beg had come across abnormalities in all shapes and sizes. A moment always came when someone stopped thinking about the consequences of his actions, the punishment that awaited, and simply followed his own nature.

Last winter, two drifters had eaten a dog. You had those who saw the animal as a pet, others who saw it as a tasty morsel—the boundaries were not the same to everyone. The dog's owner had gone into the park and split the drifters' heads with an axe. He had submitted calmly to his arrest; he was prepared to pay the price for following his own nature. 'They should have kept their dirty fucking hands off of my dog,' he'd said, and everyone at the stationhouse knew what he meant. The world was a hard place; children and pets represented a kind of final innocence—you kept your hands off that.

The general sympathy for the man with the axe worried Beg. You knew how close chaos really was when you approved of someone splitting another person's skull because they had eaten his dog. 'Hold your thumb and index finger so close together that there's barely any light between them, and you'll know how close the chaos is,' he'd told his people. They were there precisely to preserve that little bit of light, that tiny crack—to whatever extent that was possible.

His thoughts spun in ever-widening circles, until he fell asleep and dreamed things he would forget by morning. He never remembered his dreams.

In the morning, he showered and pissed into the drain. Only first thing in the morning did he piss as vigorously as he used to.

If he were converted, he would have to be circumcised. There was no doubt about that; the Everlasting demanded it.

> This *is* my covenant, which ye shall keep, between me and you and thy seed after thee; Every man child among you shall be circumcised. And ye shall circumcise the flesh of your foreskin; and it shall be a token of the covenant betwixt me and you.

Abraham was ninety-nine when he received that order. He circumcised all the men in his household and then himself. The Everlasting wanted to place a brand on the bodies of his people. He called for blood and pain: the covenant was not merely spiritual; it was also physical.

What would Zita think if his foreskin suddenly disappeared? He could hear her disapproval already. The same way she couldn't stand the table covered with books in the living room.

'Look,' he'd told her, 'you don't read this from front to back, you read it like this . . . you start at the back of the book.'

She looked as though she had just encountered a highly dubious sort of newfangledness.

The books served as run-up to the announcement that soon there would be no more pork eaten in his house, just as that announcement served in turn as run-up to a possible circumcision. He hadn't told her about his meetings with the rabbi, or about the fact that he now belonged to the Jewish nation. Things like that had to be communicated one step at a time. Slow and steady seemed the best strategy. The head-on confrontation could have undesired consequences: 'Come on, Pontus, I'm Catholic. I don't sleep with Jews! You should know that!'

It made him uneasy. What he feared most was her dead mother. From the far side, the old cow whispered bad advice in her daughter's ear. It was a sorry state of affairs when the dead started throwing their weight around over here. Let the dead see to the dead, the living see to the living.

He couldn't afford to lose Zita. There were other women he could pay for—the Morris was full of them—but they would never fit as comfortably as Zita. They would have annoying traits. Gum-chewing. Sublime figures. Words he didn't know.

He would not be able to stand their lack of interest.

Tina! Yes, Tina, but then she had quit the business. She had gone off and specialised in meatloaf.

When Zita came into his house, she took off her shoes and replaced them with a pair of slippers she kept in the hall closet. She was as at home in his kitchen as she was in her own. She wiped down the stove and boiled water to make soup. The soup steeped as she cleaned the house, so that she and the soup were finished at the same time a few hours later. Neither of them was in a hurry.

His uniforms hung in the closet, laundered and starched. She sewed the buttons on the waistband of his trousers (he wore suspenders *and* a belt, as though afraid that his pants would fall off), and every two months she put fresh mothballs on the shelves.

On the evenings when she stays over, the bottle appears on the table. The rest of the transaction takes place in a mild haze. She listens breathlessly to his stories about criminals and car chases, all of which she's heard before. Sometimes he adds a new twist to the circumstances, the setting, or the events, making the story new again. The results amaze him, too, at times. Then they watch television until it is time to go to bed.

She withdraws to the bathroom and comes back a little later in a bright pink nightgown that reaches all the way to her ankles. She goes to the toilet and then climbs in between the sheets. He follows the same route, but much more hurriedly. She lies waiting patiently for him. He turns off the light.

Now we hear only the rustling of sheets before the finding of positions, the brushing of bodies as they approach, the hurried reconnoitring in the dark, and the 'Wait just a minute, Pontus.' He feels himself becoming weighed down with desire again, a capsizing ship. Then his body is on hers, their bellies slapping together. Fumbling, he whispers: 'What have you got on under there, woman?'

She says: 'Ow! You're not a dragoon, are you, Pontus?'

But he is a dragoon. A soldier returning from war, it's been so long since he's felt a woman's body. He is the paramour of need, his deeds said and done in a matter of minutes.

29

RESTLESS LEGS

The interrogation room is on the third floor. The cast-iron radiators glow. The first prisoner's file reads 'male, nameless, age unknown.'

The man is alone in the room. He can't keep his legs still. His legs are still underway, while the rest of his body has come to a halt in the interrogation room. His cuffed hands are resting in his lap. The hands are calm. They're not going anywhere anymore.

When Beg enters the room, the man keeps his legs still for a few beats, but before the commissioner has had time to reach the table, the jittering has resumed.

Beg sits down. He places a folder on the table and pulls out a few sheets of paper. He spreads them out in front of him, and chooses a black ballpoint pen from his breast pocket. He has red and blue ones, too. The ballpoint slides out with a click.

'Okay,' he says. 'First we need a name.' He looks up. 'Your name is . . . ?'

The man looks and says nothing.

'No name,' Beg says. He takes a deep breath and leans forward. 'My name is Beg,' he says then. 'I'm the commissioner around here.'

The man stares at a spot on the wall behind Beg. His shoulders are a clothes hanger for the jacket of his tracksuit. It's hard to imagine what he would look like with flesh on his bones.

Beg has seen the washed-out tattoos on his body—the icons of the convict—and the tracks of the needle. That's why he's the first one to be interrogated. You can negotiate with junkies.

'Okay,' Beg says, as though picking up the thread of a momentarily interrupted conversation. The man doesn't move. That he still has no name makes things difficult. You can use a name to flatter and to flog; it's the start of an understanding. The game begins with a name—the negotiations. But no identification has been found on any of them.

'We found the head,' Beg says. 'Which one of you was carrying it?'

Silence.

'Was that your bag?' He snaps his fingers. 'Hey, do you hear me?'

The man's eyes pull away from the wall for a moment, but are drawn back to it right away.

'That's where we've got a problem,' Beg resumes. 'Whatever you people were planning, I can't judge that, but the head . . .'

The man says nothing, and now and again his eyes fall shut. It's as though he hasn't slept for years.

Beg recalls a sentence from a police academy handbook: 'The victim is deceased when the head has been lastingly separated from the body.'

That 'lastingly,' that was the thing. They had laughed so hard about that.

Beg scratches at a minuscule bump on the tabletop. They've been sitting across from each other for ten minutes already. It doesn't bother him. If there's one thing he's good at, it's remaining silent—waiting and remaining silent. He's in no hurry.

The creature sitting across from him, Beg had learned at the academy, was thinking back over its sins. Louder and louder, the crime he had committed was echoing inside him. It looked for an opening through which to crawl out, to shout itself from the rooftops. Even if the crime had taken place in the deepest darkness, he was seeing it before him now in the clearest of light. There was nothing else he could think about anymore. You could almost see it taking place behind his eyes. His body seemed to do its utmost to drive out the crime, to be shut of the guilt; only the spirit was still resisting. But his body would betray him. It made the spirit ripe for capitulation.

Beg looks at the man across from him, and has his doubts. It seems as though the man isn't even here, but somewhere far away.

'Smoke?' Beg asks.

He lights a cigarette himself and slides the pack with the lighter on top of it across the table. A junkie rarely has only one addiction.

The man reaches for the pack with both hands; but because his cuffs are chained to a ring on the table, he can barely get to it. Two fingers on his right hand are missing. He takes a cigarette from the pack and puts it between his lips. The wheel scrapes across flint, and then comes the flame, and the quiet crackling of paper and tobacco. He keeps his eyes closed as he sucks the smoke into his lungs. Pleasure has returned to his life, thanks to the man across from him. He doesn't know it yet, but inside him gratitude and dependence have formed a reluctant alliance—he is being made ripe for a regimen of punishment and reward. He will be thankful for either; he has earned both the punishment and the reward.

The little bump on the table is a tough one. Beg can't get it off with his fingernail.

There is no ashtray, and the cone of ash on Beg's cigarette is growing longer and longer. He gets up and walks to the door. Holding it open with his foot, he shouts to someone out there to bring him an ashtray.

Halfway through his cigarette, the man begins coughing violently. He sounds like he's choking.

'Been a long time, I suppose?' Beg asks once he's calmed down a bit.

The man nods, his eyes filled with tears.

'How long?' Beg asks.

The man smiles and shrugs. Long ago. 'A few months? Six months?' Beg asks.

The smile fades. An expression of endless melancholy takes its place. He leans forward and puts out the cigarette in the ashtray. The question dissipates along with the smoke.

'Where are you from? Is there someone we can inform about your being here? Wife, children, family? Isn't there anyone who wants to know where you are?'

'No family,' the man says in an unsteady voice.

'And where do you come from?'

He shakes his head. 'The thicket . . . of horrors.'

'What's that?'

'The poacher says . . . he says we have to pass through that, that then we'll get home.'

'Who's the poacher?'

The man remains silent.

'Do you know where you are right now?'

But he has sunk back into himself already, to a place where Beg can't reach him.

'You're here because a man's head was found in the baggage of someone in your group,' Beg said. 'You are all suspects, unless you tell me who crushed that man's skull. If you do that, you'll be a free man soon.'

The man says nothing.

'This thicket you were talking about, what does it look like?' Not a word. Beg raps his knuckles on the tabletop. The highest row of windows is as grey as a television screen. It snowed again last night. When he left the house, the morning was windless and cold.

The man's chin has sunk to his chest. His breathing is deep. Has he fallen asleep again?

Earlier that morning, as he came into the office, Oksana said to him: 'The mayor's here.'

There could have been no worse way to start the day. Oksana rolled her eyes.

'He's down in the cellar.'

Whenever she rolled her eyes, Beg knew, it meant trouble.

Blok had arrived with two of his men and made someone take them downstairs. When Beg came in, he had just summoned the prisoners. They were standing lined up in front of him, shivering.

'Pontus!' Blok shouted.

The door fell closed behind him with a click. He stood there and looked. Looking had a way of slowing down the events, of giving you time to think about what to do.

'What a bunch of beanpoles, man,' Blok said. 'And what's this I hear? They were carrying a *head*? A *head*? Pontus, listen . . . why don't you call me about things like that? One little call, right?' He held up his thumb and forefinger to mimic a telephone. Beg made a mental note: boisterous, talkative. Red eyes; pupils like keyholes.

The prisoners stood in a wretched clump, their shaven heads bowed. Broken sunflowers.

With brusque, pent-up waves of his arms, Beg herded the prisoners back into their cells.

'Hey, Pontus, what are you doing now, man, hey?'

Beg turned. Semjon Blok came closer, as though he were planning to push Beg aside. Beg smelled whisky. They had been up all night drinking and snorting cocaine. Then they'd decided to have a little fun. The party must go on.

'And now I want everyone out of here,' Beg said. 'This is not a fashion show.'

Blok wagged his index finger in front of his face. 'No, Pontus, you've got it all wrong. This is not up to you.'

Beg didn't budge. Rage had cleared the way for him; now there was no going back. 'Shoo,' he said, 'get out, now.'

'Pontus, Pontus.' Semjon Blok shook his head, but his dash had shrivelled, he was suddenly so incredibly tired. Wasn't there someplace around here where he could lie down?

'You're a gutsy one, Pontus,' he said. 'Real gutsy.'

He gestured to his companions. The guard pressed the buzzer, and the electric lock clicked open. Laughing feebly in disbelief, Blok left the room, defeat like a monkey on his back.

The guard cleared his throat. 'Commissioner, you put them back in the wrong cells, I'm afraid.'

Beg's index finger punched thin air. This was the fucking limit. The guard's mouth slammed shut like the muzzle of a dog snapping at a fly.

Blok will never forgive him for this. Somewhere, in an unguarded moment, he will strike back, and Beg will think back on this morning.

The office of mayor has given Semjon Blok almost limitless power. Michailopol is his private domain. He parks his black Cadillac Escalade on the sidewalk, he drives too fast, he ignores all the traffic lights. During his term of office, the property he owns has doubled. No one crosses him in any way; he stands above the law.

Feathering one's own nest, giving and taking bribes, nepotism—all part of a system, true enough, but that system is defective and shortsighted. In the last ten or fifteen years, Beg has seen everything slow down, as the city's entire economic life has fallen under the spell of favouritism and greed: no land is sold, no house built, without dubious permits and money changing hands under the table—which means that, often enough, nothing is built at all. Social relations have become bogged down in the mud of corruption; no one can call anyone else to account, for they all have dirt on their hands. No one looks beyond his own interests. Not a single manager or government official thinks about the long term. It's a system that demands your participation; if you don't join in, you relegate yourself to the sidelines. In the end, it corrupts even the purest soul. This way, everything goes rotten.

This morning, he not only hurt Semjon Blok's pride, but he also ran the system off the rails. Not for long, though. It will avenge itself. It will exclude him, somewhere, at some point, not long from now. His position will be undermined, and he will have to step down. He knows that; that's the way it works. The system protects you as long as you play along.

It doesn't bother him; it had to happen sometime. In some ways, the overt hostility between him and Blok comes as a relief. He has jammed the tip of the scalpel into the abscess, and the stinking pus that wells up reminds him of a dignity he lost long ago.

Later today, Blok will get his letter.

He has the prisoners separated. Isolation will make them emerge sooner from the spell that binds them.

30

ASTRO BOY

He follows the shadow of the psychiatric hospital to the entrance. Snow chirps beneath his shoes. The plaster on the walls is flaking—the building is suffering from psoriasis. The windows are tall and arched; the entrance is flanked on both sides by sandstone knights in niches, their faces almost obscured by their helmets. The realisation that Vienna's influence once reached all the way to Michailopol never fails to amaze Beg.

The boy is in bed, in a bright, high-ceilinged room. A drip is infusing high-calorie nutrition into his veins. His skin has the dark hue of a Gypsy or an Arab. His head is on the pillows; he is asleep. The nurses have been spoiling him with candy and fondant hearts. On the bedside table is a bottle of Coca-Cola—the real stuff, not an imitation. He'd never tasted Coca-Cola before, the nurse said. They've stuck colouring-book illustrations of stags and pirates to the walls, even though he seems a bit too old for that. Their down-to-earth nurses' hearts have been touched by his story. They know that he has eaten from garbage cans. News of the severed head has reached the hospital, too, but they can't imagine that the boy—their fledgling—has done anyone any harm. The pregnant woman just down the corridor doesn't seem that way to them, either. And besides, they were travelling with a group of men, weren't they? Men are the bane of this world.

Beg looks at the boy through the little window in the door. Suddenly, behind other doors, a few crazies begin screaming at the same time—a zoo. The boy frowns in his sleep. The senseless cries of alarm cut through you like a knife.

The boy looks like he's about to die of some ancient disease, he's that skinny—translucent, almost.

'Has he been talking?' Beg asks the nurse.

She nods. 'Sometimes.'

'What about his name? Did he tell you that?'

'No. But he said other things. We wrote it all down, like they asked. Nothing very special, though. That this is softest bed he's ever slept in. And that he has a brother. He comes from a farming family. He's a good kid.'

She unlocks the door and leads him into the room. 'I've got a visitor for you.' The boy looks wide-eyed at Beg. The nurse checks the drip, and then leaves the room.

Beg has brought along a few comic books, which he lays on the bed. 'I guess it can get pretty boring around here,' he says. The comic books are Japanese—they're about Astro Boy, a boy automaton with a heart. Beg had flipped through one of them: Astro Boy fights on earth and in the cosmos against the forces of evil, and when he flies his legs look like the flame from the afterburner of a fighter plane. The boy snatches the comics and hides them under the blankets. *Scarcity*, Beg thinks.

He slides a chair up beside the bed, but doesn't sit down. Instead he stands at the barred window, his hands behind his back, looking out at a radiant white park. The north side of each tree is flecked with fine snow. Maybe, when his days on the force are over, he will become a gardener—a man with a wheelbarrow and a hoe. He knows a few things about plants and the seasons. His flowerbeds will be a comfort to the patients.

'It's been snowing,' he says. 'There's more on its way. You people got in just in time.'

He turns around, walks to the bed, and sits down. The neutral coldness in the boy's eyes feels unpleasant. Children sometimes make him feel inferior, as though he's sold out by becoming an adult. Again the faint memory returns of the boy he once was at the weir—his thin, *effective* body, still devoid of both fat and memories, pinned in place between dive and impact. That's how a fifty-three-year-old man looks at a boy of thirteen, from a distance as far away as it is close by.

These are things he can't tell the boy in the bed, because he wouldn't believe him if he did. In the boy's world, grownups have always been the way they are now; earlier manifestations are too hard to believe.

'What's your name?' he asks.

No reply.

'Where do you people come from?'

Somewhat to his amazement, he hears the boy say: 'I don't know.' He has a high, clear voice, almost like a girl's.

Beg leans forward, his elbows resting on his knees. 'What do you mean, you don't know? You know where you come from, don't you?'

The boy shrugs his skinny shoulders—a sparrow's bones. Then he says: 'I saw you when that man shaved off my hair.'

'That's right,' Beg says. 'I'm the boss at the police station.'

The boy runs his free hand over his shaven head.

'You have no idea how filthy it was,' Beg says. 'When was the last time you'd washed your hair?'

'We didn't have any soap,' the boy says, offended.

'That's true,' Beg says. He clears his throat. 'But now, I still don't know who you are or where you people come from.'

'You weren't there,' the boy says. 'So you don't have to know.'

Beg grins. 'I wish I could say you were right, but we found a human head in your baggage. Did you know about that?' The boy remains motionless.

'One of you beat that man's brains in,' Beg says, 'and then cut off his head. That puts you on my turf, criminal turf. I want to know everything about who did it, and why. Then the rest of you can go home.'

A veil has descended over the boy's eyes. 'You weren't there,' he repeats feebly.

'That's exactly why I need you to tell me what happened, because I wasn't there. The sooner you do that, the sooner you'll be out of here. You don't want to stay here, do you?'

The boy shakes his head. His gaze wanders across the wall.

'You want to go home, don't you?' Beg asks.

The boy purses his lips and shakes his head almost imperceptibly.

Somewhere, a madman begins screaming. 'Shut! Up! Shut! Up! Shut! Up!' another one shrieks.

'They scream all day and all night,' the boy says quietly. 'Why do they scream like that?'

'That's what crazy people do. No one knows why.'

The boy slides his feet back and forth under the blanket.

'What's your name?' Beg asks. 'You can tell me that, can't you?'

'No one needs to know that.'

'I do. I need to. Without a name, I'm not leaving here.'

'Nacer Gül,' the boy says.

'So your name is Nacer Gül,' Beg says slowly. 'And where are you from, Nacer Gül?'

'You said you were going to leave.'

'Whoa, wait a minute, I said I wasn't going to leave *without* a name, not that I would leave *with* a name.'

He sees the boy's amused surprise. The wordplay appeals to him.

'So then when *will* you leave?'

'As soon as I know everything.'

A sigh. 'Not before that?'

'Not before that.'

'It's nobody's business. Only the ones who were there. I can't explain it. You weren't there.' He looks at Beg. 'So you can't understand.'

Two bumps slide back and forth under the blanket at the foot end.

'Don't underestimate me too quickly,' Beg says. 'There are a lot of things I can understand. Even things that happened when I wasn't there. I've been a policeman for thirty-four years, I've seen a lot. Really nasty things, but also really funny things. In fact, maybe I'm able to understand too much.'

'What's the worst thing you've ever seen?'

'There isn't really a list from bad to worst—there are just some things you forget, and other things you keeping thinking about.'

It's quiet for a moment, then he says: 'I often think about this one girl. What we think, what you could sort of tell from the things she had with her, was that she was hitchhiking. It was summertime; she was wearing summer clothes. They found her in a ditch at the side of the road. She'd been there all winter. In her bag, there was a diary, some pictures, tickets for a rock concert. Just a girl, maybe a little more reckless than other girls . . . She took a little too much of a risk, I think. But who she is . . . we'll probably never know.'

He thinks about it for a moment, then says: 'That shouldn't have happened, you know what I mean?'

He doesn't know exactly what it is about the story that affects him so. The lost innocence, perhaps; the unfulfilled potential, maybe . . .

'Her father and mother don't know where she is?'

Beg shakes his head. 'They're still waiting for her. A person who doesn't come home isn't dead. The door stays open a crack.'

'Yeah,' the boy says.

'Yeah,' Beg says, too. He lays a finger on the boy's nose, pushing it to one side a bit. 'And what about you?' he asks then. 'Someone's waiting for you, too. I heard you have a brother. Your parents—are they still alive?'

The boy nods.

'I'm sure they'd like to know where you are. I could let them know that you're safe.'

'Who says I'm safe?'

'I do. I say that. Maybe you don't like it here, but you're safe. A thousand times safer than out there.'

'I hate it here.'

'I can imagine.'

'At night, the screaming is even worse. I don't know why I'm here. I didn't do anything.'

'That's good news. So then the only thing I need to know is who actually *did* do something. If you tell me that, I'll help you to get out of here as quickly as possible. Once you're fixed up a little. Once you've got your strength back.'

'I didn't do anything,' the boy says resentfully. 'So why do I have to stay here?'

'That's kind of a technical thing,' Beg replies, 'but I'm allowed to tell you. You people were trying to get across the border, right? Without passports or anything. Crossing the border illegally is a crime. It's punishable.'

The muscles tense around the boy's jaws.

'But that's not the worst thing. If it was only that, I wouldn't keep you here too long—so many people try to do that. The black man's head, that's what it's about. That's a much bigger problem. I can't be lenient about that.'

The feet slide back and forth restlessly under the blanket.

Beg says: 'There are things you're not telling me because you're afraid of the others. Am I right?'

He sees nothing that looks like confirmation.

'You're safe here—there's nothing to be afraid of. The others can't hurt you.'

The boy shakes his head.

'What?'

'It's not like that,' he says quietly.

'What's not like that?'

'Nothing. Forget it.'

Beg repeats his question, but the boy remains silent.

'Then you're staying here,' Beg says as he gets up. 'I can't help you if you don't cooperate.'

He walks to the window again and stands there, his hands folded behind his back. A pack of glistening snow falls from the branches every now and then. Otherwise, the park is devoid of motion. Fresh snow—this is what the world on the seventh day looks like.

Behind him he hears the deep breathing of sleep.

When the monotonous whistling in his ears begins again, he leaves the room and quietly pulls the door closed behind him. The nurse gets up from her chair in the hallway and comes to him on creaking rubber soles. The jangling of her key ring echoes in his ears. She locks the door. Metal against metal, the sound is amplified many times over.

31

REMEMBER WHAT AMALEK DID

'Do you play chess?' the rabbi had asked him once; since then they would sometimes play as a distraction from spiritual affairs. The hours with Rabbi Eder were dear to Beg; they constituted his only physical tie with Judaism. They drank black tea from Krasnodar, ate sweet cookies, and thought about the moves to come. The bulbs on the ceiling shed little light, so the difference between the objects and their shadows was hard to see.

The rabbi sacrificed a knight.

He's just shaking up the board, figured Beg, who had never won from him. One draw, on one occasion—that was all. Now that Beg was in a good position for once, Eder had to go and do something unexpected, like this. Frustrated, he sipped at his tea.

'A peculiar move,' he murmured.

'Then you don't understand the essence of the game,' the rabbi said.

After a long silence, Beg asked: 'And what might that essence be?'

'The essence consists of leading your opponent into a dark forest, the forest where two plus two is five—and the only path leading out of that forest is broad enough for only one of you. That's how Grandmaster Tal put it.'

'Ah-ha, I see.'

He lost that game, too. The rabbi had left the forest, but Beg was still wandering around in it.

They arranged the pieces of the board. 'You don't seem to be focusing well,' the rabbi said. 'Usually you put up more of a fight.'

Beg told him about the talk he'd had with the woman that afternoon, after he had left the boy. His reconstruction took form slowly.

'Try to figure it,' he said. 'They all pay a huge chunk of money to cross the border. They spend hours hiding in a dark trailer until they get to the border. Dogs, guards, they're shitting their pants. When the truck starts rolling again, they feel like screaming in fear and joy. It's night out, dark, by the time they leave the truck. The driver points them in the direction they need to go, says they'll find a city out there. Morning comes, they walk and walk but never get to a city. They're in doubt; they fight. All they see are the steppes, nothing else. The group splits up, a few of them go back, most of them push on. Westward, all the time. But they never get anywhere. There is no civilised world anymore; they've ended up in the wilderness. Without water, without food. They have nothing to shield their heads against the sun by day or their bodies against the cold at night. People die. That's the way the woman put it: one after the other died, and any one of us could have been next. In the end, there are five of them left. They wandered across the flats for months.'

Beg shook his head.

'They even made it through the winter. It's a miracle that they survived.'

The memory comes to him of the woman, describing the journey in a feeble voice, monotonous as the steppes themselves. Her pregnant belly was heaving beneath the blanket, a hideous deformity on her emaciated body. When he'd asked who the father was, she hadn't answered. She remained stubbornly silent when it came to the black man's head. That he had been with the group from the start, that was all she would say.

'I don't understand,' the rabbi said. 'They crossed the border, that's what you said.'

Beg slid his chair back and sat up straight. 'What I'm going to tell you now . . . it's almost unimaginable.' He stood up and paced around the kitchen. 'A border, that's right. The woman says they crossed it; the boy saw barracks, border guards, barrier gates, and dogs. He described what he saw to the others. And the others heard it, men and dogs—there could be no mistake about it. Still, they were nowhere. They'd wandered through a no-man's land the whole time, under conditions we can't even imagine.'

He was standing in front of the rabbi now. He could smell the old man—a damp mattress, a coat that had been worn too long. 'And then they reach civilisation,' he said. 'Houses, cars, people—and their worst nightmare comes true: they never crossed the border at all . . . there is no new country. All that time they were *just here!*'

'So what about the border?' the rabbi asked impatiently.

'There was no border! There was only the product of an evil imagination: a copy of a border, a fake border. A replica of a border built by people-smugglers. At the real border you have to bribe people, get lucky—all risks you'd have to take.'

'People . . .' the rabbi murmured.

'The brilliance of something like that! Faking a border. Someone had to *come up* with that.'

'It sounds as though you admire it.'

'No, not at all. Or yes, disgust *and* admiration.'

'It's perverse to admire something like that.'

'Only because of the imagination it would take, nothing else. The same way I admired your decision to sacrifice a knight. But this . . . evil is an art, I'm afraid.'

'You give evil too much credit. That puts you outside the pale of the Torah.'

'Excuse me for saying so, but the volume of crime one sees in the Torah . . .'

'Crime *and* punishment. Crime is depicted so that the Everlasting can determine His punishment. By way of the crime, He imposes His laws. Without evil, there is no way for us to know good.'

'You know what man is like,' Beg said. 'You know that there are thousands of ways to get around a prohibition. He always finds a way out.'

'Which means that he breaks the law—your earthly law and my law, which comes from heaven. Man is a born delinquent. Our laws are meant to keep him on track.'

And how powerless we are with our laws against the limitless fantasy of the transgression, Beg thought. He sat down and placed his hands on the table. 'I have looked murderers and child-molesters in the eye,' he said, 'and the bizarre thing is that you can never tell. There are no special traits. There's nothing that makes them recognisable. The only thing, perhaps, is that sometimes you notice something missing. You notice that you're staring into empty space. How are you supposed to recognise the vacuum inside a human being? How can you measure it?'

'They say that Rabbah bar bar Hanna once made a journey by ship,' the rabbi said. 'When the sailors saw a bird standing with its ankles in the water and its head reaching to the sky, they thought the waters were shallow and fit to refresh themselves in—until they heard a voice from heaven warning them not to enter the water; seven years earlier, a carpenter had dropped his axe in the water there, and it still had not reached the bottom! So bottomless, too, is reprobate man, whom you know better than I do.'

'And then you've got the situations as well,' Beg said. 'The alcohol, the heat, the man who loses control. He has suspended his humanity for the moment; he acts like a beast, as a colleague of mine says. Later on, he looks back in amazement and shame, and thinks: *That wasn't me—that was the beast.*'

He thought for a moment. 'But personally, as far as I'm concerned . . . a new high point, or perhaps, rather, a new deep point, is imitating a border. And then sending them out onto the steppes, knowing they're going to perish there. Something like that . . .' He shook his head. 'No, I wouldn't have thought that was possible.'

The rabbi leaned across the table. 'Then you have forgotten what Amalek did . . .'

'And what was that?' Beg asked.

The rabbi recited the lines from the Torah:

> Remember what Amalek and his tribe did to you along the way when you came out of Egypt. When you were weary and worn out, they met you on your journey and attacked all who were lagging behind; they had no fear of God.

He took a breath and went on:

When the Lord your God gives you rest from all the en-
emies around you in the land he is giving you to possess
as an inheritance, you shall blot out the name of Amalek
from under heaven. Do not forget.

'Amalek attacked us when we were weakest,' he said. 'His name
is a curse.'

For the rabbi, the past didn't exist, Beg thought. It was as alive to
him as the present; the low tricks of a tribal chieftain in the wilderness were reflected in the treachery of the people-smugglers he had
just encountered. The day before yesterday, or three thousand years
ago, it made no difference to him.

This mysterious timelessness overcame him, too, when he read
about the lives of Moses, Aaron, and Joshua in the desert and knew
himself connected to that in some mystical fashion. He was no longer
so alone. Others had gone before him, just as others would come after
him. Whether he would strap the phylactery to his arm each morning, he didn't know. But with every word he read and every visit he
paid to the rabbi, he sensed—with a certainty that touched him—that
he was approaching his destination.

He didn't know if it was allowed, but even more than to the Everlasting, he was drawn at times by the desire to be immersed in the
mikveh, the niche of stone deep in the earth, where the living water
would renew his soul.

32

AKMUHAMMET KURBANKILIEV

When they came to the edge of the city and realised where they were, the poacher began to weep. He couldn't stop. The woman couldn't stand to see his sorrow; the tears washed down her cheeks as well. It was like a contagious sickness: they infected each other, they were all crying now, their tears kept flowing. It had all been for naught. All of it. They had crossed the wilderness to a new country, only to discover that it wasn't a new country at all—only the nightmare of the eternal return.

Right after seeing the boy at the psychiatric hospital, Beg visited the woman there, too. He pulled up a chair beside her bed. He heard three names.

The boy's name was Saïd Mirza.

'He told me it was Nacer Gül,' Beg mumbled.

Nacer Gül, the woman said, was the man who had almost sent them to their death. Nacer Gül with his white BMW and his sunglasses that he wore even at night. Nacer Gül—the betrayer, the faithless one.

She knew Vitaly's name, and the boy's, but not those of the others. There had been no call for names.

'You were already pregnant when you left?' Beg asked.

A brief glare. She shook her head.

'Who is the child's father?'

She kept her eyes averted.

'You don't know who the father is?'

When she remained silent, he exhaled through his nose in disgust. 'Then I see only . . . three possibilities, am I right?'

But although she told him all about the fake border crossing, Samira Uygun remained silent on two counts: the life inside her, and the death of the black man.

Beg bought cigarettes, a pack of chewing gum, and a couple of bottles of energy drink. He climbed the stairs to the third, because the elevator took forever to travel from floor to floor. Beg mounted, holding the railing with one hand. He needed to do something about the shape he was in, he thought—not for the first time. There was a little gym on the first floor. It was slowly filling up with broken office furniture and crates of empty soda bottles.

In the interrogation room, he arranged the things on the table. He put the chewing gum in his inside pocket. He slid the cigarettes and plastic bottles around until he was satisfied. It was no mean feat to make things look as though you hadn't thought about it.

The toothless man was brought in. Beg tried to estimate his age; he could have been forty, but just as easily fifty-five. The man was leaning over, so that he could reach his chest and scratch at it. His fingers clawed frantically at the fabric of his sweater. The handcuffs rattled. Beg looked on in amazement at how he lost himself in his scratching, his eyes fixed on the floor, in a sort of trance.

After a while he seemed content, and sank back in his chair.

'You ready now?' Beg asked.

The man nodded. Beg pulled out the blue ballpoint. 'What's your name?' he asked.

'Akmuhammet Kubankiliev.'

The tip of the pen remained hanging above the paper. 'Run that by me one more time,' Beg said.

'Akmuhammet Kubankiliev.'

'Why don't you write it down for me yourself?' He slid the pen and paper across the table. The man's hand shook as he wrote his name.

'Where are you from?'

'Ashkhabad.'

'All the way from Turkmenistan.'

'From the madhouse.'

'You're a long way from home, my friend.'

'The farther, the better.'

The man raised his left hand to scratch at his right shoulder. *Man, this guy has it bad.*

'Fleas?' Beg asked.

The man shook his head. 'Skin condition.'

'Ah.'

Forearms crossed at the chest, he tore at his upper body. Beg tried not to watch, but it was impossible. The hands dug at the sweater like starving animals.

'Do you think you could stop that?' Beg asked.

The man shook his head. 'If I could . . .'

'But?'

'It went away for a while . . .' He closed his eyes, as though trying to remember something. 'I left that nuthouse so that I would get better. The farther away I got, the better it was. The whole trip—never bothered me for a moment.'

'And then?'

The man shook his head. 'This. Here.'

'What?'

'Just the sight of that uniform, I start itching.'

'My uniform makes you itch?'

Kurbankiliev nodded. 'That, the walls, you people. Everything.'

'I'm afraid I can't help you on that score.'

'That's what I figured.'

'I could take my coat off, if that would help.'

'No, forget it.'

'We're going to talk about the head,' Beg said. 'We found it in the baggage. What can you tell me about it?'

The man shrugged. 'Nothing.'

'One of you killed him. Someone cut off his head. What can you tell me about that?'

'I wasn't there.'

'This is your one chance to get yourself off the hook, if you're innocent.'

'I want my teeth back.'

'Your teeth?'

'They were in my pants pocket. I was keeping them.'

'I'm afraid . . . your clothes . . .' Beg shook his head.

'What?'

'We threw it all away. They were so filthy.'

'They took our clothes, then he stole my teeth.'

'Why would someone want to steal your teeth?'

'Gold, what do you think?'

'I'll have them check it.'

'First I want them back, man. They're my teeth. He has to keep his mitts off of my teeth.'

'Who do you mean by "he"?'

'That guard, the fat one.'

'Just a minute,' Beg said.

He went out into the hall. In one of the rooms he found a phone and called downstairs.

It took ten minutes before the elevator doors opened and the ward stepped out. He was holding something wrapped in newsprint. He handed it to his superior. Beg unwrapped the package and saw Akmuhammet Kurbankiliev's almost entire set of teeth, the gold molars and teeth set in a gold retainer.

'These are the ones,' the ward said, his head tilted hen-like to one side.

'What were you thinking . . . ?'

The other man shrugged. 'I was keeping them for him.'

Beg looked at him, while the warder clasped his hands and waited.

'Dismissed,' Beg said, and the man vanished in relief into the elevator.

In the interrogation room, Beg laid the packet on the table and slid it over. The man leaned forward and opened it. He slid a finger between the teeth and molars, feeling them. He looked up. 'These are mine,' he said.

'Take a better look if you like,' Beg said.

The man nodded. He seemed pleased to see his teeth again. Beg averted his eyes, to not see the brown roots. He lit a cigarette and ran a hand over his jaw. The stubble on his chin felt like sandpaper. 'Okay,' he said, 'let's get down to it.'

The man refolded the packet carefully. It remained on the table.

'What am I being held for, actually?' Kurbankiliev asked.

Beg leaned back and folded his hands on his stomach. 'Attempting to cross the border illegally, and first-degree murder. And desecration of a corpse. But because you're not from around here, the first charge will probably be dropped.'

'That's nice.'

'But of little import. The other two charges, that's what I'd worry about if I were you. You've been assigned a lawyer. You have a right to that. Only thing is: he's not coming. They couldn't get hold of him.'

'So when's he coming?'

'Sometime.'

Kurbankiliev nodded in resignation.

'The head,' Beg said.

'I don't know who did it.'

'That's impossible—you people were on the road together for months.'

'I'm sorry.'

'Whose head is it?'

'Africa's. The Ethiopian's.'

'Why did he have to die?'

'Don't ask me. Because.'

'Let's not have any misunderstandings,' Beg said. 'It's not wise to underestimate me.'

That wiggling again. When Kurbankiliev wasn't scratching himself, he was shimmying with his legs.

'Ethiopia,' Beg said.

'Only because that's where he came from, at least that's what we understood. Almost no one ever talked with him besides that, I don't think. Except for the tall guy, for a while.'

'Who's that?'

'I don't know him. We knew almost nothing about each other. I think he mentioned his name once . . .'

'So where's "the tall guy" now?'

'Dead, right? Dead as a doornail.'

'How did it happen?'

A pitying look. 'Starvation, all of them. Our own natural cause.'

'How many of you were there?'

'Fourteen, fifteen when we started. Two of them walked back right away. They were smart—they had it figured out. We didn't. We walked in exactly the wrong direction.' He nodded. 'There were fourteen of us, not fifteen.'

Beg wrote down the number fourteen, and retraced the ciphers with his pen. Then he drew a circle around them. He asked: 'Why is the Ethiopian dead?'

'I'm not the one to ask about that.'

'I'm going to ask you one more time.'

Beg tapped the tip of his pen on the table and looked at the man from beneath his eyebrows. 'Why is he dead?'

'Man, I don't know. I didn't have anything to do with it.'

'Goddamn,' Beg said calmly. He slid his chair back, got up, and left the room. When he returned, he was carrying a claw hammer. He placed it on the table in front of him.

The hammer had now become the room's burning vortex; outside it, there was nothing at all.

'All right,' Beg said, 'let's try it again.'

'What do you want?' Kurbankiliev said. 'I don't know anything about it.'

There was shrillness in his voice.

Beg leaned across the table and grabbed the packet of dentures. He unfolded it, and selected one front tooth from among the rest. It was circled by a frame of gold. The root was stained brown. He picked up the hammer.

'Okay, here we go again: who did it, and why?'

'I really don't know, man,' Kurbankiliev said. He frowned deeply. 'What is it, do you want me to make something up?'

The hammer came down with a bang, shattering Akmuhammet Kurbankiliev's front tooth.

'Aw, fuck!' he screamed. He tried to jump up, but the manacles around his wrists pulled him back down. 'Why are you doing that? Aw, fuck!'

The tooth was now a little heap of gold-veined powder. Carefully, Beg laid the hammer on the table. He folded the paper back around the teeth and held the little package in the air. 'You wanted this,' he said, 'and then you were going to tell me what was going on. Instead of that, all I'm hearing is bullshit.'

'My tooth, man,' Kurbankiliev whimpered. 'Aw, fuck.'

'You should abide by your promises. Then things like this wouldn't happen. Smoke?'

He slid the pack across the table. Kurbankiliev took one and lit it. The coughing that followed bent him over double. After a bit, teary and red-eyed, he sat up straight and took another drag. He was able to suppress the next coughing fit.

'How's that taste?'

He nodded. 'Good,' he said in a pinched voice.

Beg looked at the pack of cigarettes. 'Marlboro. Freedom.' He flipped it over and read the back. 'You think it's really as harmful as they say?'

Kurbankiliev sucked on his cigarette and said nothing.

'Such freedom,' Beg said, 'especially if it kills you.'

The face across the table was veiled in a column of smoke. That was the way the Everlasting had spoken to Moses on Mount Horeb, from inside a pillar of cloud. He longed for Him at times—a sudden, ecstatic longing that he didn't understand and that frightened him. This was the image: a ship is pulling away from the dock, and there, he, Pontus Beg, comes running, waving his arms because he is on the verge of missing his destination. The gap between the ship and the quay widens. He screams, he leaps . . .

Maybe the dream meant that He was calling him. That he was on the right road. That he was almost ready to be immersed in the mikveh, the water that awaits him, the dark niche into which he'll lower himself until the living water closes over his head.

But then again, maybe not.

He put the pack of Marlboros on the table. 'A striking similarity, isn't it?' he said. 'That you wanted to be free, and that it almost killed you. Just like these cigarettes.'

Kurbankiliev ground out the cigarette between thumb and fore-finger, above the ashtray. He sniffed at his fingers.

'Anything was better than that,' he said. He nodded at the back wall, with the transoms in it. 'Anything.'

'Even dying?'

Kurbankiliev scratched his chest. 'I think so, yeah.'

'And the same went for the Ethiopian?' Beg asked.

'I don't know why he was on the road.'

'It wasn't his longing for freedom that killed him,' Beg said.

'I wouldn't know.'

Beg glanced at the packet of teeth.

'Vitaly had the head with him the whole time,' Kurbankiliev said. 'He was the bearer.'

'Why Vitaly?'

'He was appointed.'

'Who appointed him?'

'The black man.'

'I don't get it. The Ethiopian announced who was supposed to carry his head after he was dead?'

'While he was still alive, yeah. That's when he appointed him. On top of the hill. He burned the truth into him.'

'And then he said: "I want you to carry my head once I'm dead"? Get off it.'

The man was leaning back in his chair, his eyes travelling across the ceiling.

'Hey!' Beg said. He snapped his fingers. 'I asked you something.'

'I heard you.'

'So answer me already.'

'He pointed him out. With his finger. He burned a big old hole in his arm. You can still see it. That's the way it went. There's nothing more to tell.'

'And who beat his brains in?'

'It was necessary.'

'Why?'

'There was no other way.'

'Why not?'

Silence.

'Why not?' Beg repeated.

'He had to go so that we could go on.'

'That's what you figured? And then you killed him?'

'No.'

'So who did? Come on!'

Kurbankiliev shook his head slowly, almost pityingly. 'I didn't do it,' he said, and laughed bitterly. 'We all did.'

33

WE ARE THE DEAD

On the morning before the last suspect was questioned, Beg received a call from Inspector Matuszak, and frowned. Because this was also about frontier-running, the fugitives had been reported to the National Investigation Service. Matuszak had wasted no time in jumping on the case. Beg had never thought the service could exhibit so much get-up-and-go.

The inspector wanted to hear all about the fake border. There had been suspicions for a long time: bodies found out on the steppes, some of them kneeling in the sand; others with their arms still raised in supplication to the skies, sculpted in death. But this was the first time survivors had been found.

'I'll put in an order to have them transferred,' Matuszak said. 'We'll get them out of your hair.'

Beg said that the woman still had to give birth. The others were sick and malnourished.

'So when do you think you'll be finished with your investigation?' Matuszak asked.

'Depends,' Beg said.

He told him about the head, about which he still knew so little. 'They agreed with each other not to talk about it,' he said.

He knew what the man at the other end of the line must be thinking: *Stupid hayseed, can't you do* anything?

He didn't care; he just wanted to get his work done. His life had become bound up with the refugees, with the road they had travelled. They had wandered through the wilderness like the Jews, and like the Jews they had carried the bones of one of their own along with them . . . Beg's reasoning came to a halt at the glorious analogy. They had carried a head with them, just as the Jews, three thousand years earlier, had carried the bones of Joseph—Joseph, who had died in Egypt, and was then embalmed and placed in a box.

> God will surely come to your aid, and then you must carry my bones up with you from this place.

Hundreds of years went by, but the promise remained unforgotten. A proof of fidelity, the rabbi had called it.

Carry my bones from this place—that was how the history of Beg's ancestors was bound up with that of a group lost on the steppes.

Three thousand years ago, or the day before yesterday. What was the difference?

The rabbi had said that every Jew, wherever and whenever on earth, had to see himself as a refugee out of Egypt, a wanderer in the desert; that's how important the escape and the forty years lost in the wilderness were for the people of Israel. Every step a Jew took was a reminder of the exodus, and carried him back to the birth of a people in the desert. That was where God had given them his Commandments, and where their belief in Him had assumed concrete form.

In some mysterious way, the interrogations brought the exodus closer to Beg. History was being projected before his eyes—he sometimes had the feeling that the refugees' story had been spun specially for him. The Everlasting was so close at such moments that he was seized by joy.

But what did Inspector Matuszak know about any of this? He only did his job; he had no idea what such things meant.

'In three or four weeks,' Beg said, 'they'll be strong enough for transport. My investigation will be finished by then, too.'

'Today . . . two weeks from today, on December 22, I'll have them picked up.'

'With all due respect, Inspector Matuszak, the period I mentioned was not negotiable. On January 1, they'll be all yours.'

'You have no authority to impose that delay.'

'You should see them—then you'd understand. Someone here described them as "the Jews in the camp." Their condition prohibits it.'

Before they hung up, Matuszak said he would call again in a couple of days. And so their first confrontation ended in a draw.

Beg sat in the interrogation room, his arms folded across his stomach. The final prisoner would be brought in after lunch. Beg's eyes slowly fell shut.

Only now, at rest, did he become aware of the noises in the building. He heard the elevator cables meowing in their shaft, and the gurgling of air and water in the heating. Somewhere, there was a ruffling he couldn't place. Somewhere else, slamming doors, and voices floating down the corridor. He had been walking around in this building for almost twenty years, but he had never before heard the way it sounded like an organism gasping for breath.

When the final prisoner was led in, Beg awoke from his catnap with a start. As he watched them chain the man to the metal ring, he twisted the top off a bottle of energy drink. He gulped it down. The police guard left the room. The two men were alone.

'You're the last person in the group I'll be talking to,' Beg said. 'I already know a lot, but maybe not everything. This is your chance to tell your side of the story.'

When the other man said nothing, Beg slowly screwed the cap back onto the empty bottle and said: 'Do you understand what I just said?'

The man nodded.

'Good,' Beg said. 'Your name, age, and occupation, please.'

Alexander Haç had left his tiny village in the Urals to find a better life elsewhere. A butcher could get work anywhere, he'd figured. He was forty-seven.

'You've been charged with attempting to cross the border illegally,' Beg said, 'but seeing as you were never even close to a border at all, I guess that charge won't really stick. What *will* stick is the man's head we found in your baggage. Murder—I think that's what the prosecutor will call it. And desecration of a corpse, if he's particularly pissed off.'

The man shrugged. 'You know what they say. The law is a serpent that bites only those who have no shoes.'

'I suppose you're right, but you're forgetting the head. You'll be prosecuted for that.' He scratched at the little bump on the tabletop. It looked like a clump of dried glue. He looked up. 'Unless, of course, you tell me that's not the way it was.'

'I can't do that,' Haç said. 'I'm guilty. Just like the others.'

'What are you guilty of?'

'What I'm charged with.'

'Accepting the charge is not the same as the crime itself,' Beg said. 'What exactly are you guilty of?'

Haç kept his mouth shut. The hair on his forearms was standing straight up. The room was much too warm, but he had gooseflesh. He was still nothing but skin and bones, so every trace of warmth flowed right back out of him.

'You know,' Beg said, 'they say I'm a patient person. I usually question people mildly. My colleagues laugh at me because of that. After all, violence is so much more . . . effective. Soon the National Investigation Service is going to interrogate you. They know what pain is all about. They went to school to find out. If they want, they'll make you remember the date when your grandparents got married. And then you'll wish you'd answered me, instead of letting things get to that point.' He sank back in his chair and laid his arm on the table. 'What are you laughing about?' With his knuckles, he began tapping out the rhythm of 'Chopsticks.'

'You say I'm the last one you'll talk to,' said Alexander Haç. 'So how come you still don't know who you're dealing with?'

'So who am I dealing with?' Beg asked in irritation.

'You have no idea how often we fell asleep in the certainty that there would be no tomorrow. We're dead people. You can't get to us.'

Beg stifled a belch. The sweet chewing-gum taste of the energy drink swirled in his mouth. 'Let me tell you something weird,' he said. 'I really don't care all that much who murdered him and who cut off his head and all that. They'll find out all about that when you get there. For me, the point is . . . what I want to know . . .' He was silent for a moment. 'Maybe I should ask this first,' he said then. 'Do you believe? In a god?'

The man's eyes clouded over. He shrugged.

'I,' Beg said, '. . . not so long ago, I myself found the way that leads to the Everlasting. Lots of things still aren't clear to me, but I have to say that I . . . well, that I've embraced a faith. It's a long story, it's all still pretty fresh, but what matters to me is this . . .'

Then he told the man about the exodus. How the Israelites were led by a pillar of cloud by day, and a pillar of fire by night. The sea had parted to let them through. For forty years, it had rained food, always just enough for one day at a time. 'We all know the story,' Beg said, 'but what I *didn't* know was that, all that time, they were carrying the bones of one of their forefathers. Joseph, who had made them promise to bury him in the Promised Land . . . hundreds of years later, and they still remembered . . . that kind of faithfulness, that kind of breathtaking faithfulness . . .'

He felt his eyes burning.

'So?' the man asked. 'Did they bury him when they got home?'

Beg nodded. 'He entered the Promised Land. He did . . . but not Moses, who had the most right to. The reason I'm telling you this, though . . . the Ethiopian. Why was it necessary for him to die? Why was it necessary for you people to keep him with you? It must have been important to you, otherwise you wouldn't do something like that. Tell me what importance he has for you people. Only that.'

Haç sat motionless. It looked like he had stopped breathing.

'We lived with wonders all around us,' he said slowly. 'Once they started, we never doubted that we were going to be saved. These things are impossible to talk about. They're only important to the ones who were there—those who passed through the thicket of horrors.'

'What is that, this thicket?'

'You keep on asking questions, as though there's an answer to everything.'

'You're the one who started talking about the thicket of horrors. I'm asking you what it means.'

But the man across from him was sunk in thought. He seemed to be wandering amid his memories, a bit amazed at the things he saw there.

Beg's suspicion of idolatry grew and became increasingly concrete—a thing they couldn't talk about, because every faith shivers and shrinks under the cold lamplight of inspection.

'After we killed him,' the man said suddenly, 'the boy's dreams started. He dreamed the way for us. The woman said they came from him. She could interpret them. The boy told them, and she understood them.'

'So you're saying . . . who did these dreams come from?'

The man grimaced. 'From Africa. Who else? He sent them so that we would know the way. I swear, we walked straight to it.'

'To what?'

'The woman said we had to start going south. All that time we'd been heading west; now suddenly we had to go the other way. I didn't want to—once you choose a direction, you have to keep following it, otherwise you go completely nuts. But they were so sure of themselves. I figured . . . well, what if it's true . . . that he's the one telling them . . . who am I to . . . then we found the village. That's what saved us.'

'So you're telling me the black man *sent* those dreams?'

'They started once he was dead.'

'Then why did he have to die, if the things he did were good?'

'You don't get it. It wasn't always like that. At first, he was in the service of evil. He did bad things. He ate from the tall man's body. He was covered in sores, because of him. We saw all of that. And Vitaly's arm almost fell off, at the place where he'd touched him. It rotted all the way through. If you think back on it, that whole trip . . .'

'He *ate* from someone else's body?' Beg asked. He tried to suppress his disgust—and his deep-rooted bafflement.

'He sank his teeth into it, oh yeah.'

'And you all saw him do that?'

'Cannibals, right? The blacks. Always have been. Couldn't have been anything else.'

Occasionally, Beg was granted a glimpse of the thicket of horrors—flashes, already gone before he could actually feel the despair.

'Tell me about the village,' he said.

34

THE ROOSTER

Three of the four had been for it; only he, the poacher, was against. Vitaly didn't count anymore; lightning had struck in his head. For the first time in weeks, they turned from their route and walked south. They were following a dream, a vision of salvation—if they found no deliverance, the men would kill the woman and the boy. Winter had started, and in the mornings their bodies were covered with frost.

As darkness began falling on the fifth day, they saw rows of trees rising up from the plains—the tall trunks of poplars, the civilisation of trees. Someone had planted them, and the current in ditches had watered their roots. They stood there like that, an outer ring of protection against the wind and sand off the steppes.

But the trees were dead.

Behind them they found abandoned farmhouses. They wandered through the streets of the hamlet, the wind blowing through windows and doorways. There were no lights anywhere, not a living soul in sight. The wind had piled sand against the walls; grass and bushes had advanced into the streets themselves.

They built a fire on the dirt floor of a house. They warmed their hands at the flames. Why had the people abandoned their homes? What disaster had made them flee? Where had they gone?

Their shadows danced on the walls. They had found nothing to eat, but this night, they would not freeze to death.

It was still dark, the final coals glowing amid the ashes. They pricked up their ears in their sleep. The sound they had heard was unmistakeable.

A rooster. Somewhere a rooster crowed. And again.

Somebody fumbled around, trying to sit upright. The others moved restlessly on the floor.

They had heard a rooster—the last living rooster in the world.

'Fuck,' the poacher said in the dark.

With a groan, he rose to his feet and left the house. The woman laid wood on the fire, and fanned the coals. One by one they rose, shattered, stiff; the underfed body cannibalises itself, devours its own muscles.

Grimy light was coming through the windows; outside, they occasionally heard the cock's crow. In the attic, the man from Ashkhabad was ripping up planks for the fire; it was hard work. Downstairs, the others sat in a cloud of black, sticky dust that clogged their windpipes. The fire leapt up. Vitaly raved.

The poacher came in, cold sweat on his forehead.

In the distance, the rooster crowed.

'I can't get hold of him,' he panted. He rested, his hands on his thighs. 'Someone else has to go with me. That bastard is in good shape.'

He shuffled up to the fire, enraged by his defeat.

After a while, the boy spoke up. He asked: 'So who takes care of the rooster, anyway?'

The cold splinter between their eyes was their realisation that poultry could not survive the winter alone, that there was someone who fed them and locked the run to keep the predators out at night. They left Vitaly beside the fire and searched the houses and sheds. They fed themselves silly on half-frozen, rotting fruit they found at the feet of a few tangled trees. The boy threw down the apples still hanging on the branches. The fermenting fruit made them light in the head.

They gathered wood, and the boy found a wooden rake with two tines. They combed each house and every shed. It was impossible to tell whether the inhabitants had left in a hurry, or one by one over the course of years.

When they saw a brood of chickens pecking at the ground on the bleaching green outside the village, they froze. Here was a prospect of plenty. Euphoria welled up within them, but they didn't know quite where to start. It was too much all at once.

'Oh-oh-oh,' the man from Ashkhabad said.

They were reeling—they would never be fast enough to catch them. Grubbing about amid his harem was the cock, a champion rooster with long legs and a fiery red comb. This was where his life would end; their teeth ached in anticipation.

Then they saw the house.

It was a little way outside the village, half-hidden behind a mound. A few sparse poplars surrounded it.

From the chimney came a thin wisp of smoke.

In none of their imaginations had their salvation ever looked like a fairy tale.

They moved towards it hesitantly, afraid it would vanish before their eyes as they approached. The clay walls had once been white, and the farmhouse's blue could still be seen on the shutters and sills. The doors and windows were all slanted, as though the house had shifted and was slowly sinking into the earth.

At the door, they stood indecisively.

'Anybody home?' the poacher shouted.

He pushed open the door and went inside. The others followed. They found themselves in a low-ceilinged room full of shadows. The stovepipe leaked smoke; the walls were covered in soot. It was as though they had entered the inside of an old, dented kettle. At the back, beside the pump, stood an old woman. Her hair was in pigtails. Her toothless jaw had dropped open.

'Food,' said one of the ghosts who had invaded her house.

'Food,' the others said now as well.

The woman stood with her back pressed against the washbasin. There were red wooden cherries attached to the elastic bands in her hair.

'Food! Food!' the ghosts now shouted, all at the same time. They raised their hands to their mouths in an eating gesture. They pulled tins of food out of her cupboards, tore them open, and dug out the contents with their bare hands. Goulash. Beans. Pilaf. They drank milk sweeter than they had ever tasted. They gobbled and scoffed until they lay writhing and groaning in pain on the floor, amid their own vomit, their hands clutching their bellies.

All this time, the woman had not moved. Then she tied an apron around her waist and, stepping over the bodies on the floor, went out the door. She ladled grain from a barrel and shouted, *Heeere, chick-chick-chick! Heeeere, chick-chick-chick!* Clucking pitifully, the chickens came running up to pick at the grain around her feet.

One by one, the ghosts left her house. She watched as they climbed the mound and walked to the house farther along, their arms clutching cans of food and packs of pasteurised milk—her supplies for the winter.

The fire was out. Vitaly was gone. They poked at the fire, and hid the booty in their satchels.

Vitaly had left his own satchel behind. The thing lay between them, a clump of plastic bags, one pulled over the other, muddied, stained: a disgusting hide from which the animal itself had fled. The boy pulled it over and picked at the rope that kept the satchel closed. He yanked it free and dumped the contents onto the ground. Something heavy fell out of it, hitting the floor with a dull thud.

He shrank back with a strangled cry: lying between his legs was the black man's head. He scuttled back away from it, on hands and knees. The dead face was looking at him, its one, intact eyelid half-open.

The woman buried her face in her hands.

'Fuck,' the poacher said for the second time that day. He took the thawed head by the hair, walked to the door, and tossed it into the street.

The woman stood up, wormed past him through the doorway, and came back carrying the head.

'Have you forgotten,' she panted, 'how he brought us here? Is that your thanks? For this? A roof over our heads, the fire, the food in your stomach?'

She held up the head for him to see. Thin, colourless fluid dripped from the wound at the neck. 'He steered Vitaly's hand to cut off his head, so that he could be with us. Even in death he hasn't left us.'

The boy took a breath to say something, but choked back his words. The poacher stared into the fire.

'There's something to what she says,' the man from Ashkhabad said haltingly. 'Our luck has changed so much since we started going south, it's amazing.'

'That's no accident,' the woman said.

The boy looked at the poacher. He wanted to know what he was thinking.

The woman pointed at the boy.

'And have you people forgotten his dreams?'

They had not forgotten his dreams.

'I'll admit,' the poacher said then, 'I was against it. But we were definitely being pointed in the right direction.'

The others nodded. The thought gave them a sense of comfort and security.

The woman spoke, explaining the signs to them. Since the death of the black man and the boy's first dreams, time had acted as a helpmeet; the situation had suddenly changed in their favour. The doom that had lingered over their heads from the start had dispersed and blown away. The oppression, the stone on their chests, was lifted. Who could point to any other cause than the black man's death? She had found none; it was his death that had redeemed them. He who had brought on the oppression had lifted it, too.

'I don't understand it completely,' the man from Ashkhabad said. 'But, at the same time, I don't see what else it could be.'

'You don't have to understand everything,' the woman said. 'It's enough that it happened. It's impossible to understand everything. All we have to do is be grateful.'

'That we . . .' the poacher murmured, 'we, of all people . . . get to experience something like this. It's just . . .'

The others nodded; yes, they had been chosen. The boy looked around wide-eyed, and saw how a shared conviction took hold of the others, how they came together around the black man's head. His death united the opposites. A feeling of euphoria overtook him, too. Everything had, of necessity, led to this outcome. Everything had happened so that he could see it happen, so that he could tell about it later.

The poacher shook his head. 'Who would have believed it?' He poked at the fire and said: 'So what now? What's expected of us?'

'That we follow him,' the woman said, 'and not doubt.'

She said that the head would lead them; they had to fear it and honour it, and not forget what they had been through.

At the heart of their little community, they reshaped his image: mercurial and ambiguous. His cruelty, but also his mercy.

How he had nourished himself with the dead.

Suddenly, in a shrill voice, the boy said: 'At first, I couldn't believe it, but the longer I thought about it . . . what else could it be?'

The woman nodded. 'He nourished himself with us.'

'That's why he lagged behind all the time!' the boy cried.

'It was him or us,' the man from Ashkhabad said.

His death was inevitable, the way seed had to fall to the ground and perish in order to bring forth fruit again in spring. The poacher, the woman, and the boy come from farming families, so they know how that goes. They know about the eternal cycle. How new life sprouts from the dead.

They sit around the fire and tell each other what they remember: on top of the burial mound he had picked out Vitaly—with his finger, he had burned his sign into his arm. They talk of the corrosive mange that had appeared on the tall man's body; how he had conjured food out of nothingness, after they had left the tall man for dead; and how he had sown fear and conflict among them.

What luck that they had killed him! Such wisdom! In life, he had destroyed them; in death, he was their salvation. In thankfulness and in repugnance, they looked at the head beside the doorpost—that abhorrent, knowing thing.

Vitaly! Where's Vitaly? They can't lose him now, now that they know that he is the bearer, that they are saved.

By the time the poacher found him, in the graveyard outside the village, it was already dark. Between the listing headstones he had dug a shallow pit in the cold ground. His eyes closed, hands folded across his chest, he lay waiting for death. And death would certainly have found him if the poacher hadn't chased him out of his grave before night set in.

Now he is sitting hunched by the fire. He occasionally dips his hand into a can of beans and licks his fingers. He's beyond hunger. To their questions, he gives no reply.

35

WE WANT HIM BACK

'The poacher's lying,' the boy tells Beg. 'He did it himself. After we went back.'

'Back where?'

'To Africa.'

'Why?'

'We almost couldn't move. Like we had lead in our shoes. He didn't want to let us go.'

'Haç, the one you call the poacher, says that you dreamed the things that made you people go south.'

The boy crossed his arms grumpily. The new comic books Beg had brought with him were lying on the bedspread. His fingertips slid across their colourful covers. His skull sported a fine down of black hairs.

'Geese,' he said then, for the sooner Beg left, the sooner he could start on his comics.

'Geese,' Beg repeated.

'Just the things I saw up in the air. I dreamed about that a couple of times. First geese, then airplanes. They asked me what direction they were going in. That way, I said. That's what happened. Her grandma used to dream about geese, too, she said. She wanted to know everything.' He snorted. 'She's nuts.'

'Was that before you went back to the black man's body, or afterwards?'

'Around the same time. I don't remember exactly.'

'And when you got back, Haç cut off his head.'

'Yeah.'

'You saw him do that?'

'Yeah.'

'You were all there?'

'Yeah.'

'Everyone saw it?'

'Yeah.'

'How did he do it?'

'With Africa's knife. He found it in his pocket. It used to belong to the tall man, that knife.'

'So why did his head have to be cut off?'

'Ach.'

He flipped one of the comic books closed and put it back. 'The woman's the one who said that he dreamed inside my head, not me.'

'And was that true?'

The boy lowered his eyes. Beg repeated the question.

'Have you got a better idea?' the boy said. 'If you look at everything that happened after that? All the good luck we had all of a sudden? She said we had to keep him with us, that he would lead us and stuff. But we couldn't take all of him along. So . . .'

Beg nodded. His understanding was not feigned; he understood their desperation. Their gods hadn't answered their pleas. Deaf and mute, they had looked down on them. So they had replaced them.

'He was still lying there,' the boy said, 'but don't ask me why. Animals had eaten their way right through his ribs. They picked at his liver, his organs. Blecch.'

'Who beat his brains in, do you know that?'

'I wasn't there. I only found him.'

'Who do you think it was?'

The boy shrugged his skinny shoulders. 'Anybody could have done that. It's not all that hard.'

Intuitively, they seemed to have realised that silence was the best policy, Beg thought. That way, all five of them were guilty, just as all five of them were innocent.

The boy leaned forward. He wanted to say something, but hesitated.

'What is it?' Beg asked.

'Nothing,' the boy said.

'Just tell me.'

'Where is he now?'

'Who?'

'The black man.'

'In a cooler. The same place where the dead girl is.'

'Together?'

'In the same space, yes.'

'Oh, okay.'

'Why do you ask?'

'What are you going to do with him?'

'Nothing. Bury him, after a while, I guess. If we can't trace his identity.'

The boy shook his head slowly. 'You people don't understand . . . we want him back.'

Beg burst out laughing.

'He doesn't belong to you,' the boy said. 'He's ours. We want him back.' His black eyes glistened.

Beg had stopped laughing. 'What are you going to do with him?'

'We want him back.'

'That's not an answer.'

The boy's upper lip curled in a sneer. 'Tough shit.'

'If you talk to me like that, I'll take these along with me.' Beg picked up the comic books from the bed and rolled them up. He had trouble disguising his disappointment. He had become fond of the boy. He felt compassion for him. Beg wished the feeling were mutual. Friendship with a child made you a chosen one.

We want him back.

Even now, the head was exercising its magic power; it was still keeping them more or less together. Maybe that explained his fascination, Beg thought, being so close to that. That he was witnessing the start of something. Primal ground. *Get thee out of thy country, and from thy kindred, and from thy father's house, unto a land that I will show thee.*

There were too few of them, and the times were not suited to it, but in a more distant century it could have happened. Something new, a sacred mystery: blood, retribution, salvation.

The start of a sharply delineated faith.

And immersion, purification. Why not?

The snow in the treads of his patrol boots had melted into little puddles on the linoleum.

'The woman had a child last night,' Beg said after a while. He looked at his watch. It was December 19.

The sisters had told him when he came into the ward that afternoon.

The boy nodded. 'I heard her screaming. They took her away.' He sniffed loudly and scratched his leg under the blanket. 'I didn't know that was what was going on.'

'Premature, but healthy. It's unbelievable,' Beg said. How could a skeleton bear a healthy child?

'Can I have my comics back?'

Absently, Beg laid the little bundle back on the bed. The boy opened one and began flipping through it.

The baby still had no name, the nurses had told him when he came in. They'd asked how he was supposed to be registered.

'Saïd Mirza,' he'd told them. It was a flash of intuition, a hunch. They looked at him in surprise. He said: 'You wanted to know what to call him, right? Saïd Mirza, that's his working name. So write it down, already. Who cares if there are two of them?' The nurse wrote 'Saïd Mirza' on a sheet of paper and asked no further.

'I'm going by to see her,' Beg told her.

'You don't have much time,' the nurse said. 'She's in intensive care.'

And so it happened that there were suddenly two Saïd Mirzas in the same hospital.

Saïd Mirza the First stared intently at his comic. *Does he actually know how to read*, Beg wondered. He could handle a slingshot, he knew how to plant corn and tend goats, but was he familiar with the written word? Who would have taught him that, up in those mountains? If he couldn't read, there was no life for him outside his native village—washing dishes, perhaps, or lugging merchandise at the bazaar, but that wasn't why he'd undertaken such a journey. He wouldn't have risked his life for that, to be a drudge. It would be a real loss; the boy had brains. Without writing, without civilisation, he would be only a talented predator, suited for nothing but a life of petty crime. For quick scams and the occasional trouncing.

'Do you actually know how to read?' Beg asked.

'Of course I can read,' the boy said without taking his eyes off the page.

Beg went to the window. The park lay in white innocence at his feet. It was growing dark; the shadows were leaving their hiding places. Yellow light fell from the windows onto the snow in the garden. The trees stood white and heavy, taking a time-out. From behind him, now and then, came the sound of a page being turned; the rustling of paper wings. Later he would go visit the rabbi in his consecrated den, amid the moulding relics, and burden him with the things that were troubling his heart.

It looked as though nobody was lying beneath the taut sheet. There were dark rings under her eyes. Every gasp of breath sounded as though she was surfacing from the deep. Beg shivered involuntarily. She had gone to the very limit for the child she was carrying, and now she was going to die beneath that sheet. And she knew it; Beg recognised the look of the animal that senses its life slipping away. Despair and resignation flow like layers of cold and warm water in a single stream.

'My son,' she says, 'where is he?'

He nods. 'I'll ask them to bring him.'

He goes back out into the hall. In the distance he sees a nurse, and he calls to her. She presses a finger to her lips in warning. He gestures to her, tells her to get the child.

'We can't . . .'

Beg shakes his head. 'You have to. Now.'

'The baby's premature,' the nurse says. 'Seven or eight weeks too early! It's very vulnerable.'

'I'm sorry, but that's the way it is.'

'Then it's *your* responsibility,' the nurse says, her mouth as sharp as paper.

A few minutes later, the baby is brought in, wrapped in a cotton cloth, only its little head sticking out like a doll's—a waxen, pale little face, black hair in brush strokes against its scalp. It looks as though it hasn't opened its eyes yet. Long, syrupy tears slide down the mother's cheeks. She rolls slowly onto her side and takes the bundle in her arms.

Beg stays in the room with mother and child, deeply aware of his heavy, indiscreet presence. The woman makes quiet, soothing sounds at the impassive baby. Outside of this union, nothing exists. Beg averts his eyes as she bares her breasts, wrinkled sags of skin. She raises a nipple to the child's mouth. The lips do not part; the baby is asleep. She wrings the nipple between his lips. Now, led by one of the first assignments given him by nature, he begins to suck; feebly at first, and then with increasing force.

The woman closes her eyes, and she smiles.

The baby starts crying weakly—a bleating, lonesome wail.

'Shh, shh,' the woman hushes.

When the child keeps crying, the woman looks up at Beg in a quandary.

In the hall, he finds no one. He comes back, empty-handed.

The child's disappointment is unbearable; the baby is inconsolable.

'Take him,' the woman whispers.

Beg swears under his breath. 'How . . . ?'

'Take him!'

Beg reaches out with his big hands and scoops the baby from its mother's embrace. He holds it away from his body. What discomfort—how long ago was it that he last held a child?

Slowly, he raises the little boy to his chest and rocks it; he is a dancing bear, beneath coloured lights by the river.

36

SHABBAT

More and more often these days, Pontus Beg looked at the grey sky of snow, and thought of God. This was a thought beyond his control, but not an entirely useless one. Firm faith, he felt, was based on cast-iron repetition. Repetition forced you to your knees.

He often thought only on the word 'god,' because he didn't really know how to think of God Himself, the Jewish god of countless pseudonyms, nor did Beg know how He truly differed from the Christian-Orthodox god of his countrymen, other than in His special preference for the Jews.

He noticed that he had gradually come to imagine Him in a different setting—not the jubilant pomp of Orthodoxy, but the blistering heat of the desert; his god wandered among eroded rock formations, pillars of red granite, the restless plains of sand.

The rabbi had said that the Everlasting was not subject to questions of shape and definition. He was unlimited—a statement, the rabbi said, that limited Him, too, which meant it couldn't be true, either.

To his regret, Beg was unable to herd his image of godliness towards the immaterial; his god always assumed a human shape. Even more disappointing was that he seemed unable to think of Him without a beard. In the face of these childlike projections, he stood powerless.

Beg's blood was what riveted him to the God of the Torah, which—as the realisation of being Jewish became more firmly anchored in him—also removed many senseless doubts. He was a Jew, consisting of one part coincidence and two parts resignation. He learned to pray in Hebrew, and entered into the exalted universe of repetition. He knew that repetition could summon up ecstasy, and that ecstasy brought the mystery just that much closer. He had no Jewish life in his surroundings, no exemplary lives. He had only his rabbi to follow, but the rabbi himself no longer held services, and had stopped sticking so closely to many of the directives. He was tired. The yoke of repetition had fallen from his shoulders, and all he waited for was death.

'You will have to say Kaddish for me,' he told Beg. 'Those are all things I still have to teach you.'

'You'll go on living for a long time.'

'Longevity is hardly a virtue. Spare me. Have you ever seen a *happy* old person? A *contented* old man? Age is a precarious business. It's as though all the disasters are waiting to pounce on you at the same time.'

With his right hand he formed a claw that snatched at thin air.

Before the evening meal, the rabbi shuffled into the depths of the mikveh. Beg waited in the synagogue. The door to the bath stood ajar; a stripe of yellow light lay across the floor.

The curtain before the Sacred Ark hung in shadow. In the candle-light, the gold-and-silver brocade glistened. Angelic hands bore the Ark up to heaven.

From out of the shadows, figures approached him. Mother, why are you hiding from me? Why don't you say something? Grand-mother, where do we come from? But they passed him in silence—he sat in the pew, bent at the waist, his head in his hands. His fingers felt their way across the skullcap, slid over the seams where the cloth was hemmed in, the half-crumbled velvet. He felt so ridiculous at times, a bad actor before an audience of centuries—an audience that didn't even deign to *laugh in his face*. Staring into the half-light like this, he was a Jew made of one part doubt and one part shame.

The door swung open. The rabbi bustled around the room first, and then, after a while, came and stood in front of Beg.

'Aren't you going in?'

'What do you mean?'

'Into the mikveh.'

'I can't do that . . . I . . .'

'Why not?'

Beg was confused. He'd thought that definitive proof of his Jewishness had to come first, before he could descend into the pool.

'It's the Shabbat,' the rabbi said. 'Lots of Jewish men enter the mikveh before the Sabbath arrives.'

'I'd rather wait,' Beg stammered. 'I hadn't realised that I could already . . . Better some other time.'

'Whatever you like,' the rabbi said. 'There's no obligation.' Beg stared at the tips of his boots. He thought again about the time the rabbi had asked him how he cleansed himself of the world's filth, how he became clean again. Then, before he had known about the holy place deep in the earth, he had still thought that some filth could never be washed away. Maybe it wasn't like that.

But he wanted to wait for the right moment to undergo his immersion, perhaps until news came from the rabbi at Brstice (he had been waiting so long already). Maybe until he had stopped seeing his transition as a fraud.

The bread was in a basket. It was normal, unbleached white bread, not the usual braided kind. Still, Zalman Eder had blessed it. They ate soup, spoons ticking against porcelain, the rabbi bending over with his mouth just above the bowl. That was how they celebrated the start of the Shabbat. Beg's lips had moved along with the song of blessing at the start of the meal. The rabbi's voice grated; the melody hovered:

Shalom aleichem, malache hashores malache Eilyon,
mimeilech malche hamlochim Hakodesh Barech Hu.

If I hadn't been here, Beg thought, *no one would have known he was still around.* But then the old man would still have been sitting here, by the light of two candles—a phantom, having grown translucent in his loneliness. One day, someone would have thought about the old

Jew, and they would have found him in his bed or at the bottom of the steps leading to the bath . . . and no one would have known that, with this, an end had come to six hundred years of Judaism in Michailopol.

For the second time, he helped himself to Chinese noodle soup from the terrine and said: 'The woman died last night. Fortunately, I had a chance to talk to her—she wasn't much more than a shadow. But her child seems healthy. His mother lived off of air and earth, she *bore* it all . . . I can hardly imagine it, it seems like too much for any one person. But she saw that it was good, that her child was going to live.'

'Because of her sacrifice, the world started all over again,' the rabbi said. 'The Talmud says that he who saves a life, saves humanity. It actually says "a Jewish life," but why shouldn't that apply to the goyim, too?'

Beg thought about the boy-child who had cried so loudly in his arms and wouldn't stop. Only when Beg, at his wit's end, remembered about the nursing reflex in calves, how they clamped down and sucked on your hand with their slimy, toothless mouth—oh, that suggestive sensation, down to and including the shiver that ran through your scrotum—had he stuffed the tip of his little finger in the child's mouth, and suddenly all was still. The woman looked at him, too exhausted for any expression. Her sharp cheekbones and pointed nose were already those of a corpse. She had come through the thicket of horrors, but had delivered her child safely to the other side.

Beg used his foot to slide a chair up beside the bed and sat down, so the baby could be close beside her. He slowly rocked the little bundle in his arms. Sometimes the woman's eyes closed, but she forced herself to open them again. This was all the time she had with her child.

Finally, she lost the struggle to exhaustion, and slept.

Beg sat with the little boy in his arms and rocked him.

The rabbi had blessed the wine, too. Beg was not used to drinking wine. It pinched his cheeks from the insides. The level of the bottle descended quickly. Beg had slid his legs half under the table, and he saw the reflection of candlelight in the silver belly of the samovar. He said: 'You told me that the Shabbat is also meant as a reminder of the flight out of Egypt . . .'

Fitfully, in a voice that sometimes raced ahead of his thinking and sometimes lagged behind, he talked about what was on his mind. Wasn't it ironic, he said, at this very point, just as he was taking his first steps in the direction of the Everlasting, that something like this should happen to him? A group of people who had, in a certain sense, relived the journey of the generation in the wilderness, with nothing over their heads but the empty sky? They had fled from poverty and repression; the generation in the wilderness had escaped from the slavery of Egypt. They were different, not to be compared, but still the same. Mankind lost in the wilderness, looking up in despair: Lord, help us, protect us.

Lord?

He had no trouble imagining the despair of those who had remained below, when Moses failed to return from the mountain. The rebellion and the euphoria. The dancing and screaming and exorcism of fear in a wild rite.

'And what if Moses really hadn't come back from Mount Horeb?' Beg said. 'Would we now be worshipping a golden calf? Why not— organised religions have worshipped *everything*: fire, the sun, bulls, demigods . . .'

'All down the tubes,' the rabbi sneered. 'Show me one existing religion based on the *sun*, or *fire*. Or anything like that. Just one!'

'They went down the tubes,' Beg said, 'but only after hundreds, maybe thousands, of years. And all that time they provided people with comfort—comfort, reassurance, and a life after this one. Everything you and I long for, too.'

The rabbi jabbed a finger at the air. 'You're staring so hard into the distance that you can't see anything anymore! Thirty-five hundred years ago, the Everlasting gave us his Torah, which contains everything a person needs. That's what you should be investigating. He lacks for nothing.'

'But those people out on the steppes didn't receive any answer; the heavens remained silent. Their imagination shaped a holy monster, or a monstrous holy-of-holies. I'm only thinking out loud about circumstances at some other point in history, unlike this one, when something like this . . . could have had a greater *impact*, if it had the chance to spread throughout entire tribes.'

'But it *didn't* happen, for heaven's sake!' The fire of the wine lit up in the rabbi's eyes. 'You should be taking into account what exists, not the nonexistent! There's plenty of room for doubt and discussion within the boundaries of the Torah itself. To deal with doubt we have *Lernen*, learning. That's the way, *lernen*! Explore the beliefs, not the unbelief.'

Beg shrugged. 'I thought that's what I was doing. That's all I do, I mean. But thoughts go where they will. How could I not see the similarities?'

'I take it you know the story of the heathen who came to Rabbi Shammai and Rabbi Hillel?'

The rabbi told him how an unbeliever had come to Rabbi Shammai and asked him to teach him the Torah in the time he was able to remain standing on one leg. In a rage, Shammai sent him away.

Then the man went to Rabbi Hillel and asked again: 'Teach me the Torah while I'm standing on one leg.' Rabbi Hillel replied: 'Do unto others as you would have them do unto you. That is the whole of the law. The rest is interpretation. Go now and learn.'

'Go now and learn,' Beg repeated. He nodded. 'I'll keep doing that. But I can't close my eyes to the exceptional . . . the exceptional fact of a faith that arises almost *before my eyes*. A seed . . . a sacred moment, and four or five people who follow it. Who truly *believe* in what they think they're seeing . . .'

'What you're seeing is idolatry. Humans worshipping another human, their equal—a consecrated perversion of themselves. I hope your interest is strictly intellectual.'

Beg grinned. 'Let's drink to a long life in good health. For just as you stopped being a Jew when your cook died, I will stop being a Jew once you're no longer around.'

Zalman Eder laughed and shook his head. He raised the glass to his lips and drank. He was enjoying himself. He was awake.

37

FRIED CHICKEN

They had taken up housekeeping with the chicken lady. They gorged themselves on her supplies, and didn't worry about the long winter to come. The floor was littered with empty cans, boxes, and cardboard packaging. They had pillaged her closet and spread out all the textile they could find around the woodstove. There they lay, purring like bloated cats. Her bed in the little niche behind the stove, with its ticked mattress of straw and its featherbed, had been appropriated by the poacher. The chicken lady herself had withdrawn to an old easy chair; through eyelids narrowed to slits, she watched the skinny ghosts who had invaded her home. They were hungry and sleepy. They stoked the stove till it glowed, bringing in wood from the lean-to outside, and wringing the neck of one chicken after the other. The blackened pan on the roaring stove was the epicentre of their contentment. There could be no more wonderful smell than the odour of a chicken hissing and popping in lard.

Afterwards, they fell asleep again around the stove.

Outside, in a bag on the doorpost, hung the thing that had led them to this abundance. They nodded to it upon leaving or entering the house, and murmured words of thanks.

Sometimes the woman knelt out front, laying a wreath of charms and incantations around the doorway. None of them doubted the power the head emanated. They had expelled the black man and killed him by orders of an implicit group will; now they lived on intimate terms with his head. It lived; it sent signals. The woman understood his messages, and arranged them into a tightly knit cult. The others followed hesitantly. Even the most stubborn atheist among them, the man from Ashkhabad, sank down before the head and raised his thoughts on high.

Vitaly was the only one who didn't take part, rarely emerging from the mist of his ghost realm.

The poacher paid respects to the head in the same even-keeled way he did everything: with dogged conviction and to the exclusion of anything that might distract him. He talked at times about the thicket of horrors, the never-ending suffering at the hard hand of circumstance. You had to steel yourself; you had to learn how to bear up.

They spoke quietly to the head, each on their own, beneath their breath and unintelligibly to the others, jointly sounding like a dull buzz. Along that humming, resonating web, they sent him their dreams and lamentations by airmail—their supplications for a good end to their journey.

The chicken lady stepped around the bowed figures on the little wooden porch and went on living imperturbably, as though nothing had happened. They heard her voice only when she called her chickens; she spoke to them in soothing sounds in which no human language could be discerned.

Inside the little house, the lady and the new inhabitants slipped past each other like fish in a pond; whenever someone asked her the name of the village or where the other villagers had gone, she was so startled that, after a while, they stopped asking at all.

The poacher had found tyre tracks outside the village. The deep, frozen ruts disappeared in a westerly direction, in a route crossed by other tracks here and there. The village was being visited from time to time by someone with a jeep—someone who brought the chicken lady her supplies.

The poacher stood staring worriedly at the graphite-grey sky to the north. A growl of disapproval rose from the back of his throat. They had talked about it before, about whether—and if so, when—they should move on. They would have to be quick about it now, the poacher said, before the tracks disappeared under the snow.

Now he and the boy were standing beside each other at the edge of the village. The hard-frozen grassland stretched out before them, white and crackling with cold. The poacher scratched at his beard and squinted. His eyes fixed on something in the distance, he said: 'We can't wait any longer.' The steam from his nostrils scattered quickly.

'So?'

'So I'm leaving tomorrow morning, early.'

He turned and walked through the tall grass back to the house. The boy watched him go, his chest filled with impotent rage at this desertion. The poacher could leave them behind without a trace of regret. Before the day was done, he would have forgotten them. He lived with his eyes on the horizon, tolerating the others with the patience of a pack animal.

The woman and the man from Ashkhabad had pressed to stay longer, to regain their strength, but the boy had more confidence in the poacher's common sense. If the snow came, they would be stranded in the chicken lady's house, without enough food to survive the winter.

'And what about Africa?' the boy yelled after the poacher.

He turned. 'He's for the living,' he shouted back, and was lost from sight.

That evening, the poacher prepared his journey. He sewed two burlap bags together. He would carry them over his shoulder. The bottom was tied to his waist with a rope, so the bags wouldn't get in the way as he walked. He filled them with canned food and a jar of blanched vegetables. In the light of the oil lantern, he looked like the ghost of some saint. He worked silently and efficiently. When he removed the satchel from his shoulder and vanished into the frozen night, the boy said: 'We're taking Africa with us.'

'No you're not,' the woman said.

'He's already gone.'

He was right: the head had disappeared.

The poacher came in with a couple of chickens in a sack. He wrung their necks and began plucking them, paying no attention to the woman's angry looks. At last she said: 'Where is he? Give him back—he's ours.'

'Snow's coming,' the poacher said without looking up from his work. 'The living are moving on; the dead will stay here.'

'There, out there, that's exactly where death is,' the woman shrilled. 'Walking without knowing where you're going, that's death!'

The poacher shook his head slowly. 'He serves the living. Fine if you people want to stay here, but how are you going to survive for four or five months with only enough supplies for one person? There are only a couple of chickens left. The rest are in this bag. So you do the arithmetic.'

Now the boy left the room. He took a few steps outside, and the cold snapped at his legs. Feeling his way, he went into the coop, the tingling odour of chicken shit and sawdust in his nostrils. One foot in the front of the other, he shuffled through the darkened coop until he got to the roost. He tried to feel which ones were the fattest; he had no use for scraggly pullets at this point. Slowly, so as not to startle the huddled hens in their sleep, he lifted the first one from the roost. Clucking quietly, the bird slid to the bottom of the sack. 'I am death,' the boy whispered. 'I come by night.'

He took four chickens, and closed the coop behind him. The earth crunched as he walked past the bare poplars to the house. The chimney smoke rose against the frozen opaline glass of night. How would they survive these nights out on the steppe? They would freeze to death, their rock-hard corpses impervious to bacteria and predators. Only in spring would the snow and frost release their corpses, the sun shining in their dead eyes . . .

No! He had to have faith! The black man would help them, just like he'd helped them before. The Ethiopian would point the way, and they would reach the civilised world. He wasn't afraid. He wouldn't be afraid. *Don't be afraid.* He had come this far already . . .

In front of the stove, he wrung the birds' necks, plucked them, cut them open, and pulled out their guts. The house floated on the aroma of frying chicken. The woman and the man from Ashkhabad were united in a stationary covenant, running doubtfully through their options. Vitaly lay sleeping beside the stove. The chicken lady was snoring in her armchair.

'I think,' the man from Ashkhabad said to the woman at last, 'that we should go along. There's no other way.'

'Why?' the woman shouted. 'We could . . . maybe someone will come along. For her, someone who . . . family, her children?'

'Those victuals were fresh,' the poacher said from across the room.

The boy piled the last of the supplies on the counter, and took his share. The man from Ashkhabad began to move. He gathered clothing and put it on, layer by layer. The boy, too, grabbed pieces of clothing from the piles on the floor. A competitive eagerness arose, the start of a conflict over a pair of woollen tights the boy had his eye on, and then the man from Ashkhabad pulled back his hand.

Sulking, the woman began preparing for what would be the last stage of their journey. She didn't want to stay behind on her own. The prospect of slow death by starvation frightened her more than dying under the wide-open skies, on the vast steppes.

The man from Ashkhabad pulled some clothes out from under Vitaly. 'Get your lazy arse off there,' he murmured. He handed the woman a sweater and some rags to bind up her shoes.

They slaughtered all the chickens. It was the rooster's turn as well now. The stove glowed as new pieces of chicken were added to the spattering fat, one after the other. The night was filled with excitement and a certain fateful cheeriness that could exist as long as they were still close to the warm stove. Everyone gathered clothing and food; together they assembled enough warm clothes for Vitaly. He was the one who would carry the head, the light that would lead them through the endless night. The poacher withdrew to the bed behind the stove, his provisions within arm's reach. He was ready for the last leg. The others checked to be sure they were properly armed against the cold—whether their satchels were sturdy enough, whether the weight was distributed evenly.

'A few days, no more than that,' the man from Ashkhabad said. 'Can't be any longer.'

'We have the tracks,' the boy said confidently. 'We've never had tracks before. If they start somewhere, they have to end somewhere, too. Has to be.'

'If that's His will,' the woman said.

The man from Ashkhabad pointed at the chicken. 'It's ready now.'

The boy lifted the bird from the pan by one leg. It was not nearly morning yet.

38

SNOW AND ICE

'And the chicken lady?' Beg asked. 'You just left her behind?'

'What else could we do?' the boy said. 'She was really old.'

'That's a cruel thing to say. You owe your life to her. Couldn't you be a little more grateful?'

The boy's legs dangled over the edge of the bed. He'd been taken off the drip; he could move around the room freely now.

'So what do you think happened to her?' Beg asked.

'How should I know?'

'But you can probably guess, can't you?'

'Probably. But why should I?'

'Because you people plundered her supplies and then left her behind, that's why.'

'She was crazy.'

'Oh, so that justifies everything? Then it's okay?'

The boy shrugged. He was in a brazen, recalcitrant mood. 'You don't have to act like it was easy. It was either her or us, you know?'

He was skating across the linoleum floor on his bare feet.

Touché, Beg thought. He had let himself be carried away by his pity, by the thought of the slow, lonely death of an old woman with wooden cherries in her hair.

The poacher had said something else, a clarification, a clue that revealed something about the head's character, its *personality*. When the subject of the abandoned woman came up, he said: 'We were able to go on because she was there. What do you think—you think we were in a position to turn that down?'

'I don't think anything. I asked you.'

The man across from him closed his eyes and massaged his forehead with his fingertips. 'There was a good reason for us to be there,' he said after a time. 'We took what was coming to us. She was there for us, so that we could go on. Like in the field, where the prey exists for the hunter. That's how I see it.'

'That's still how you see it?'

After a while, he said: 'Yeah.'

'He took you people to her . . .'

The poacher nodded.

'So that you could survive.'

'That's right.'

'As a sort of sacrifice? An involuntary sacrifice?'

The poacher closed his eyes. 'Words, words,' he murmured.

'He was on your side; he was only there for you people. Not for some feeble-minded woman; only for you. He allowed you to rob her of everything she had because you people were his favourites, am I right? Or I have got it all wrong?'

'Go ahead, make it all sound ridiculous, I don't care.'

But this was precisely what fascinated Beg. The god who favoured his people above all others: he wasn't there for all people; no, only for *his* people, rather like the nepotism of Semjon Blok. As far as Beg's own god went, it was no different: he had also picked his darlings. Thousands of years later, that warm light fell on him, too, on Pontus Beg—a pleasant feeling, to be honest, one he wouldn't have wanted to do without. No one deals lightly with his own redemption.

They left her house in the early-morning hours. The old woman was asleep in her chair, her mouth hanging open. The elastic bands had come loose, so that her grey hair hung in strands against the backrest. The floor was a carpet of feathers and down and innards; there were no chickens left.

The boy was the last to leave. He closed the door behind him.

'Fuck,' he said, stamping his feet on the porch. He and the others stood there a bit indecisively, as though unable to believe that they had actually left the warmth inside. The poacher had already disappeared. Like sheep ill at ease in new surroundings, they began moving, and felt how the cold took them in its grasp. Wasn't starving beside the stove preferable to freezing to death on the steppe, the boy wondered. The cold was a physical opponent—you had to be strong and fit to stand up to it. But they were skinny and feeble; they were no match for it. These last few weeks of gorging themselves made no difference.

They walked through the village. The poacher appeared from a half-collapsed shed, carrying the bag containing the black man's head. They formed a conference of shadows, and then the poacher stuck Vitaly's arm through the shoulder strap and hung the bag around his neck. This was how it was meant to be: the head and the bearer united, in a passing but sacred moment. A dash of hope trickled through their insides, a rarefied outlook—the prospect of things ending well.

'It's time,' the poacher said, his voice muffled by the scarf covering his face. He took Vitaly by the arm. He let himself be led along willingly, an obedient servant.

They reached the edge of the village. There they stopped, as though to muster up the final crumbs of courage. They had tied rags around their shoes, and cloths around their necks, their steaming nostrils sticking out of the textile. The world wore the nocturnal blue of enamel; ice-crystals had settled on the stalks of grass. The steppe opened up wide and dark before them. They had to brace themselves against that piercing emptiness, as much as against the cold. They started moving, the boy taking up the rear. He kicked holes in the hollow white ice between the tyre tracks.

Their footsteps crunched on the frozen layer of snow. The cold slipped through their clothes, felt its way along their limbs, and slid into their muscles and bones. It had only just started to grow light, and they were already as cold as stone. The village had dissolved behind them, a luxurious mirage. So much happiness, all that comfort—it was already more than they could imagine.

The thin snow lit up with a blue sheen at first dawn. A gradual light spread itself across the world, the sun itself remaining behind the ashen cover of cloud. Out in front went the poacher, keeping Vitaly close to him. The others could barely keep up. The head dangled against Vitaly's back, summoning them to move on. But as the day proceeded, the distance between them grew. The boy was sent up ahead as the liaison, to ask the poacher to slow the pace until the others could catch up.

Only when darkness came did they find each other. The poacher and Vitaly were sitting by a little fire in a dip beside the road, and didn't look up when the others approached, groaning, holding out their yearning hands until they almost touched the flames. The poacher melted snow in a pan. They drank greedily.

They ate frozen chicken and beans until their jaws burned. They didn't have a yardstick for divvying up their supplies, because they had no idea how long their journey would last. And because surviving for more than a few days was unthinkable, they ate until they could eat no more. Then they unfolded their cardboard and mats on the frozen ground, and buried themselves in loose ends of cloth and blankets. They crawled close together in the dip. Above them, the sky was cloudy and dark—there were no stars—and beside the dying embers lay the black man's head. They sent it their pleas and detailed imageries of salvation. The boy lay at the outer edge, not wanting to be beside Vitaly. Even though Vitaly's brains had been ground to mush, the boy remembered who he had been. He was still inside there somewhere.

He slept very little. The hard, cold ground hurt his bones. He tried to think about the house where he would live when this was all over, the big house for his whole family—if only he could remember the faces of his father, his mother, and his brother! They kept escaping him; there was only the flash of an eye, a laugh, his mother's skirts. And the vultures riding the thermals over the valley, he saw, but not the people themselves.

Where are you? he shouted in silence. Come out!

But he had been away from home too long already; his new life had buried the old one. Only his heart wept. Real tears would have frozen right away and rolled from his cheeks like pearls.

One day, he promised himself, once he was safe, he would dig up his old life; it was waiting for him beneath the sand—immovable, unchanged.

Stiff as string puppets, they stumbled through the day. They heard geese in the sky above them, but didn't see them. A bit of snow fell that afternoon. For a few hours, tiny flakes whirled down from heaven. They were still following the frozen tyre tracks, their lifeline. They had to go somewhere, because they came from somewhere.

That was how they crawled forth across the frozen planet, an icy stone. The sky grew more and more compact. Snow fell from it uninterruptedly now, grey as ash. They peered into the lightless day through a crack in the cloths protecting their faces. The snow whirled before their eyes. It had been the worst mistake of their lives, to move on again. The head had stopped bringing them luck; his candle had guttered.

But there was no going back. The village was already too far away; they could move only ahead.

They rested for a few hours, mere snowy bumps on the plain. Their account of time had been reduced to days, hours.

Long before the new day began, they were on their feet again. They ploughed through the heavy snow. Still following the track, the poacher cleared the way before them. When they stopped for a moment, the silence pressed against their ears.

The snow had covered the world and its sounds.

Before their eyes, the picture shattered; they could see for only a few metres.

Vitaly sank to his knees in the snow and stayed there, unable to take another step. He would have frozen in that position had the poacher not gone back to pummel him to his feet and drive him out ahead, cursing. Behind them came the woman and the man from Ashkhabad. The boy brought up the rear.

Hour after hour passed. His eyes averted, he followed the footsteps in the snow. That was why he was the last to see it: the light in the distance, light that was unsteady and casting about in the darkness and the driving snow.

A car.

First, a car. Then, for a long time, nothing. Then the city.

Spring

39

LITTLE MOSES

The soil had come unfrozen, the cold afternoon sun shining through the light-green leaves of the poplars. In the distance you could hear the deep, continuous barking of dogs. The pope cleared his throat. He had buried a nameless girl. The scant information he'd had was given to him by the other man at the graveside—the police commissioner. In a level, earnest tone, he had told the pope about the anonymous girl. The commissioner had a boy with him. His son? Why would he bring his son to a sad occasion like this?

The weak breeze rolling across the graveyard held traces of winter and the cheerful warmth of spring. It was full of old scents that reminded your old heart of desires from long ago—vague but oh-so-strong. It led young people into the worst of blunders and the greatest of happiness, so you could imagine how the girl had left her parents' home on a day like this to go her way, heading for adventure. *Don't!* Beg shouted straight through the years, *Stay home, please, the world is a dangerous place!* But she didn't hear him. Her heart pounding in excitement, she took up her position along the road, and it wasn't long before the first car stopped . . .

They parted at the end of the lane, close to the Polish graves. The pope watched them go, the stocky policeman and the dirt-poor boy with eyes like a doe's. Then he returned to the chapel, his black skirts flapping around his body.

● ● ●

Beg left the city behind, and they drove through open countryside, past dilapidated sheds amid tall bushes and weeds—the tail ends of town. With his window open a crack, the wind seized at his doleful thoughts about the girl and blew them away. The boy toyed with the knobs on the radio, alighting on snatches of voices, metallic jangling, and a music station from beyond the border. The boy liked contraptions, as long as they had buttons. The noise didn't seem to bother him. At Beg's house, he hadn't been able to keep his hands off the TV and sound equipment. Now, Beg reached out resolutely and turned off the radio, so that they heard only the toiling of the engine and the hiss of wind through the window.

'Don't you like music?' the boy asked after a while.

'Yes, but not that loudly.'

'So you could have turned it down, couldn't you?'

Beg didn't reply; instead, through the windshield, he looked at the hills in the distance. The road climbed gently.

'I want to show you something,' he said. 'It's not far now.'

'Did you bring any bread along?'

That was the other thing: the boy was always hungry. He seemed to have a hollow leg. Beg looked over. 'We'll buy something on the way back.'

The boy opened the glove compartment. He found handcuffs and sunglasses, a pair of binoculars, a citation book, pens, and sheets of paper—but nothing that could still his hunger.

'Why do you have such an old car, anyway?' he asked. 'You're the boss of the policemen, right?'

Beg glanced over. 'A long story,' he said.

They drove into the hills. Beg avoided the potholes. At a turnoff, broken graders stood rusting in the open air.

Beg crossed the road and drove up a dirt path beneath the trees. They went downhill again, the car jolting over stones. The woods thinned out before Beg parked the car on a little promontory. They climbed out.

It was quiet, and cold air streamed from the woods. Sand and stones crunched beneath the soles of their shoes as they walked to the edge of the bluff. The range of low hills was nothing but a blip in the flats; at his feet, the vast landscape began anew. The steppe in front of them stretched as far as the eye could see. The dead, yellow grass was making way for new shoots, so that the landscape was shot through with a green haze. The wind swept it, and the grass billowed. Rays of sunlight fell between the clouds. The horizon was hazy, uncertain.

The boy looked up at him. Where were they? What were they doing here?

Beg pointed at a line in the distance. 'The border,' he said.

Neither of them spoke.

Far below them, the border meandered. Once it had been heavily guarded on this side. In those days, refugees were shot down by snipers. Now it was the other side that had thrown up new defences.

Beg took the binoculars out of the car and handed them to the boy. He looked through the lenses, and then held them a little way from his eyes.

'Here,' Beg said, 'you have to turn this until the focus is right for your eyes—no, hold them up to your eyes . . . and now turn it. Until everything gets clear.'

'Is that a fence?' the boy asked after a while.

'This section of it is a fence. Farther up, north of here, they work with infrared, mobile teams, even satellites. They have night glasses. It's watertight.'

The boy snorted. 'Not for me.'

'Yes, for you, too.'

'I can make myself real small . . .'

'But not invisible.'

The boy peered at the horizon. 'Houses!' he said in surprise. Never had the promised land been this close. It looked like you could touch it; all you had to do was reach out . . .

'Cars! Over there!'

What seemed to surprise him most was that life on the other side looked just like it did here—the same grass, the same cars, the same houses. He sighed. A cloud slid across the sun, and the steppe faded to an ashen grey.

Little Moses, Beg thought, *come so far, and now at last he sees his destination.*

It was sheer torment, for this was where the road ended for him.

Still holding the binoculars to his eyes, the boy asked: 'Is it really that difficult?'

Beg nodded. 'Very difficult.'

The boy was soaking up the world on the other side. He had no greater desire than to be there—there, where there were no problems. It was impossible for there to be problems, no matter what anyone said.

'Have you ever heard of Israel?' Beg asked.

The boy shook his head.

'It's a country, too, far away from here.' Beg waved his hand, in a gesture that went far beyond the horizon. 'A sunny country, beside the sea.'

'So what about it?'

'Maybe you should think about going there. It's a civilised place. Not like here. They've cultivated the desert, they grow dates and grapes and mangos. Later on, I can show you some pictures.'

Deep thought was traced on the boy's forehead. 'How would I get in there, into . . .'

'Israel.'

'Is it really far away?'

'I've been thinking about it a bit lately,' Beg said. 'Imagine for a moment that you actually did get across the border here. One day, I'm sure you'd make it—maybe the first time you tried, maybe the tenth, but you'd make it. You're smart enough; you're not the kind who gives up. But after that, you'd still be nothing more than an undesirable alien. They don't want you over there; they really don't. It's important that you realise this. There are so many people like you over there. You're going to have to put up with humiliation. Maybe you'll sell newspapers in front of a train station, or lug boxes at a market, or wash dishes in a restaurant. There's a good chance that you'll have to share a room with seven other men; you'll have to take turns sleeping.'

He saw that his words were not touching base. He was describing a reality that lay in store for others, not for the boy. He was the anomaly, an illusory exception to the countless others, immune to statistics and probabilities.

'All right,' Beg went on, 'so imagine that what I'm saying is true. Just try to imagine that, okay? Over there, you're an illegal alien. You could be picked up and deported at any time. You'll have to have eyes in the back of your head, live like a criminal. You don't want that, do you?'

The boy shook his head impatiently. All he wanted to hear was where Beg's thoughts were going, not how they got there.

Beg nodded. 'That's what made me think of Israel,' he said slowly. 'Completely different from what you were planning, I know. A different route. But a hundred times better than what you were planning at first.'

'So we do that, right?'

'There's just one hitch: you have to be a Jew in order to live in Israel. Do you know what a Jew is?'

The boy shook his head.

'Just like you've got Russians and Americans, you've also got Jews. They live in Israel—that's their country.'

'Oh.'

'All right then,' Beg said. 'You're not a Jew, so that means you have to become one.'

The boy's frown said: *I'm not following you, old man, you're ranting.*

'That's what you need to think about, whether that's what you want,' Beg said. 'To become a Jew.'

'I want anything,' the boy said. 'Tell me how.'

Beg stared at his boots. This morning he had polished them to a high shine. There was already yellow dust on the tips.

'So?' the boy insisted.

'To start with . . .' Beg said. 'How do I explain this? There's an administrative problem. To become a Jew . . . you'd have to be my son . . . become that, I mean. To apply for an Israeli passport.'

He felt as shy as a schoolboy. He said: 'I'd have to be your father. Not your real one, of course, just on paper. Because you're not a Jew, and I'm not a father. We'd both have to become that. It's possible. I mean, it can be arranged. Administratively. To have you be of Jewish parentage. My rabbi is a wise man; he understands the world. We could make that happen, the administrative side of it. You've already escaped once on paper.'

The boy looked up. The two of them grinned at the shared memory—how he, Pontus Beg, had presented a two-week old infant by the name of Saïd Mirza for transport, and the detectives' relief when they were allowed to leave the baby behind at the hospital. That way, one Saïd Mirza entered the books as a newborn and was left behind in the hospital at Michailopol, while the other Saïd Mirza moved beyond the range of prosecution and the eyes of the world. By the time they found out—*if* they ever found out—he would be long gone.

'And that's it?' the boy said.

'Unfortunately,' Beg said, 'there's another hitch. You'd have to learn Hebrew. You can't go to Israel without knowing Hebrew. They'd see you coming a mile away . . . I'll try to teach you, but it's pretty difficult. My brain is old, yours is still young, and you can learn faster than I can.'

He narrowed his eyes and looked at the boy. 'You'd make a good Jew, Saïd Mirza. You've spent your time in the wilderness already—you know what it's all about.'

'And so once I'm a Jew, what then?'

'Every Jew, anywhere in the world, has a right to an Israeli passport. That means you can hop on a plane—you're legal, you don't have to live like a fugitive.'

The boy sighed like a mournful dog. 'A plane? Do I have to?'

'You can't walk all the way there.'

'I could.'

'Yeah, you're right, you probably could.'

'What about you, are you going, too?'

'Me? No, let me stay here. I'm used to this mess. Send me a card every once in a while, and let me know how you're doing.'

'I will.'

'But first, learn Hebrew.'

The boy nodded.

'Become a good Jew.'

The boy nodded again.

'A chip off the old block. Hardworking, smart.'

'All right, sure.'

'And when I die someday, maybe you could come back for a few days and bury me.'

'All right already.'

The wind murmured across the slopes. It had grown chilly all of a sudden. Beg zipped up his jacket. The boy felt no cold. He stood there with the sun of the promised land on his face, and stared out across the waving grass in the distance, the yellow sea.

ABOUT THE AUTHOR

TOMMY WIERINGA is one of the bestselling authors in Dutch history. His novels include *Little Caesar* and *Joe Speedboat*, which was short-listed for the 2013 International IMPAC Dublin Literary Award.